DISCOVERING
LITA

A Novel

By

Angie D. Lee

Copyright © 2018 by Angie D. Lee

Editors: Christaina Jones, Angie D. Lee
Book design by ADL Marketing

ISBN 978-1-7328641-0-8 (paperback)
ISBN 978-1-7328641-1-5 (ebook)

www.angiedlee.com

Reggie, Ramiyah, RJ, Mommy, Daddy and Trice, thank you for your unwavering love and support. You continue to encourage me and allow me the space to grow.

CHAPTER

~~~~~~

1

When I met Lawrence, aka "Law" which is what he said his college buddies used to call him, I knew then I wanted to know more about him.

Lawrence was tall, six foot three to be exact, which towered over my five foot five frame. With a shiny bald head that I could see my reflection in and a salt and pepper goatee, he was a man's man. He was strong, and he came from an era where men knew how to fix cars even though he wasn't a mechanic. I was thirty-two years old at the time, and he was twenty-six years my senior, but he didn't look like it. He had his alpha ways about him, but he was so gentle and sensitive towards me which is what attracted me to him. His voice was deep, yet comforting and reassuring. And his hugs swallowed me and my pussy would throb with an eagerness and longing for him to enter me. He was a successful entrepreneur who knew what he wanted and was unapologetic about who he was. I envied him at times because he seemed so free and not bound by the societal norms I allowed to cripple me all my life. To say I desired him was an understatement. I wanted to be engulfed by him with every opportunity. Law was *not* my husband. Law was my soulmate because he helped me take a long hard look at the lie I had been living. He was my drug of choice even though I didn't know I was addicted. As soon as he would look at me, my panties would come tumbling down. And so did his face, directly between my thighs.

"Excuse me, Miss; I think you dropped your scarf." A deep voice said from behind me. I turned around to see a very intriguing man.

"Oh, thank you. I didn't even realize it wasn't around my neck anymore. I nervously stuttered over my words while reaching for my scarf.

"If you don't mind my asking, what perfume are you wearing? I noticed the scent from when I picked up your scarf."

"It's actually one of my faves by Jimmy Choo. That reminds me, I need to catch Ulta before they close, so I can pick up some more."

"Well, it smells delightful on you, and you wear it well. But I must admit, your beauty overpowers it all."

I was smiling extremely big in the inside at that moment, but I was also very nervous for some reason. I could sense the attraction between the both of us and even though I loved my husband Mike dearly, I wanted to know this man.

"Thank you for the compliment; it's greatly appreciated."

"No doubt, it's my pleasure. Have a great evening sista and hopefully I'll see you again."

As he began walking away, I kept saying to myself; I want to know this man. What if I never see him again? But seriously, Lita, you're married. You can't just go picking up random dudes off the street, even if he does look like Idris Elba's long lost brother. Get it together Lita, snap out of it.

"Excuse me!" I yelled out loudly because we were surrounded by many chatty groups of people in the book store and I really wanted to get his attention before he got out of my sight.

He turned around and looked at me with a confused look on his face.

"Can you come here?" As I was motioning my arms and signaling him to come over to me, he was smiling while walking briskly my way.

"Is everything alright, sista?" I loved the way he said sista the first time and then again the way he said it this time. It was like a term of endearment and respect for me being a black woman. Almost as if black women were truly his choice over any other ethnicity.

"Can I be completely honest with you? And please don't look at me weird." I said with hesitation.

"Sure," Mr. Elba said with a slight grin.

"I've never said this to anyone before, but I find you extremely intriguing and attractive. I just wanted you to know that." I couldn't believe the risk I took in saying that.

With that same grin on his face, he said, "Well, thank you. Immediately when I locked my eyes on you, I was thinking the same thing. When I saw that you dropped your scarf, I said to myself, here's the perfect opportunity to speak to this beautiful woman, but when you reached for it, I noticed your wedding ring, so I didn't want to overstep."

Dammit! I thought to myself; *why do I keep wearing my ring when Mike acts like he's my husband only on paper?* "I definitely understand, and I appreciate the respect."

"What's your name beautiful?"

I could tell he was totally getting comfortable with me.

Even though I had never stepped out on my husband before, I had plenty of practice flirting, and I could tell he was really into me at that moment. "My name is Lita. How about you?"

His eyes were piercing into my soul.

"My name is Lawrence, but everyone calls me Law. And I must say it is definitely a pleasure meeting you."

I was so giddy inside. I couldn't contain myself, trying to think of what to say next so that he would stay right there in the bookstore with me. And before I could get the words out---

"Well, I don't want to take up too much of your time. I'm pretty sure a woman as beautiful as you are, your husband is always in a good mood knowing you're coming home to him."

Humph, puleeeze. Mike was probably too busy working on a spreadsheet or getting ready to criticize me for not cleaning up after the kids even though they're seven, nine and twelve, I thought.

I ignored his statement, "How good is your memory?"

Law chuckled, "Well, it's not exactly the best, but I have a funny feeling yours is."

At that moment, I knew we were in sync, he knew exactly where I was going with that question. "My number is…." and he leaned over and whispered in my ear.

I smiled and looked up at Law and said "Thank you" with a sweet yet seductive grin.

"I really look forward to hearing from you, Lita."

As I turned away, I could feel him staring at my silhouette as I walked to the door. I could imagine him calling for me and us meeting at the Palmer House Hilton down the street. I couldn't believe these thoughts were already racing through my mind about a man I had only met once. But it felt so good to feel that excitement. It was even more exciting to have someone I found interesting to look at me the way Law did. I could already imagine how amazing the sex would be. I totally couldn't wait to get home to use my vibrator that night. Law had definitely turned me on.

* * *

"Mama! Mama!!!" It seemed like Sheree was screaming at the top of her lungs at the ass crack of dawn.

"What is it, child?"

Sheree busted into my bedroom. Mike was still sound asleep as if he was in a coma. I just love how Mike can barely hear a peep nor be bothered by his beautiful children when they want something, in my usual sarcastic thoughts.

"Mama, I'm trying to figure out what to wear tonight with my girls to the movies." She had the biggest smile on her face, but it was just too early for this.

"Sheree, seriously, its nine o'clock on a Saturday morning.

This is one of the first Saturdays we've had in a long time that we've all been able to sleep in. Between your brothers' football games and piano lessons, and of course me constantly chauffeuring you around with your friends, I haven't been able to rest like this in a long time. And why are you talking about your outfit now, the movie doesn't even start until seven this evening?"

Sheree was my oldest, as she was twelve. Mike is not Sheree's biological father, but he's been present in her life ever since she was two years old. Sheree is such a fashionista, and extremely creative. Some of the things she comes up with blows me away at times. She's incredibly smart and a pretty cool kid. Honestly, as much as I complain, I don't mind taking her and her friends out. It keeps me in the loop of what's going on in her life. Many of her friends don't share that same closeness with their moms. And now that

Sheree was almost as tall as me and developing more and more into a lady these days, I decided it was best to keep a close eye on her.

"Mama, come on now, you know how I am about my clothes and I refuse to let Tasha try to take away my shine tonight. She's talkin' bout she gonna wear her new skinny jeans and them Jordans her brother sent her last week while he was in Cali. I can't come up in the show looking like I ain't got no stylist." Sheree was dead serious with her hand on her hip.

"Sheree straight up, you follow them celebs too much on Instagram and Snapchat, talkin' 'bout a stylist. Need I remind you that you can't even afford a stylist let alone a pair of draws?"

"Mama, why you say that? We got money!"

"Ha! That's funny. Your dad and I have money, you and your brothers ain't got jack."

"Uugh, mama, you sound so old. And why you gotta go all savage on me like that? If you let me get a job, I'll make enough money—"

"Sheree let me cut you off right there. First of all, legally you're not old enough to get a job. But I offered you some suggestions on how to make some money. I told you that your Auntie Niecey said you could help out at her salon over on 111th."

"Mama, first of all, Auntie Niecey be wantin' me to come over there and slave all day on Saturday and only pay me like twenty dollars! What imma get for twenty dollars? Plus, it's straight hood over there on 111th."

"First of all, I'm from that neighborhood, so watch it. And just because we live in the South Loop, doesn't mean you're better than anyone. Honestly, you and your brothers are so spoiled. Back in the day, I would've been too happy with making that twenty dollars."

"Exactly mama, back in the day. These ain't old times no more. I can't stunt with no twenty dollars."

"And that's precisely the problem, always trying to stunt but ain't got nothing to stunt with. You don't need to do all that. You're too smart for this, Sheree."

"Mama, ain't nothin' wrong with beauty and brains. All I wanted to know was what I should wear? You know I think you got good taste mama." Sheree was clearly giving me that smile like she always does when she's trying to butter me up.

"C'mon child, go and get dressed. I'll take you over to Akira in Hyde Park so you can pick out something to wear for tonight."

Sheree started jumping with so much excitement. "Ooh thanks, mama, I love you!"

"I love you too baby," realizing yet again I totally gave into her.

"Lita, you do that all the time when it comes to Sheree." Mike was grumbling as he was waking up.

"Oh, so now you decide to wake up? It would be nice if you could handle the kids when they come barging into our room as opposed to me doing it all the time."

"Lita, seriously not now. I'm tired."

"Wow, so you're just waking up going in on me huh?

Anyway, I'm not going there with you this morning. I need to take a shower and get dressed."

"You know how sexy you look when you're upset?" Mike said while trying to ease my frustration.

"Whatever Mike."

"Whatever Mike? I'm trying to set the tone and get you in the mood so you'll be ready for tonight. Ain't that what the article you were reading the other day said?"

Uggh, I hate when Mike starts copying things I've read instead of just paying attention to me and listening to what I'm saying. Typical Mike, all he wants to do is the same thing. Sit up and watch some long ass boring movie while he rubs my thighs, then kisses me and signals me to go down on him. He doesn't return the favor because his feelings got all hurt when I told him he wasn't pleasuring me the way I liked. He always wants to have sex missionary style with the lights off. Which I can't understand seeing that Mike works out and has a really nice body and let's just say, I ain't doing too badly myself. I'm a size twelve, but I'm what you would classify as thick fit as I too workout and keep myself pretty toned. I can't do this with him anymore. I'm so over how lazy he's gotten during sex. Mike used to have me climaxing back to back. We used to have sex any time and any place we could think of, but I'd be lucky if he even lasted long enough to wait for me to get mines. I'm always asking him what he wants and needs in bed, which is always a turn on to him but as soon as I even mention toys or a little role playing, I get the "Baby it's getting kind of late, we both gotta get up for work in the morning", so I stopped trying. I have sex with him at this point just to make sure that he's satisfied, but when I get a moment to myself, I'm usually using one of my toys to get off. Honestly, a trip to Akira sounds way more exciting than whatever "tonight" is supposed to bring. I don't even mind if he goes into his office to work while I pleasure myself and think about Law.

"Hey, Lita. What else did you do while you were at the bookstore last night?"

My back was turned to Mike when he asked that question as I was trying to get my clothes out of the closet, but it made me a little nervous there for a second. Why did he ask me that?

Had someone seen me talking to Law and then told Mike? Lita, get a grip, Mike knows nothing and especially because he barely pays attention to you. I slowly turned around to look at Mike with the best poker face I could come up with.

"Besides going to the bookstore, I went to Ulta afterwards. Why do you ask?"

"Hmmm, I don't know, it was just a random question. You've been a little stressed lately with work and I know we haven't exactly been in the best place and usually, your mood reflects that. But last night when you came home, for some reason you just didn't seem as uptight. As a matter of fact, when you were in the kitchen putting away the dishes, I actually saw you smiling a couple of times. I was just thinking damn; she must've come across some really good books." Mike said with sort of a confused chuckle.

And now all of a sudden he wants to pay attention to my mood? Where was this Mike when I told him I felt like he was constantly putting work ahead of our marriage and how it brought me to tears?

"That *is* interesting. I must've been thinking about something funny that happened at work the other day." I really don't think I've ever been the best liar, I was thinking to myself. "Well, like you said you've noticed that I've been a little stressed, but I would think it was a good thing if my mood seemed lighter and that I was smiling right?" I said while trying to deflect the previous question from myself. I knew Law was occupying my thoughts. I was so intrigued by him. I guess I couldn't contain myself at that moment.

"No big deal Lita, I was just making an observation as I was curious about what was making you smile like that so I can figure that shit out and do it to you."

Mike had his moments, and even though he was no Law, he was looking kind of good right now. It would've been nice to lock the bedroom door and just make love right then and there even though the kids were home. But lately, Mike hasn't exactly been open to being spontaneous and I just didn't feel like being disappointed. Since I was taking Sheree to the store, I didn't want to appear upset. She was my mini me and she would be able to sense my frustration. I just didn't want her to start worrying.

"Look, Lita, I know things have been a little rocky between us over the past few months, but we're good. I wanna take you out tonight. That new jazz spot about ten minutes away just opened up. How about I call my mom and ask her to watch the kids? Sheree will be at the movies with her friends, and Rashad and Tariq will be doing what boys normally do; eat, fart and play video games. My mom can pick up Sheree when the movie is over because I know how you're always on her, making sure she's not doing anything she ain't got no business doing. I'll take you to that seafood place you like, and we can spend the night at one of your favorite luxury hotels."

Wow, I was impressed with Mike but then again, he's never been a cheap date, that's for sure. Mike has always liked the finer things in life, and he would honestly buy me anything. The lifestyle does have its perks though. Mike is the senior vice president of a construction company and is quite close to making $200,000 a year. We have an extremely nice home, beautiful cars, clothes, electronics, full bank accounts and nice retirement plans. Mike was raised by both of his parents who are still happily married. They both have Master Degrees, and they instilled a strong sense of independence in Mike and his younger brother. Mike's dad retired from the very same construction company about two years ago, and ever since Mike learned how to walk, his dad was putting a hammer in his hand and showing him the ropes. Mike has had a pretty good life.

"I really like the way that sounds baby," I said with a school girl smile.

"Oh, now I'm your baby huh? Cause you like that monaaayyy." Mike was trying to sound hip. It wasn't working, but I let him think it was by laughing.

"Anyway," I said while rolling my eyes jokingly. "Thank you for making time in your schedule for us. I really need this." And I was so serious when I said that because when I met Law yesterday, I was really feeling some kind of way but maybe Mike is truly making an effort here and I want to make sure that I do the same.

"So, you got one of those freakuum dresses you can put on tonight? Like something kind of short with your back out and your titties sitting up just right?" Mike was seriously motioning his hands to his chest trying to demonstrate how he wanted me to look in that dress.

"Yes, I can pull out one of those dresses. It may have a little dust on it since you haven't taken me out since the Bulls won a championship." I said in a funny and sarcastic tone.

"See there you go running your mouth trying to be cute.

You were nothin' but a lil' girl in elementary school when the Bulls won a championship. Girl don't come for me with the sports; you know how I get down." Mike said laughing.

This was cool, we were having a moment like back in the day when we used to clown each other and joke for hours. I think I'm really looking forward to tonight.

* * *

"Mike, this spot is nice!" Mike held my hand and escorted me into the newly opened, yet dimly lit *Jazz Bar*".

Finding a nice spot in Chicago for the over 30 crowd was always a treat. I mean, I'm all for a little clubbing here and there but being able to chill in a nice, quaint place like the Jazz Bar was ideal. It was in the heart of Bronzeville surrounded by local black owned mom and pop shops. There was an underground feel to this place but not seedy. The music playing was sultry, and earthy aromas filled the air. The vibe was cultural and eclectic with pictures of Duke Ellington and Miles Davis on the walls but also pictures of Jill Scott as there was an open mic night set taking place every Sunday evening. The people in this place were beautiful! With Chicago being known for quite some time for being a segregated city, it was nice witnessing people in the Jazz Bar from all walks of life. There were professionals, freelancers, black, brown and white people just enjoying each others' company and listening to great music.

Mike kissed me romantically on my cheek and whispered, "Anything for you Lita Baby." He affectionately called me Lita Baby when we were in a really good space. Mike let out my chair and positioned me to take a seat. He bought me a drink and we began listening to the sounds of an amazing band who was backing a local spoken word artist.

Mike was looking so good tonight. I couldn't put my finger on it. Maybe it was because we hadn't been on a date since forever, or maybe it was this Long Island Iced Tea that was kicking in, or maybe it was just the simple fact that Mike was taking the lead and making a conscious effort to wine and dine me. All I knew was the atmosphere was amazing. I was wearing one of my favorite dresses that hugged my curves in all the right places, and I felt extremely sexy and adored.

"Mike, I don't wanna miss a thing, but I need to run to the ladies room." I was pulling down my dress to prevent others from practically seeing everything my mama's genes blessed me with.

"Okay take your time baby. Damn! Lita, you look so good!" Mike said with a sense of urgency as if he couldn't contain himself. I liked when he looked at me like that.

After I left the bathroom, I decided to go over to the bar and get Mike a double shot of Captain Morgan. That was one of his favorite drinks, especially when he would meet with some of his business associates. I just wanted to show Mike that I was thinking of him.

"What can I get for you beautiful?" A very handsome bartender said to me.

"A double shot of Captain Morgan, please."

"Okay, I see you! You look like the type that can handle it and who's 'bout her business too!"

I was flattered. He was looking good, and he had that eclectic, creative style going on. His arms were tattooed, he had a fresh haircut and a Tupac style nose ring. But I wasn't in the mood to entertain this man. It was finally all about Mike and I tonight. My mind was already in a place of hoping the night would get even better especially once Mike and I headed back to the hotel.

"Aww, thank you, but it's actually for my husband." I was feeling proud to say that because this night felt like Mike deserved that level of excitement and respect from me.

"Damn, lucky man. Well, you all enjoy. There's supposed to be a surprise guest tonight." The bartender said in a somewhat disappointed voice that I was unavailable.

"Thank you." I smiled a little flirtatiously as I still couldn't help myself. "Excuse me, Lita?"

I turned around totally caught off guard to see Law's sexy self. His freshly bald cut, with that salt and pepper beard and some of the straightest white teeth ever known to man. I stuttered a little.

"Wow, hey Law? Oh, my God, I didn't know you were going to be here?"

"Well, how would you have known, you hadn't called me yet? Let me get a hug beautiful."

And before I knew it, Law hugged me strongly but not forcefully. His body was warm against mine, and he smelled so good like a mix between Versace cologne and some damn good incense.

I happened to look over and the bartender kind of gave me a look like *oh I know what time it is.* I didn't want it to come off that way like I was cheating especially since I just told the bartender I was married. I really didn't want to run into anyone I knew either and them seeing me talking to and looking at Law the way I was looking at him.

"So where are you sitting? I can come sit with you. A few of my partners are here with me, but I'd much rather be sitting with a fine woman like yourself instead of one of the guys."

Law was looking into my eyes, and everything went out the window regarding Mike. I was wishing I was here by myself so that I could enjoy this beautiful evening with Law and seriously vibe out to the music and poetry. I hated to have to tell him I was with Mike but I had no choice, and I didn't want Mike to come looking for me.

"Law, I'm actually here with————"

Before I could finish my sentence, Law took me by the hand and said, "Lita, I am doing my best to remain the perfect gentleman right now, but looking at you in this dress, I'm seriously having thoughts. The kind of thoughts grown ass men have."

God, why now? I desperately thought to myself. I loved the way Law was being flirtatious but not too pushy, insinuating sex but not in trap music kind of way but in a 70s Marvin Gaye kind of way.

My panties were literally soaked right now. I wanted to leave with him and let him play out all those thoughts he was having, but I had to go and ruin the moment.

"Unfortunately, I can't sit with you." I was so disappointed while trying to still give a sexy look, but in turn, it felt like a pitiful, sad puppy dog look.

"What's wrong? I'm so sorry if I came on too strong, please accept my apology."

"It's not that. I'm here with my husband," I said as if I wanted his sympathy and understanding.

"Oh wow, yeah this was definitely not the best time for me to approach you the way that I did. No worries at all. Again, I sincerely apologize. You did tell me at the bookstore the other day you were married. For a minute, I just got my hopes up especially seeing you in that dress. But please, still enjoy your evening. And again, your husband is one blessed man. Low key, I kind of envy him a little bit." Law said with a smile but was starting to stand up to go back over to the table with his guys. I was trying to get up from the bar stool without showing all my goodies.

"Let me help you up. Wow, you are truly wearing that dress well." Law gave me that look like he was wishing I was his woman.

"Thanks again." I gave a sort of half smile, but before I started walking, Law looked at me and mouthed "Call me, whenever you're ready."

Just when I thought Law was actually about to throw in the towel, he does that. I must admit, I get annoyed when guys insist on pursuing me even after I've shot them down, but I really liked being pursued this way by Law. He didn't seem desperate at all but was still letting me know he was there whenever I was ready. It made me even more turned on by him. It felt like an ocean between my legs at this point. How was I going to get back into the frame of mind I was in with Mike after this?

I began to walk back to my seat. I knew wearing these five inch stiletto heels would make me walk upright and stick my butt out. Again, I felt Law looking at me as I walked away. I could only imagine what sex would be like with him. Like seriously, would Marvin Gaye come up from the dead and just start singing? Yes, it was that serious.

"Lita, are you okay?"

"Yeah, baby why?" I asked while a little out of breath from my heart racing while thinking about Law and walking in these five inch heels.

"You were gone for a while. I was about to say don't let me have to open a can of whoop ass on someone if they're trying to push up on my wife."

"You're so crazy, why would you think someone is trying to push up on me?"

"Have you not seen yourself in this dress?"

"Aww, babe you're so sweet. I may have to dress like this more often to get this kind of reaction out of you."

"Well, baby I'm just calling it like I see it. You are so damn hot, and I know plenty of men that would want to be with you. I've caught a few of my business associates looking your way from time to time. But see, you're all mine." Mike lifted my chin up to kiss me. All I could think to myself was, I hope Law isn't anywhere nearby to see this.

"Since we've had dinner earlier and we're enjoying some great music, let's cap this night off by taking a walk on the Lakefront. And after that, I'm taking you back to the hotel, and I'm gonna make sure the neighbors know my name."

What was I going to do? All I could think about was Law touching me. What if I said Law's name while making love to Mike? That definitely can't happen. I need to focus on Mike, especially because he's making a huge effort to make this night so special.

But Law has already gotten me so confused right now.

* * *

"I'm really glad we've had this chance to just have a night together. You know I love our kids, and of course, I seriously value my work, but I'm loving this walk with you on the Lakefront right now. This reminds me of the old days when we first started dating."

"Huh?" I said as I had just checked back into our conversation. My mind was so consumed with seeing Law at the Jazz Bar. His eyes, his teeth, his scent and the way he held me just did something to me. I wanted to get to know him on every level.

"Are you okay? You seem preoccupied ever since you came back from the restroom." Mike appeared concerned.

"Oh baby, I'm fine. I think I'm just overwhelmed with the night and how everything has been so amazing." I tried to sound convincing.

Mike grabbed me by the hands and looked into my eyes.

"It definitely has been enjoyable. Let me take you back to the hotel and take off all your clothes, wash your body, give you a massage and touch you in all the right places. I want to bury my face in all of that wetness down there because you know how you can get."

Mike was so serious while talking to me and explaining everything he wanted to do to me. I haven't seen this side of him in a long time. Are we really getting back to the way things used to be? I really miss those days.

"I really wanna hear you scream my name tonight. I need to be reminded that body is all mine." Mike started to gently kiss me on my neck and rub the small of my back which really turned me on. I was happy he was making me feel this way again. Maybe tonight would help me get that absurd thought out of my head about Law and being with him. It was just a minor setback, one of the many bumps in the road in our marriage but we're fine, more than fine now. I was trying to convince myself.

I placed the palms of my hands on Mike's cheeks and looked him in the eyes.

"Nothing would make me happier."

We couldn't get to the hotel fast enough. I was so ready for my husband. It felt so good to have this feeling with him again.

After we checked in at The Ritz-Carlton, Mike and I held hands walking down the hall to our room. I know Mike's taste, so I was certain everything was going to be high class. As we walked into our Presidential Suite, I felt so lucky to have Mike as my husband. He's always taken care of me and the kids and given us the best of everything. I felt like royalty. But right now, I needed some passionate sex. I wanted to be dominated; I wanted my hair pulled, I wanted my ass slapped, and I wanted to be put to sleep. I needed that so badly, and my body was craving for that. Mike wasn't exactly the aggressive kind of lover. While I always appreciated how he respected me sexually, he just never hit the mark. Yes, I always had an orgasm with him but that's because I know my body and I knew how "to arrive." But I needed hot, sweaty, talk dirty to me sex, which typically wasn't Mike's thing. I've always loved going down on Mike too and while I could totally tell he enjoyed it, he just always gave me this look as if to say "How many people have you done this to in order to become such a pro at it?" It always made me a little self-conscious being totally free with Mike as he always viewed me as a "good girl." But maybe, just maybe this would be the night we could change all that.

"Baby, why don't you get comfortable and put on one of those robes while I run some bath water for you."

While I appreciated Mike's romantic side, I kind of needed to be treated like a whore tonight. I just wanted Mike to throw me up against a wall with my back facing him. I wanted him to reach up under my dress, move my thong to the side and fuck me as hard as he could while asking me how much more I could take. But who was I kidding? That's just not Mike's style. But when I say I needed that, I so needed that right now.

"Baby, why are you just standing there? Get comfortable?"

"Well, I wanna try something different tonight," I said seductively.

"What's that babe?"

"I want you to take the lead tonight. I want you to take control." I said seriously.

"Now you know I can do that for you," Mike said confidently, even though I was thinking naw nigga you can't, that's why I'm asking you, but I gave him a chance to prove it to me tonight.

"Come here," Mike was attempting to show his dominant side.

"What are you about to do to me?"

"I want you to get on your knees and beg for it," Mike said in a somewhat demanding tone. For a minute, I was thinking; here we go again, I'm going to give Mike incredible head and then I'm going to get weak sex yet again.

"Okay Mr. Payne, I can do that." I was pretending I was a high class escort and Mike was my client.

I stripped down to nothing but my thong, I threw Mike up against the wall and I began giving him the best head of his life. I caressed every part of his dick with my mouth and when I began to deep throat, I glanced up at Mike to see his eyes literally rolling to the back of his head. I loved doing this. I always felt so in control when I sucked his dick. But before I knew it, I was doing tricks with my tongue and mouth that I hadn't done in a long time and I zoned out and began to think about Law. I could imagine how his dick would feel in my mouth and how much pleasure he would receive from all that I had to give. Oh my God, what's going on?

"Damn you not playing no games tonight," Mike said as if he was losing his breath.

I just smiled and moaned while I continued pleasuring him.

"Baby, I wanna take you over to the bed."

"How about you bend me over that desk instead?" Oh, I was going to get mine the way I wanted, even if I had to guide Mike every single step of the way.

"Damn. Okay, I see what you're on tonight."

Mike proceeded to bend me over the desk in our suite; he moved my thong to the side like I hoped and began to thrust into me. I felt so wet, but Law began to pop into my head again. This time, I couldn't snap out of it. I just let the thoughts ride while attempting not to yell his name. But to my surprise, thinking about Law while I was having sex with Mike was the most enjoyable time I had with him in a long time. I was so open, it was ridiculous. I knew the climax of this one was going to be through the roof. I could see, smell and feel Law all over me and I kept imagining him because it made the sex so much more intense.

"Yes, yes, yes!" I screamed.

"Oh, you like that huh, Lita?"

"Oh my God, yes!"

"You feeling that daddy dick ain't you?" For some reason Mike saying daddy dick kind of threw off the mood but I needed some multiples in my life right now, so I let my mind return to Law.

"Yes, I do!"

"Then scream my name. I don't give a damn about this hotel. Scream my name!" Mike was insisting.

And even though I appreciated Mike's excitement, I had to pace our little sex-capade because I knew once Mike came, it was going to be a wrap. And I'll be damned if I didn't get mine tonight. I'm putting in some of my best work. My back will be blown out even if I have to strategize through this whole thing to make that happen.

"Say my name, dammit!" Oh, I could feel Mike zoning out now. His dick was getting harder, and because Mike and I have been having sex for eleven years, I know him, and I can tell when he's about to blow.

"Ooh, Mike," I said while slowing down the tempo. He was getting way too excited, and even though I was getting close to getting mines, I wasn't quite there yet, and I needed this. Like I seriously and desperately needed this. I was still bent over, doggy style, but I moved Mike's hands towards my breasts so that he could caress them while we made love. I always enjoyed doggy style, but sometimes that didn't always hit my spot, so I needed some additional stimulation, and when he caressed my breasts, I knew that would definitely get me there. I avoided talking dirty to Mike anymore because I knew that would just send him to the moon, so I just kept moaning instead. As Mike kept thrusting, I kept imagining. I kept seeing Law's face and to say I zoned out was an understatement. I could feel my heart racing faster, I became extremely wet, and before I screamed, I kept saying Mike to myself while thinking about Law as to not slip up and say the wrong name.

"Miiiiiikkkkkeee!" I screamed, I moaned and trembled as the orgasms began to come intensely and frequently. Shortly after, Mike orgasmed after me, and he grabbed my hips from behind, holding on for dear life as if that was the most invigorating sensation he had ever felt. I was so content and satisfied, but I couldn't help wondering if I had not had Law on the brain would I have had such an enjoyable experience.

"Lita, fuck! That shit was hot!!! Goddammit!." Mike was singing my praises. He could barely move from behind me. That *was* good, but now I'm starting to feel weird about this whole thing. Physically it was a great experience, but I still didn't feel connected to Mike as I had hoped. The whole time all I thought about was Law. Shit, why? What was I going to do?

Mike practically stumbled into the bathroom after we finished making love. I pulled back the thick covers to the comfy king sized bed and immersed myself in it. Even though I felt like I put in some work, I wasn't tired. My mind was preoccupied. I was a little confused. I was kind of upset that I was having these feelings.

For a long time, Mike and I have not been on the best of terms, and it seemed like this would've been a step in the right direction, but I was starting to wonder if the way I was feeling had almost nothing to do with Mike and was all about me.

I just couldn't wrap my brain around what was going. I am married to a handsome, successful man who makes six figures. And even though I don't have to work, I choose to because that's who I am and who I've always been. I'm independent, as I've always had to be. I practically took care of my baby sis when my mom decided to up and leave our family when I was only thirteen, and my dad pretty much worked around the clock to take care of us. So that left me to be a "mommy" in a sense. I've always had to work hard, hustle and make sure that we were good. My daddy depended on me. And when I got pregnant with Sheree, I was only nineteen. I had to survive, and I had to provide for myself and my daughter. I relied upon family and friends as much as I could so that I could finish school, but even then I knew, folks were only going to help out so much. Those times were hard, very hard but I made it. I'm no stranger to the struggle, unlike Mike.

I won't say that his life was perfect but damn near in comparison to mine. He's provided us with such a so much, but I feel like, with his cushion-y life, he missed the mark somewhere. Mike's mom spoiled him rotten. Every girlfriend he's ever had practically acted as if he was doing them a favor by being with them and here comes me, this firecracker. I was the one who could read through all the bullshit; I wasn't so quick to fall for the okie-doke. At the time I met Mike, I was no millionaire, but I was holding my own, and I was taking care of my daughter by myself. Sheree's biological dad, Lamont hadn't been too fortunate in the financial department, and honestly, I had never even really pushed for child support because he always made an effort to see Sheree and spend time with her which meant so much more to me.

Since Sheree and I were really in a good place financially after I'd married Mike, I never bugged Lamont about money. He appreciated that about me, and we always remained friends.

Mike also appreciated the way I handled things with Lamont and would tell me it's rare to actually witness a woman be the way I was with Lamont, especially because he couldn't really afford to provide for Sheree.

I came to the table with something so to speak, and I know that impressed Mike. Even though I had gotten pregnant before marriage, which is not as taboo these days, people always viewed me as a great example and just chalked my experience up to being "young and dumb" even though I didn't see it that way. I just always viewed that as part of my story. One that I could share and empower others with. But Mike liked how much of a go-getter I was, and he always said it was a breath of fresh air in comparison to all of the other "birds" he had dated. His words, not mine. And Mike was a catch as well in comparison to some of the thugs that kept approaching me. I loved the fact that I would not have to end up "taking care" of Mike. Hell, he was destined to be successful before he was even born. By the way his lineage was set up; he practically walked right into a career after graduation. I can honestly say I have been so good to Mike. I've loved him, understood him, gave him those sons he always wanted even though I was quite fine with just having one child, and I honestly put my dream of leaving my job and building my own marketing firm on hold, just to make sure that I didn't appear to be gambling our money on something that was not a "sure thing", as Mike would say.

I think I've always resented Mike for that because I know I can do so much more. I told Mike, we have the money to spare and I really wanted to start a business for myself. When I was in school for non-profit management, I learned a thing or two about marketing and that sparked my interest more than the nonprofit sector itself, but hey, when everyone is convincing you to get a degree and get a job since you are a single parent, you start listening to the nay-sayers. And since I did have another mouth to feed, I went with the "safest" route. So I've been doing my job diligently as Fundraising Coordinator because I have to work. It's in my blood. My daddy always taught me to be able to handle my own and never get too comfortable depending on any man. But I crave more than working this job, and I crave more from my husband. He always seems so satisfied with where we are in our marriage when I am secretly longing to connect with him on a deeper level. He feels that because he provides for me and the kids and because he's not hanging out until three in the morning every night, or not banging me upside the head, I should be totally fine. But I'm not, and I'm borderline angry that my head was not in the game tonight. All I thought about was Law, and I don't even know him, but I feel connected to him in some way.

"Lita Baby, oh my God, tonight was amazing!" Mike slid under the covers and held me from behind. "Me rubbing up against you like this could seriously have me going for round two."

Surely, I wasn't trying to go for round two. I was good. I just needed time to think.

"Listen, you're always wet when we make love but girl you were feeling like the Pacific Ocean down there tonight! Got a brotha wanting to take *your* last name?" Mike chuckled with amazement.

Mike didn't even have a clue that there was a change in me. He didn't even recognize it. He didn't even sense my mood. I could totally have gone for round two, three and four but I just wasn't in that space. This is crazy. Maybe I'm crazy. Maybe I need to get this whole "I need more shit" out of my head. There are women out here that freaking pray to God everyday for a man like Mike, would beg to marry a man like him and worship the ground he walks on just to have him in their life. And no doubt, I see how women respond to him. But I've never been jealous when it comes to Mike. I've always been secure in who I was as a person and I've never felt the need to compete. I can never share these thoughts with anyone because people would practically stone me for even thinking this or on the other end of the spectrum, a woman would see it as an open invitation to come into my life and disrupt all my shit, so I play the role of supportive wife. I tend to his needs, but I wish Mike could understand my needs and tend to them as well.

"Baby, I'm so glad you enjoyed tonight, I did too. I think I'm going to go off to sleep."

"See that's what I'm talkin' 'bout! You know I put you to sleep with how I put it down tonight." Mike was so confident in his abilities, but honestly, I just wanted to go to sleep to avoid having these thoughts continuously racing through my mind.

"Okay baby, I know you're tired." Mike kissed my forehead, smacked my ass and said, "I'm going to head up front and watch a little TV."

Why am I not surprised? Mike didn't even lay with me long enough to rub or caress me as I drifted off to sleep. Sometimes, I just wished Mike would be more in tune and really explore me. Uugh, I guess tomorrow is a new day.

CHAPTER

2

I'm so preoccupied this morning, but I've got to wrap up these last minute donations. For the fifth year in a row, I've been spearheading my company's Leadership Gala here at Global Connections which is a non-profit agency that connects foreign exchange students with surrogate families in the United States. At first glance, it almost looks like a foster care program and I can see why many people would think that, but many of the students attending school here are from other countries who do not have the financial resources to continue their educational pursuits. The program consists of students applying to American colleges and universities along with completing the necessary paperwork to be considered for "Family Sponsorship." Once accepted, the students are then paired with the most appropriate placement that is in alignment with their goals for education, creativity and their career pursuits, as well as maintaining their cultural identity.

Many of the families are well-versed in the students' background and are able to connect them with the most appropriate resources. We have students from all over the world, including; Asia, Africa and South America just to name a few. The families that sponsor our students are not always of the same culture but they are required to attend trainings and workshops to ensure they are the best fit for our students. Now more than ever, we are gaining a larger gay, lesbian and transgender population into our program, so I'm always on the hunt for additional financial support to attract more suitable families. We provide stipends for our families to support our students and obviously, we can't provide those stipends without fat wallets. So my job is to connect with the bigwigs in various industries and make magic happen.

The Leadership Gala that's coming up this Saturday is my biggest fundraiser to date and we have some major power players expected to attend like NBC Channel 5 anchors here in Chicago, some amazing actors and actresses who make huge donations to our organization yearly such as Sheryl Lee Ralph, Steve Harvey's wife, Marjorie Harvey, and actor/comedian Corey Holcomb who is a native of Chicago and an absolute riot. He told me he was going to be on his best behavior though because he definitely speaks on controversial topics regarding relationships specifically in the black community. To my surprise, my bosses love him! They always want to take him out to lunch when they know he's in town. They say he is extremely funny and they like his "candor", which we crack up laughing about all the time.

"Lita, it's only 5 days away from the Leadership Gala and that guest list you put together is the truth! As a matter of fact, the whole evening you have planned is nothing to play with. People ain't ready. You the shit girl! Damn, I wish I had your skills and connections." Val said while making some coffee in the break room.

Val was one of the first people I met when I started working for Global Connections as an intern. She was already an employee here, but she quickly became one of my closest friends. She was my candid, straightforward Polynesian/African blended friend who was about eight years older than me, and she grew up in the hood in Chicago just like me. Val was actually a foster child. Her mom was from Polynesia and being that her dad was African, Val's mom never had the support of her family regarding her relationship with her dad, so she ended up moving to the States after Val was born. Unfortunately, her dad began abusing alcohol and also began abusing her mom shortly after they relocated so her mom left and decided to raise Val on her own. Being a single parent at the time, Val's mom worked several jobs to make ends meet. Val was the only child even though she'd heard stories that her dad fathered other children. When she was only five, Val's mom died of cancer which is how she ended up in the foster care system. Val never had the best relationship with her foster parents and she quickly became that "rebellious teen" as she would often times skip school, get high and she started having sex at a pretty young age. She never really grew up with a sense of family but she and I were family in every sense of the word.

At times, I wish I could be as blunt as her with my feelings, but Val said that one of "us" had to be present at the top and that she could never be that person due to her "big mouth". She says we balance each other out and that I'm the politically correct friend while she hangs out in the "slums" and deals with the "real people". But Val always seemed to like that role. She said white people in suits made her itch and then she would say really *all* white people made her itch which is why she carries calamine lotion with her to work daily. She said the only white people she could stomach was her neighbor Bob and the singer Pink.

Val said Bob seemed to only sit on his porch and walk his Golden Retriever all day, but he graces her with a substantial amount of compliments including if he was forty years younger, he would turn her out with his Italian-bred dick. Val said after that comment, he was alright with her. She said she liked his "sauce", which was a newer term for swag.

Val had also been a fan of Pink. She said Pink had spunk and was a real woman in her eyes, not conformed to the societal norms of what a "girl" should be. Val was definitely a feminist and a free spirit. She wasn't gay, she loved men but said she just enjoyed kissing girls from time to time. She said there's always a sense of comfort being that close to a woman because women are more engaging and understanding. Val said men were better fuckers and she definitely wasn't the one to turn down good dick but she looked to women for real conversation and companionship. Whenever Val and I would go out, so many people would assume we were a couple because we had so much fun together. Our chemistry was clearly visible but we were never attracted to each other romantically. We're too much like sisters and that would've seemed incestuous. And let's not negate the fact that I definitely didn't find comfort in kissing women; that was Val's thing, but I respected her and she respected the way I chose to live my life.

What I love about Val is even with her adventurous life, she doesn't look at me as boring or wasting mine by being the dutiful wife with kids. Val says that she respects where I am in my life and all anyone wants in this world is real companionship and love from another human being no matter the package. And then she later says *Lita, girl, I already know you a freak, but I get that you don't want the whole world to know that.* And we always laugh because Val knows so much about my life that no one else knows. Val is definitely my kindred spirit.

"Val, you are too kind. Hmmm, let me take that back, yeah you're right, I am the shit." I was feeling myself a little.

"And it's about damn time you admitted that. I've been telling you that for years ever since you started interning here. I was like; oh she's gonna turn this place out. She be movin' and shakin' like she knows all the Hollywood secrets. You always had that way about you. When we started talking about the hood during our break on your first day here, I was like; oh she's the real deal, I wanted to kiss you!"

"And uum, I'm glad you didn't."

"Ha, I know you don't do all that, but don't get it twisted, you and I had some fun back in the day making these niggas run wild."

It was so comforting having Val at the job with me. All day long, I've always had to have the "white people voice on deck" like all black people who work around corporate snobs.

"Yeah, those days are long gone. Plus, I never had the dudes going wild that was you."

"Okay, yeah, I probably slept with more of them, but they were always buying *you* shit, wanting to take *you* on extravagant trips. Hell, what did I get? Just a free trip to the clinic because I got pregnant by the executive director at the time."

"Yeah girl, now *that* was wild. He was an ass though because anyone could see he was so into you. He was ready to leave his wife and everything, but when the CEO found out and threatened to fire him, he flipped the entire fuck out."

"Yeah, but hey, it is what it is. I don't think I would've been a good mom anyway."

"I don't know why you say that. Honestly, I think you would be one of the best moms ever. You're so pure—"

"Bitch, did you say pure? Now that's the funniest shit I've heard all day, ha!"

"Listen, I'm talking about pure in the sense that you are who you are, you make no apologies for it. You're transparent and you're honest with yourself. You flow with life, not against. It just seems like you and the universe work together in tandem."

"Aww shit, you make me sound so earthy. That's hot, Lita! You betta write that book!"

"You are a whole fool, but you know what I mean."

"I hear you, but you acting like you ain't rocking the shit outta life right now. You are killing it here at Global Connections, still got these men wanting to take you on trips and shit at the job knowing full well you ain't interested in they asses. You got a fly ass husband who loves and adores you, your kids are so stinking cute they actually make me almost second guess wanting to adopt a few myself cause you know I can't hold out for that whole six weeks after the birth thing, what the fuck is that about? You have an amazing crib with everything you could ever want. You know you 'bout that life."

"But, Val, there's just so much more that I want."

"Girl, like what? I just named everything. What you want somebody to drink yo' bath water too, cause I'm pretty sure Mike would if you asked him with his extra whipped ass."

"Ha, funny," I said sarcastically. But seriously, I've been wanting to start my own marketing firm. You know I would be the one to fuck with especially here in Chicago. The people I know and the moves I make sis, the sky's the limit."

"And like I told you before, start that shit now, ya'll got the money."

"Yeah, but when I talked to Mike about it, he shot that down real quick. He started saying he didn't want to put his hard earned money into a hobby. He just doesn't understand me and what I'm capable of."

"Lita, listen, babe, have I not taught you anything? Now you know how men get. Mike used to date them hoes back in the day before ya'll met, so he's used to chicks trying to always take. Now I know that ain't you, and he knows that ain't you, but he's a solid dude, and he probably just wanna make sure you and the kids are straight, that's all. In his own way, he's just looking out for ya'll. But this is what you need to do. You need to put it on him so heavy one night that the nigga be singing Beyonce' while his toes curl and then ask him again for however much money you need for your business."

"Like I did the other night." I kind of mumbled.

"Oh watch out, what you talking 'bout, you put that, Lita, on him?"

"You don't know the half."

"Well, shit tell me, don't have me waiting. You know Greg is gonna come up in this break room looking for me in a minute because I told him I would be back in my office in like fifteen minutes and it's been damn near thirty. I know I said I wasn't gonna sleep with nobody else at work after the whole clinic fiasco, but shit, when we met up after that work party the other night and we were both drunk, he gave me that spaceship to the moon head and I was like; oh he's a keeper. You can never go wrong with having a dude that supplies the head regularly, no questions asked. He got that white in him you know? They love doing that. But that black side of him, good lord, that Mandingo side!" Val had totally checked out of the conversation as she normally does when she starts talking about good sex.

"Uum, earth to Val, how you gone start talking 'bout Greg? I thought we were talking about me?"

"I know, but damn you were taking too long. Anyway, so tell me what happened?"

"Well, Mike and I went out for some seafood and then he took me to that new jazz spot."

"Oh yeah, the Jazz Bar right? I know one of the drummers who performs there."

"Yeah, that one. It was so nice. And then we went back to the Ritz-Carlton."

"Okay, seriously this just sounds like some rich people shit. Get to the damn good part."

"You always talking that rich shit, you ain't too poor yourself."

"My rich is different than your rich. I only have money because of the time I married that dude in Vegas only after knowing him for like two seconds. Shit, we were so high, I didn't even know his last name until after we said "I do" and I didn't even know he had money. I didn't want to assume just because he was Arab and owned a few gas stations, that he was plugged like that. Who would've known he was gonna be my Arab version of the Prince of Zamunda? We got an annulment like a week later because we knew it wasn't gonna work. The only reason we lasted that long is because we were literally both high for the whole damn week! We were so high that we would be out on the Vegas Strip making up stories about how we were childhood friends who met in the sandbox and played on the swings. And because everyone else on the Strip was drunk and high too, they were listening to that shit. Damn, that was a wild week. But basically what I'm trying to say is he didn't owe me a thing, but he said he felt bad for "using" me, ha! You know that's funny, a bitch like me can't be used. But yes, he sends me a $50,000 check every month, but who knows when he'll say fuck this shit. So I just save it. I don't know what imma do with it yet."

"Damn, you done went through that whole story yet again."

"Well, you were acting like you ain't remember my struggle so I had to give you the play by play of how I got 250K sitting in my bank account right now."

"Anyway, like I was saying, in a nutshell, I wore Mike's ass out but that ain't the issue."

"So what *is*, Lita?" Val said while anxiously awaiting the juicy parts of the story.

"Long story short, I met a guy and while Mike and I were having sex——"

"Shut the entire fuck up! Mike let you bring another dude into the mix?" Val sounded too excited.

"Uum hell no, Val, that's your thing, not mine."

"Well, don't knock it until you try it."

"C'mon you've got to be kidding me."

"I'm just saying having sex with two guys is some hot shit. Sorry I just got a little excited there for a minute. Got me thinking about calling a few folks so I can have some fun, but that's beside the point."

"Girl, if you interrupt me one more time."

"Damn, sorry, I'm listening." Val was attempting to look innocent and attentive.

"So as I was saying, a few days ago, I met this guy at the bookstore and he was hella fine. He was tall, bald, salt and pepper beard, he smelled good and I told him he was attractive and I asked him for his number."

"What?" Val seemed disappointed. Maybe I had made a mistake telling her. I mean I know she's a free spirit and all, but she loved Mike like he was her brother and she always said we were a good fit. I knew I should've kept my mouth closed.

"Let me explain," I said nervously.

"You ain't gotta explain. I saw this coming some time ago."

I was confused, what was she talking about? "What did you see coming a long time ago?"

"This." Val was waving her hands all around me as if she was doing some energy cleansing or something.

"I don't get it. What are you talking about?"

"Look, I'm your best friend and I love you." Val actually seemed serious for once like she was about to break some bad news to me. "You and Mike been at odds for some time now, you want to leave your job and start a business, you've been making more time for yourself which I love and which you deserve and honestly, you want your back blown out. You're opening up to life more and you're accepting it the way it comes. It's all in your limbs right now. I can see it."

And this is why Val is my girl. I can't hide anything from her even if I tried.

"Please tell me, how did you pick all that up like that?"

"Well, damn you are married with three kids, your life looks pretty good on the outside. Women like you don't go asking sexy tall bald men for their number unless there's some other shit going on."

Val had a point, but that's precisely the problem. I'm trying to figure out what's going on with me.

"So I bet when you and Mike headed back to that hotel, all you could think about was the guy you met and you ended up fucking the shit outta Mike?" Val said as if she was a true psychic.

"Damn, you're on it today. Well, that's part of it. I actually ran into him at the Jazz Bar while Mike and I were there."

"Wow! Damn, what did you do?"

"Well, Mike didn't see him because I saw him at the bar and it was extremely dark in there. But Val, when I tell you!"

"Aww shit, your pussy was a swimming pool wasn't it?"

"That's an understatement."

"So how in the world did you deal with that?"

"Well, I was totally caught off guard. He wanted to sit with me but I told him I was there with Mike. He knew I was married when we met at the bookstore so he was surprised but not surprised. I honestly thought he was going to just let me walk away but then he mouthed to me to call him whenever I was ready. I have yet to call him. How does he know I'm going to call him?"

Val chuckled, "Girl, he sniffed that out when he met you. The question is are you going to pursue that?"

"I can't do that. Mike is a good man. I can't do that."

"You've got some things to think about honey because I can see how excited you are right now. It's all in your eyes. Yeah, Mike is a good man to you, I see that myself, but your soul ain't on fire. Well, no matter what, I'm here for you. You know there are no judgments from me at all. So what is this mystery man's name?"

"His name is Lawrence, but he goes by Law."

"Damn, he sounds sexy. How old is he?"

"I'm not sure. He looks to be about forty to forty–two, but something about him wreaks of an older man as if he's in his mid to late '50s."

"Well, watch out for them older guys, they always trying to woo some young thang and then dominate her. Not saying you're all that young. You're in your '30s now. You damn near got one foot in the grave."

"Shut up. I'm very much in my prime and who said I *would* mind being dominated?"

"Oh, okay, I see what this is all about. You on your fifty shades of grey shit. Well, yeah you ain't getting that outta Mike, he's too straight-laced for that. Well, if you decide to entertain Mr. Law, you betta give me a play by play of the details cause you know I love a good sex story."

"You crazy, you the one with the stories."

"But what's crazy is you haven't heard one from me in a while besides Greg, but that ain't nothing too spectacular. The sex is mediocre at best, but the head is very nice. Oh, I think I hear Greg's crazy ass coming down the hall now. I better go. Ooh, I almost forgot to tell you about me and Bob the other night."

"Oh don't tell me you had sex with your seventy year old neighbor," I said unfazed.

"Girl naw, for the first time right? Ha! But no I didn't have sex with him, but I did go over his house the other night and we talked for hours about my childhood, my life in general. It was some deep shit, but I really enjoyed it. But let me go now, Greg is coming."

Greg walked into the break room and Val immediately flipped the script and turned on her "white voice" so that our colleagues wouldn't suspect a thing. But knowing Val, when she's alone with Greg, she probably starts to role play and breaks out her real voice and it probably has Greg seeing stars. Oh, how I loved me some Val. I don't know why I felt nervous telling her about Law, but now I'm glad that I did.

* * *

"Lita, great work gathering our corporate sponsors and guests for the gala for this upcoming Saturday. I'm always impressed with your work." Don said.

Don was the Executive Director of Global Connections and also the man who broke my Val's heart even though she tries to act like he didn't. Don was definitely a good looking man though, I'll give him that. Don was about five foot ten, I believe he's German and Irish and still had a head full of hair even though he was sixty years old. He had charisma and honestly every woman in the office wanted to have sex with him at some point, but he was so in love with Val. Val called him out on his shit, but she did it in a way that Don loved which included her rawness and realness. He actually loved that he had to do more than flash his money, suits and title to impress her. Val was able to get Don to loosen up like the time she got him to do karaoke at the staff Christmas party last year which was hilarious. But I really liked them together. I knew he was married, but from what Val told me, it sounded like his wife was already out the door anyway. She felt that Don travelled too much for work and she just never felt connected to his lifestyle. She was always so antisocial at work events and quite honestly she had no style, and no ass, which I think is a "no-no" if you're going to be the wife of a fine ass executive director. Val really appreciated Don's work ethic and even encouraged it. She was Don's cheerleader even though she had to do it behind closed doors.

"Well, thank you, Don. I'm always appreciative of your confidence in me and letting me have free reign over the Leadership Gala every year. There's always this unspoken dialogue going on between Don and I. Many times I'm thinking, so you gonna just fuck my girl, get her pregnant and leave her high and dry to get an abortion because you didn't want to lose your job? He gave two shits about his wife, but he loved his job and he loved that paper. He always wanted to be seen with the who's who of the corporate sector. He was definitely a fuckboy in my eyes, but he was also my boss so I had to be cordial and professional at all times even though I wanted to rip his head off.

"Lita, can you close my door?" Don asked seriously.

As I began to close Don's door, I started to take in the gorgeousness of his office seeing that I didn't spend much time in there. Don had a sweet set-up in his corner office on the 19th floor overlooking the Magnificent Mile. The skyline of the city was absolutely amazing even during the day time. Even though I was born and raised in Chicago, I was always taken aback by how beautiful my city was. Don was a jazz head so he always played a little Boney James or Joe Sample quietly in his office.

"Is everything okay?" I asked nervously while sitting down and crossing my legs at my ankles seeing that my skirt was not exactly short but not long enough to hide my thick thighs.

"Actually, more than okay." Don scooted closer to his desk while folding his hands.

"Steve and I were talking and we're looking to have you head our fundraising committee over in the Atlanta office if you're interested. You have the knowledge, contacts, professionalism and appeal we need to get things really poppin' out there in Atlanta." So, the first thought that ran through my mind is my girl Val really done turned Don out for him to be using the word "poppin". But that was beside the point, oh my God, Atlanta? I love Atlanta and I sure do have some amazing contacts out there. And if Steve, the CEO of Global Connections is co-signing my involvement in this, I must be really on my way! But what does this mean for my business? If I get wrapped up in this, I really won't have time to focus on a business plan and launching my own project. And even though I liked Atlanta, will I have to move there to do this job?

Mike is definitely not looking to move to Atlanta. He is very secure in his work and I just can't see him giving up any of his career goals for mine.

"I don't know what to say?"

"How about yes." Don flashed a bit of a smile and at that moment, I could see what drew Val to him.

"I'm extremely flattered, but the first thought that came to my mind was; will I have to move?"

"Not at all. There is a bit of travel involved but we are well aware of how much your family means to you. I really respect your husband Mike as a businessman and I truly appreciate the contributions Chase Construction has made to Global Connections. Steve and I talked extensively about how to make this work for you because we really value you here and your role as Fundraising Coordinator. We've even designed a specific itinerary for the days that possibly your husband and kids can travel with you."

Wow, now this was a side of Don I had never seen before. He always seemed pretty uptight and honestly, not as caring. But it was really refreshing to see him in this light but this offer just seemed too good to be true. I needed to know more details.

"If you don't mind my asking, I thought this would be an assignment for Natalia, seeing that she is the SFC?" which was an acronym for Senior Fundraising Coordinator.

"I appreciate your concern and being quick on your feet for recognizing that. Natalia has had some hardships between you and I. It's not exactly public knowledge, but she has decided to resign due to some health challenges. We just want to get a head start on filling that Senior Fundraising Coordinator position and we would like you to be the one to fill it." Don stated with a concerned yet we need to move on this quickly tone.

I couldn't believe my ears. Natalia always seemed like the beacon of health. She was the gorgeous model type, size six with curves in all the right places, hazel eyes and the most beautiful accent as she was from Panama. Natalia was always a big advocate of working out and she and I even hit the gym in our company's basement during our lunch hour sometimes. Now, I wasn't a size six, but don't get it twisted, Lita Baby kept it tight and right, but I just had a thicker frame. But I respected Natalia and learned a lot from her. I felt like I needed to talk to her first before even considering the job, but Don said it was not yet public knowledge.

"Don, thank you so much for the vote of confidence. Can I have some time to think about it? I want to discuss this with Mike first and just weigh everything before making my final decision."

"Of course. I totally admire the relationship you and Mike have and the way you think about your family's needs while still pursuing your career goals. It's very refreshing to see that those kinds of women still exist." Don stated as if he was deep in thought about something. I wasn't sure where this conversation was going but it was starting to feel awkward because I could tell he was thinking about the dissatisfaction with his wife considering everything Val told me.

"Thank you so much, Don. This sounds like a great opportunity for me so I will definitely think about it."

"Okay, well don't think too long because I don't want you to talk yourself out of it," Don laughed. "And we have to make a decision by next Monday so how about you give me an answer at the gala on Saturday?"

"Sounds like a plan Don, and again, thank you."

"No, thank *you* for your hard work and dedication to this organization. You've helped raise a tremendous amount of money for the students we serve so you deserve this Lita." I was really impressed with Don and I felt like I was beginning to really see his human side.

"Oh, one more thing". I said to Don as I stood up from my chair.

"What's that?"

"Is there a pay increase associated with this promotion?"

"I was wondering when you were going to ask," Don said with a smile.

"Yes, there is a significant pay increase. I believe you are currently at $75,000 a year correct?"

"That is correct," I said confidently while awaiting the increase in my new position possibly.

"You will get a $50,000 a year increase along with an expense account for travel and a new office down the hall here on the 19th floor."

I was blown away, I didn't expect this at my age. I was only thirty-two and I was really making some great gains. Even though I had not experienced any financial worries since being married to Mike, I spent a lot of money building up the kids' college funds, and paying for my dad's bills since he had that bad accident at work which left him jobless and on disability. The disability checks were barely covering his expenses, so I was the only one taking care of him. My sister would give him money when she could, but she had only owned her salon for two years and she was a single mom raising her daughter with no help from her child's father. This pay increase could possibly help me get my *own* business up and running without Mike's help.

"Your poker face is quite amusing. It's okay to be excited." Don said with a smirk.

"Oh, you noticed that huh?" I said in a nervous tone.

"I did, but its fine. Again, we just feel that you're the best person for the job."

"Thank you."

"No problem at all. Oh, Lita——"

"Yes?" I looked at Don wondering what he could possibly have to say after giving me this news.

"Can you please tell Val I said, I'm sorry?" Don looked extremely concerned, yet sincere.

Oh, this totally caught me off guard. I did not expect this, especially from Don, so I pretended to act like I didn't hear him.

"Excuse me?" I said trying to collect my thoughts.

"Like I said earlier, you have to work on your poker face," Don said while smiling. "I know that you know about Val and I. You all are the best of friends. Not only do I see that but she told me she confided in you and I appreciate your discretion with everything that has happened."

Little did Don know, I did that for Val, not for him, but I appreciated his sincerity.

"Without going into too much detail, I know Val is avoiding me and not returning my calls and for good reason. I totally deserve it. For lack of better words, I was an ass for how I handled the situation and how I let her go as easily as I did. She tries to pretend it doesn't bother her but I know it does and I hate that I was the cause of it. I eventually filed for divorce from Amy as I've known for a long time it needed to be done. Val was never intimidated by my marriage nor did she judge me for my choices. I just needed to file those papers for me so that I could move on. Hopefully, Val will consider coming back into my life. Either way, I knew I needed to get some things straight with myself. I chose this job over her and I know that hurt her tremendously. I can never take that back. I just hope she'll forgive me one day and again, if you can tell her I'm so sorry, I would greatly appreciate it."

Don seriously threw me a curveball and even though I felt like I saw a different side of Don just now, I began to wonder if that's why he offered me this job to get back into Val's good graces because he knows how close we are. But I will not forget how hurt she was about all this. He chose this fancy life over her, he continued to flaunt "Frumpy Amy" in front of her here at work, and he convinced her to get an abortion. But after thinking about what Don said, it almost sounded as if he didn't convince Val to get that abortion. Oh my God, was this really Val's decision and not Don's? I needed to talk to Val!

"No worries Don, I'll see what I can do." I wanted Don to get the impression it wouldn't be that easy to get my girl Val back and that he would have to do a lot for her to even consider listening to a word he said.

* * *

As I approached the expressway on my drive home from work, I could see the traffic that stretched miles ahead and immediately I felt a sense of exhaustion. Thankfully my sister has a pretty flexible schedule and is able to pick up my kids from school and get them started with their homework seeing that I typically don't get home until close to six o'clock every evening. Most of the time, Mike doesn't get home until about eight o'clock so having my sister get the kids settled is always helpful. I wanted to call Mike to talk to him about the job opportunity Don proposed to me earlier just to get his take on things. I guess I could wait until Mike got home from work, but I know Mike, he'll drop his briefcase and shoes at the door, say hello to me and the kids, plop down on the couch, turn on the sports channel and zone out. He won't appear interested at all in what I have to say until he's awakened from his "nap" around ten at night and then he'll become preoccupied with working in his office. I really want Mike's undivided attention when telling him about the new position as Senior Fundraising Coordinator. Part of me is a little torn between taking the position as I want to focus on starting my own business, but at the same time, taking the job would mean more funds for me to start my business without having to depend on Mike. An added perk of taking this opportunity would be to travel and explore on my own. I've been a parent since I was twenty years old and I've been married for almost just as long. It's been a while since anything has just been about me. I love my family of course, but I feel like everything has revolved around Mike and the kids and I just want it to be about me for once.

"Hey, Lita Baby, what's up?" Mike sounded exhausted on the other end as I called him from the car while stuck in traffic.

"You know it's always bumper to bumper around this time of day. But I have some very interesting news to share with you."

"Oh, you do? Well, I'm all ears. I just wrapped up an intense meeting a few minutes ago with one of our clients, but it's nice to hear your sweet voice." I could tell Mike was spent by the way he sounded on the phone.

"Are you sure you want to talk now? Would you rather wait until we got home?

"Believe it or not, I hate when you do that. I want to hear what you have to say. I know you can probably tell I'm tired, but tell me what's going on?"

"Okay, well, Don called me in his office today."

"Oh, how is Don doing by the way?" All of a sudden Mike's voice perked up as Mike and Don had become pretty good acquaintances after Chase Construction made that hefty donation to Global Connections a few years ago. Don had even invited Mike over to his downtown condo for a poker night with the guys, so they've been pretty cool ever since. I never told Mike about Don's affair with Val as I just thought the least amount of people knowing about their relationship the better.

"He seems fine but he surprised me today when he offered me a promotion as Senior Fundraising Coordinator."

"Wow that is interesting news. I thought Natalia was the SFC?"

"Well, that's what I asked him, but he said it wasn't public knowledge yet. He said Natalia was experiencing some recent health problems and would be resigning soon."

"Wow, I wouldn't have even thought that about her. She always looks so good."

"Uum excuse me?" I asked with a slight jealous tone.

"You know what I mean. You know she ain't got nothing on you. I was just saying that she doesn't look sick enough to resign from her job. It just seems left field. You all have worked so closely together on various projects and you never mentioned her being sick."

"Exactly, that's what I was thinking when Don told me."

"So tell me more about what the job entails."

"Well, the whole conversation started with Don giving me kudos regarding how I've planned this year's Leadership Gala and the previous galas that I've coordinated and how much money I've brought to the organization. He also told me that he wants me to head the fundraising committee at the Atlanta office."

"So he wants you to relocate?" Mike sounded concerned.

"No, actually my office would still be based here in Chicago, but there would definitely be some traveling involved, more than I've done in the past. He even mentioned that he would have an itinerary for me if you and the kids were ever able to travel with me."

"I'm liking the sounds of this so far, even though it may be hard for me to travel with you at times. It would be nice though to have an excuse to get out of town for leisure even though you know I don't really care for ATL. Well, I have to ask. Does this promotion involve a raise because I can't have people working my Lita hard without the proper compensation?"

Mike was definitely a smart businessman who knew his worth when it came to his career, so I'm not surprised he responded that way.

"Yes, Mike, as a matter of fact, I will be getting a $50,000 increase with an expense account and a new office on the 19th floor same as Don with a very nice view."

"Well, Damn! I think I'm feeling this so far."

"There's one thing though, Mike."

"What's the catch, baby?"

"There's no catch, it's just I don't know if this is what I want to do?"

"What do you mean? You are the best damn fundraising coordinator I know. You know how to utilize your contacts and just like Don said, your galas are the truth. The donations that you've brought in is because of *your* hard work. Quite honestly, it seems like a no-brainer to me."

Wow, Mike was really giving me major points. I typically don't hear him pump me up like that. I'm so used to hearing people recognize Mike for his career moves and how smart of a businessman *he* is.

"Well, I know I haven't mentioned this in a while but I still want to start my marketing and public relations firm and I think if I take this position it will consume all of me and I won't have time to work on my business goals."

"I thought we talked about this. I'm just not comfortable with backing the whole marketing firm thing with my money——"

"Wow Mike, seriously?" I found myself starting to get frustrated and typically when I began to feel like this, our conversations usually didn't end well.

"Seriously, what?" Mike said with a dismissive tone.

"First of all, it's not a marketing firm thing, like it's some kind of hobby. You just said it yourself, my galas are the truth and you know my connections are solid and I definitely know how to get people to open their wallets. So c'mon!" My voice was starting to elevate.

"I already see where this is going. I can hear it all in your voice. You're getting too emotional about this and this is one of the reasons why I just don't think you're ready for this entrepreneurship lifestyle and I will not put my hard earned money into this."

"You just reminded me of how much little faith you have in me. And honestly Mike, I don't need your damn money to start the business anyway. I'm going to take that job and I'm going to use my own increase in pay to fund my business without your help."

"Fine. If you want to waste your money on that, that's up to you. Even though I thought we agreed that we wouldn't speak in reference to *our* money ever being separate remember? You said you wanted us to share everything when we first got married."

"And maybe that's the problem. So many things have changed in the ten years that we've been married. And don't forget you just told me that you didn't want to spend *your* hard earned money on my business thing, so I'm just giving you back what you're dishing out."

"You're really tripping right now. I thought things were getting better with us. I just feel like you've been different and I can never follow what you're going to say or do from one moment to the next."

"Oh, I'm acting differently?" I was getting really upset now.

"Where has the Mike that I married been for the past three years? Oh, that's right, you've been so consumed with Chase Construction that you've been practically invisible. And it's okay for you to be serious about your career and what you want to do but it's not for me. And when was the last time you've taken the boys out and bonded with them a little bit? You want them to be little reflections of you all the damn time but you're not around to train them. They're getting older and I can't teach them how to be men. And when was the last time you lifted a finger to clean up around the house? And don't feed me that bullshit about hiring a housekeeper when the last one we hired was too busy trying to impress you with her titties that she couldn't even do the damn job so of course, I fired her ass. I can clean my own damn house. And let's not even talk about how lazy you've been during sex——"

"Okay Lita, I suggest you stop now. You're getting real comfortable saying what's on your mind and all but you really need to chill the fuck out. We'll finish this conversation when I get home, and when you've had a moment to calm your damn nerves."

And all of a sudden I heard silence, Mike had hung up on me. I was pissed! He has a lot of nerve talking to me like I was a little girl throwing a temper tantrum when he fails to realize I get this way when he doesn't acknowledge my feelings and dismisses my ideas. In one moment he's pumping me up about this job because of course it makes him look good and it keeps his relationship with my bosses tight, but then the next minute when I want to step out on my own and really show people what I'm capable of as an entrepreneur, he totally acts like it's a hobby. I'm so upset and I feel like crying but I'm tired of hurting and trying to get Mike to see things from my point of view. After I get out this damn traffic, I think I'll just go to the bookstore. That always relaxes me.

* * *

Surprisingly, the bookstore wasn't too crowded this evening. Maybe because it was a Monday night? I'm not sure why but I liked it. I needed some time to myself to regroup especially before I got home to the kids. They could always tell when something was bothering me and I just didn't want them to worry. I found a comfortable reclining accent chair that was calling my name and as soon as I sat down, every muscle in my body just seemed to loosen and relax on site. I let out a deep sigh and cozied up with a self-help book which was typically one of my favorite genres to read. Before I knew it, my eyes started getting heavier and heavier and I had drifted off to sleep. I didn't even realize I was so exhausted.

"Hey, sleeping beauty." I thought I was having a dream when I heard a man's voice.

I slowly opened my eyes to see Law standing in front of me! Shit! I tried to act like I was brushing my hair out of my face, but what I was really doing was checking to see if I had drool on my cheek as I didn't realize how long I had been sleeping.

"Oh wow, hey Law." I was feeling kind of embarrassed while trying to straighten out my top as I had gotten so comfortable one of the middle buttons on my blouse was undone.

"You must've had a long day," Law said with a smile and actually looking quite refreshed and well rested.

"You can say that. I guess I didn't realize how tired I was.

But *you*, on the other hand, look like you've experienced the luxury of eight hours of sleep." I said a bit sarcastically.

"I'll take that as a compliment." Law smiled as he revealed those beautiful, straight white teeth that I was extremely impressed with.

"Well, you should. Myself on the other hand—"

"Is as beautiful as ever." Law interrupted my statement as if he knew I was preparing to say something about myself that wasn't exactly positive.

"Thank you. You're too kind."

"So I'm curious, its eight o'clock and you're clearly taking a much needed nap in the bookstore because you're exhausted. What's going on?"

As much as I wanted to talk to Law about how I was really feeling, I didn't know him. And honestly, did he even really care? I practically threw my panties at him with all of my subtle advances when we first met. I'm pretty sure he just wants to get some. And I'm not naive, I couldn't even be mad at him if that was all he wanted but I definitely wasn't going to assume he just wanted to talk and try to understand my feelings.

"Well, thanks so much for your concern. I just had a long day at work that's all and I probably should be heading home."

"What kind of work do you do?"

So I clearly just said I should be heading home but I was loving the fact that Law wanted to know more. It didn't bother me at all that he asked.

"I'm a Fundraising Coordinator for a nonprofit organization."

"Wow that seems like a noble position."

"I don't know if I would say all that. It still boils down to trying to get people's money of course."

"Well, you have a point there."

We both kind of laughed in sync. And then there was a bit of a stare on both of our parts.

"Well, Law I really have to go it's getting late and my kids are probably wondering where I am."

"Oh, you have kids too?"

"I sure do. You sound surprised."

"No", Law chuckled. I was just thinking you're a pretty hot looking mom but I probably should've kept that comment to myself."

"I'm actually flattered, thanks for the compliment." I smiled but tried not to exude too much excitement.

"Well, before you go. I know you have my number and there's no pressure at all to use it. I just thought it was kind of nice running into you again. As a matter of fact, it was a very pleasant surprise. So do you work in this area? Maybe, I can meet you sometime and take you out for lunch? You seem like you could use a little break from time to time, if that's okay?"

God, this man was so fine. And even though I approached him the other day when we met at this very same bookstore, I knew that meeting up with Law for lunch was probably not the best idea especially with how I was feeling about Mike at the moment, but it *would* just be lunch? And we *would* be in a public place? And it *would* just look like a business meeting, right? I was really trying to convince myself that allowing Law to take me out was purely platonic even though I knew it wasn't.

"Actually, that sounds like a great idea." Wow, did I just agree to this?

"Oh cool, I honestly didn't expect you to say yes?" Law looked pleasantly surprised.

"Haven't you heard of the law of attraction?" I kind of laughed to myself when I said that knowing his name was Law but still thinking it was rather corny nonetheless.

"Yes, I have. What made you ask that?"

"Well, if you wanted to meet with me, you should have expected a yes in order to attract what you wanted."

"Well, I guess I didn't need the law of attraction then because I didn't think you were going to say yes and you did anyway which means that you were possibly doing the attracting for the both of us."

Hmmm, that was nice how he flipped that on me. I liked his quick comeback.

"Think about where you'd like us to meet up and maybe just send me a text this evening or tomorrow morning and we'll go from there."

I was really feeling this. He seemed so carefree like he wasn't bound by a schedule like myself. I wondered what he did for a living, what his life was like? Did he have kids? How old was he? Did he have a wife hidden somewhere he so conveniently did not bring up? There were so many questions running through my head. I guess I'll find out more when we see each other at lunch.

CHAPTER

3

"Hey, Lele, You look exhausted." My sister always had a way with words especially when I didn't feel like being bothered.

"Thanks, you look rather exhausted yourself," I said with much attitude.

"Heffa, I was just recognizing the obvious, but since you wanna get all stank on me right now——"

"Seriously, Niecey? Can you at least refrain from calling me a heffa in my own damn house, especially while my kids are around?"

"Oh really? Are you referring to the kids I pick up and help with homework everyday since you and Mike are so damn busy living the lives of the rich and fabulous up in this motherfucker?"

Why did Niecey always have to get so extra about every little thing? Always trying to win a damn argument.

"We're really going there right now? All I ask is that you don't insult me as soon as I walk through the damn door."

"See, sometimes we just really have different perspectives on things. I wasn't trying to make you feel bad. I just noticed you looked tired and I figured you were going to be a little out of it when you called to tell me you were stuck in traffic so I went in that fancy little kitchen of yours to make you that bougie chamomile tea with chai or whatever the hell ya'll be drinking in this house."

"There you go again. You always gotta come with the insults and talking shit because of what I have."

"Oh, if you implying a bitch is jealous, I'm not! I'd rather have my Hennessy after work anyway, but I know ya'll don't keep that real shit up in here but I'm trying to be respectful and all by making you some tea."

When I looked at Niecey's face, she actually did seem a bit hurt and I could always read my baby sis so I apologized.

"Look, I'm sorry. I had a long day. The executive director offered me a promotion with a $50,000 increase. I don't know how I'm going to do this and juggle trying to start my marketing firm. Mike is upset because he wants me to take the job even though I told him I didn't know if I wanted to."

"So, you're trying to tell me you had a rough day because you got offered a damn promotion, making more money than you already are and Mike wants you to take it? I'm sorry, I don't get what's upsetting you. Some of the things you get frustrated about, I just don't understand."

Again, Niecey and I just have different perspectives like she said. She thinks my life is so great because of how much money we have and because Mike secretly wants me to be a stay-at-home mom like his mama was. Mike knew from the jump I wasn't going for that. He is encouraging this new job offer because of the money and prestige, which is what Mike is all about.

"Niecey," I said with an exhausted tone and thinking she just wouldn't understand anything I was trying to say anyway. "What about independence and creativity?"

"So, you're trying to tell me that your new position won't afford you more independence and creativity? Look at how you've worked your magic at that old dried out place. Because of you, Global Connections has top notch donors and also because of you, they have been able to attract a new and exciting breed of younger employees. They value you and they're willing to pay you for it! And don't get me started on Mike. Yeah, ya'll argue and disagree sometimes, but what married couple doesn't? He's a good dude, definitely not like these sorry niggas I be attracting. So what if he doesn't want to spend money on you starting a business? He was born and raised in that whole corporate world. I think he could see if using ya'll money to start a business in this day and time was not a good decision. His whole damn family is like the fucking Huxtables and you see how they turned out because they're smart, they know the game. Why don't you just trust him on this?"

See, the problem with Niecey is she just assumes that if a guy is working and ain't spending all his money at the strip club, then he's a real good dude. She's never had anything better so she doesn't have too many standards. I believe in me and this marketing firm, but Mike doesn't. That shit hurts and it makes me pull away from him. I'm always supposed to support every single decision he makes and I'm tired of it. And quite honestly, I'd rather not even talk to Niecey about this because she comes off as real basic at times. I'm surprised she wouldn't support what I'm doing seeing that she owns her own salon.

"So, how's the salon coming along?" I said totally changing the subject.

"Oh, so you don't wanna talk about that no more, huh?

Okay, anyway, the salon could be a lot better. Bitches don't wanna come to their appointments on time and then wanna start shitting on us and our reputation when we start on someone else's head. I had to increase the booth rent because Chicago's business taxes are too damn high, so I've been losing some real solid stylists. I'm getting audited soon and I'm kind of nervous because I allowed Juju to use my salon a few times to clean his money. I know, it's a dumb mistake, but the salon took a huge hit and I really needed an extra come up really quick. See this that shit you don't have to deal with, because you have a degree and you have a good job and you have a good man. This owning a business ain't all it's cracked up to be but I can't have nobody running me and the only real skill I got is doing hair."

"First of all, did you say Juju?" Juju was Niecey's baby's daddy who she swore she wasn't going to mess with anymore after he slept with one of her clients. Niecey beat her client's ass but ended up giving Juju another chance when he said it was over. But then just weeks later, Niecey saw her client on Facebook referencing her new "boo" with a picture of just their hands and she recognized Juju's tattoo so she ended it for good, well at least I thought.

"You something else. I'm out here being transparent trying to vibe with your ass and that's all you heard was Juju? Anyway, yes, Juju has been coming back around but I ain't been giving him shit, I just needed some money. I told you the salon took a huge hit when some of my stylists left. I asked Juju to help me out and he did it with no questions asked." Niecey was talking about Juju as if he was the damn love of her life and that he would do anything for her.

"Of course, he was gone do it Nieceyyy, you cleaning his drug money for God's sake! Why didn't you just ask me for it?"

"So you can come in and save the day and then everyone can see how pitiful my life has turned out right?"

"Oh, here we go again with the comparisons. Ain't nobody saying that! I would rather you come to me than risk going to jail, damn!"

"I know! Do you always have to remind me of how I'm fucking up, Lita?"

"Okay, let's just take a step back. This is a serious issue and I don't want us arguing right now. We just need to come up with a plan. You know Mike's friend, Drew, right?"

"Girl, how could I forget? His fine ass was at that big 30th birthday party Mike threw for you right?"

"Yes, but stay focused."

"Uum, I am. Just because I'm going through doesn't mean I can't notice how sexy he is. Anyway, what about him?"

"Well, Drew is an accountant, he may be able to help you out with a few things."

"Hmmm, who would've thought Drew had a little street knowledge in him to help me clean this shit up?"

"I ain't talking about him helping you do some more illegal shit. But he may have some good suggestions."

"Whatever, yes, please call his sexy ass and then tell him to call me ASAP. Maybe we can get together for a drink at that spot in the West Loop that I like." Niecey had a mischievous look on her face that said that she was only trying to see what Drew was working with.

"Earth to Niecey, let's get you out of this mess before you let him hit, okay?"

"Ha! See you know me well because you know imma put it on him so he can't refuse. But honestly, I ain't got time for no sprung niggas in my life right now. I just need to make this money."

"Okay, whatever. Let me go check on my babies. And I'm sorry about earlier, I've just been having a lot going on."

"Don't even trip, I'm already past it. You just need to relax. Let somebody else carry the load for once. You work like crazy, you take care of your family and let's not forget daddy's old ass even though I love him he can be a bit much. When was the last time you've been pampered?"

While Niecey was talking, I started thinking about Law. Maybe that could be my form of pampering? I just got the sense that I could get lost in him which is probably why I've been so hesitant about reaching out to him.

* * *

"Hey, baby." Mike walked in the front door as Niecey was leaving out. Niecey and Mike were cool but Mike always kind of looked at Niecey as if she was beneath him. Even though he never admitted it to me, I could sense it. Mike and Niecey rarely had anything to say to each other. Before I could greet Mike, the kids ran up to him and started bombarding him with things they wanted him to buy.

"Kids, it's past your bedtime. Go put your pajamas on and you can talk to Daddy about whatever you want to talk to him about tomorrow."

"Thanks for handling the kids. I'm just too exhausted to answer any of their questions right now."

I didn't even send Sheree, Tariq and Rashad upstairs for him. I honestly did that so they wouldn't notice how pissed off I was with Mike right now. I didn't say a word when he thanked me.

"Oh, so you gonna give me the silent treatment?"

"I'm not trying to give you the silent treatment. I just don't know what to say. You hung up on me earlier, remember?"

"Yeah, about that, I'm sorry. I just felt like you were starting to go real hard on me and I ain't trying to argue no more. Seriously, on my way home, all I kept thinking about was how you started talking about sex and I thought we had a really good time at the hotel the other night. I wasn't lazy with how I was putting it down that night, was I?"

Again, all Mike got out of that conversation was his sex game. It wasn't just about sex! The other night was about him actually making me a priority, talking to me and basically being available to me emotionally. He's still not acknowledging me as being capable to handle my own business and it's irritating the fuck outta me!

"No, you weren't being lazy." I said that just to stop the conversation. I didn't feel like going back and forth with Mike tonight because I already knew how he felt about me starting my own business so what was the point? I began walking up the stairs.

"I'm going to take a shower right quick and head to bed. I've had a bit of a long day myself."

"Is that an invitation for me to join you?" Mike was smiling as if all was forgotten. He still didn't realize how much him not supporting me was affecting me. Right now, the thought of Mike's hands on me just made me feel uncomfortable. I wasn't open to him right now but I always made a point to have sex with him even when I didn't feel like it because I wasn't going to be the cause of him looking to another woman to satisfy his needs. I just wished he felt the same about me and gave me what I needed so I didn't seek that validation elsewhere.

As Mike laid on top of me and began thrusting, I just couldn't get in the mood. I wasn't even throwing it back to him.

"Lita baby, you okay?" Mike asked while still grinding on top of me.

"I guess I'm just tired and it's kind of thrown off my mood."

"What you need for me to do, Lita? I got you, whatever you want."

I knew Mike didn't really mean that but I was going to test it tonight.

"How about you go down on *me* tonight?"

"I mean, I've been inside you and I don't like doing that after I've been all in you," Mike said as if he was trying to get out of it.

"Mike, I can go wash up, that's no problem." I made that suggestion quickly because Mike wasn't going to disappoint me yet again.

"Okay, I'll be waiting." I heard the words but Mike didn't sound too convincing.

I washed up quickly but efficiently. I definitely did not mess with Summer's Eve or whatever that shit was that some chicks be putting up there. It can throw off your whole pH vibe so I stuck with the normal wiping the outer parts of my vagina and I always smelled and tasted my own self down there so I knew it was all the way right. It's not like I had a group of niggas running up inside me. I took two showers a day, I carried baby wipes and I always wiped front to back. I was definitely good.

"Okay, I'm back," I said with a little bit of excitement that Mike was somewhat willing.

"You all good?" Mike asked as if he wasn't sure if I really cleaned myself up properly.

"Uum yes, I'm good." I said trying to reassure him.

As Mike approached me, he started kissing me on my neck which always helped me get in the mood. Mike's face started going lower and lower until his mouth touched my pelvic area which felt really good. Mike noticed my excitement so he kept kissing my pelvis, maybe a little more than I hoped but I didn't want to rush him because I wanted him to enjoy it as well. As Mike started kissing my clitoris, he said: "Do you like that?"

"Yes, that's good Mike," I said trying to encourage him but I wanted less talking and more doing. I noticed Mike was kind of pecking the clitoris instead of massaging it with his tongue. Now, of course, I didn't want him to be too aggressive with it either as that's a big no no, but it's as if he was afraid to explore all of me down there. And I'm just lying here thinking this is pitiful. We have been married for ten years and Mike still does not know how to please me the way I like. But it's up to me to guide him so I was willing to do that tonight.

"Can I ask you to do something for me?" Mike looked up at me like he was starting to get a little frustrated as if I was about to criticize his skills. I tried to approach it as diplomatically as I could. "Can you take your index finger and your middle finger and gently spread the lips apart and lick around the clitoris as well?" I said hoping Mike would give it a try.

"Okay." Mike let out a bit of a frustrated sigh which started to turn me off but I was trying to give him the benefit of the doubt. He looked really awkward down there and it just didn't seem like he was enjoying it. I could tell he wasn't even giving it much effort. I politely asked Mike to get up.

"What is it now?" Mike said with an upset look on his face.

"Nothing, I just want you inside me that's all." Mike looked as if he knew I was lying but of course, he's not going to turn down sex so we went with it and I just suffered in silence. I wanted to be touched a certain way. I wanted to be pleased without envisioning another man. I wanted to be in the moment with Mike but I just couldn't. A tear almost fell from my eye because I was that frustrated with our sex life. But I held it in and let Mike get his. After Mike orgasmed, he immediately got up to go to the bathroom as if he knew I wasn't into it and I could no longer do this. I had always been a very sexual person, not in terms of sleeping with a lot of people, but I've always enjoyed sex. Most importantly, I had always enjoyed the prelude to sex; the talking, the flirting, and the touching. That always got me in the mood but I'm lucky these days if Mike and I even go out on a date or just get lost in conversation with each other that doesn't revolve around work, the kids and bills. I was just feeling really uneasy about my marriage at this point. Would we ever get past our disagreements and the fact that we're not connecting sexually? I was starting to feel a little worried.

* * *

"Hello!" His voice was so deep and sensual when he answered the phone.

"Hey Law, it's Lita," I said nervously while using my office phone to call Law because I didn't know if I was quite ready for him to have my number.

"Hey, beautiful. It's so great to hear your voice."

"Thank you, that really put a smile on my face this morning. My apologies for calling you so early—"

"No apologies necessary."

"I'm actually in my office right now but before I get bombarded with phone calls and work, I just wanted to see if that offer still stands regarding lunch today, only if your schedule allows. I know it's kind of short notice." I really wanted to see Law but I secretly was hoping he would say he had some things to do so I could get out of it as I was extremely attracted to him.

"I would love to meet you for lunch today. As a matter of fact, I was going to make a few phone calls myself but that most certainly can be moved around for you. Where would you like to meet?"

"Hmmm, there's a really nice bistro about five minutes from my office. We can meet there at noon. I can send you the address?" I was getting even more nervous because Law was still willing to meet and again, how was he able to just quickly rearrange his schedule like that? I was so curious about his life.

"That sounds great. And again, thanks for wanting to meet with me. I'm really looking forward to it. It's been a while since I've had a lunch date that wasn't focused solely on work. It's nice to break up the monotony."

Hmmm, Law really got me to thinking. Was he saying he hadn't been out on a date in a while? Does he meet with married women often? What was his deal? I'm not sure but I was really looking forward to finding out.

"I'm looking forward to it as well. See you at noon."

"Okay see you soon."

Law's voice always mesmerized me. How in the world was I going to make it through a whole entire lunch date with this man? One thing is for sure. I began working very efficiently and tying up all loose ends for the gala on Saturday so that I could just go home after lunch and have some time to myself before Mike and the kids got home. I'd been feeling so spread thin these days and I just needed to be in my quiet home before the kids got out of school. I honestly didn't even plan on meeting Law today. My mood was still a little down about what happened with Mike last night. To make myself feel better when I got up this morning, I put on one of my favorite pencil dresses with the crew neckline and cinched waist, my high heels with the ankle cuffs and pearl earrings. My updo was definitely not anything to sneeze at either. I had finally mastered my natural hair and figured out styles that complimented me the most. I didn't want to look like how I felt. I looked in the mirror and I saw a beautiful, strong, creative and exciting woman. I just felt like Mike didn't see me that way. I honestly felt like he just didn't really "see" me at all. He had kind of grown comfortable with me being his wife as if I was just another achievement like his many achievements at work. He didn't seem to try anymore. It was just bothering me. Maybe having lunch with Law and breaking up the routine at work was just what I needed to get unstuck.

As I entered the bistro, I was thinking to myself, maybe I should've called Law first to let him know that I was walking inside but it didn't matter because as soon as the hostess walked up to me with a menu in her hand, Law approached the hostess and said, "No need to escort her, I got it from here."

Law extended his hand so that I could take his while he smiled at me. The hostess gave me a look like "Right on girl." The hostess and I both smiled at each other as if she could tell I was being kept in good company by a gentleman and a fine one at that.

Law pulled out my chair and helped me sit down first before he took his seat.

"You look absolutely breathtaking I must say."

"Why thank you. You look very handsome yourself," I said with a shy smile.

"You know, I have seen you a total of four times including today and each time you have looked stunning. That dress you had on at the Jazz Bar was definitely top notch. But your business attire even stands out. I see you're a bad woman, Ms. Lita."

The compliments Law was throwing at me really made me feel beautiful and for once in a while adored. It was really nice.

"You're really too kind, but I'm definitely going to accept the compliment. I could use it." I couldn't believe that just came out of my mouth.

"What's wrong, hard day at work?"

"No, it's nothing. Speaking of work, what do you do?" I was trying to change the subject. Law looked like he knew I was trying to change the subject but he didn't pressure me to answer, he just answered my question which I was actually very curious about.

"Well, I'm an entrepreneur. I started an investment firm about 10 years ago and since then, I've opened 2 more offices, one in Vancouver and one in Atlanta."

"Wow, that's amazing! I'm looking to start my own business soon myself."

"Okay cool, in what capacity?"

"I want to start my own marketing firm?" I said very proudly.

"That's great to hear. I can tell you're really excited about it by the way your face lit up just now."

Wow, he noticed that? And he was actually encouraging me to pursue my dream? This was a first and something I definitely wasn't used to.

"Well, I think it's definitely a natural progression with regards to what I do now."

"Oh right, I remember you mentioning that at the bookstore. You're a fundraising coordinator for a non-profit right?"

Well, that really made me feel important considering he remembered what I'd told him I did for a living.

"Exactly. I work for a company called Global Connections, Inc. As a matter of fact, we have our annual Leadership Gala coming up this Saturday which I spearhead every year. We have some amazing guests that will be joining us including Sheryl Lee Ralph, a few Channel 5 news anchors, Marjorie Harvey and Corey Holcomb."

"Wow, Corey Holcomb is actually a friend of mine and we've done business together. He's a real solid dude and funny of course."

"I agree. I cry laughing whenever I listen to him."

"That's really cool. You must really be a confident woman not to take his jokes so seriously like some women do."

Law was looking into my eyes and I felt the chemistry all throughout our conversation but I was trying to avoid it.

"I just think he's hilarious and yes, they're just jokes and I love to laugh so it doesn't bother me at all."

"That's nice to know you're not serious all the time. I just think there's a time and place for everything."

"I agree." Law and I were locking eyes again but our connection was soon interrupted by the waitress.

"Hi, my name is Miranda and I'll be your server for today. I would've stopped by earlier but I noticed you two were definitely engrossed in your conversation and I didn't want to interrupt." Miranda said with a smile. I guess our connection was quite noticeable to anyone who might have witnessed. I was just hoping I didn't see anyone I knew. I probably should've chosen a place that wasn't so close to my job but considering I have business lunches from time to time, I would just tell someone that I was meeting with a donor.

"No worries at all Miranda and thank you so much for giving us some time. Please, let the beautiful lady order first." Law said while smiling at me. I just loved his chivalry. It was something I craved that I just hadn't experienced in some time.

"I'll take the chicken caesar salad."

"And would you like our signature caesar salad dressing with that?"

"Yes, I would definitely like that."

"And would you like to try our soup of the day?"

"And what might that be?

"We have a French onion soup served with a fresh baguette that would go great with your salad."

"Hmm, sounds pretty good. I'll definitely give it a try."

"Great choice. And for you sir?"

"Lita, do you have any suggestions? I can't lie, a soup and salad is not going to do it for me right now. I'm a pretty solid guy so I need a little more than that." Law said with a slight grin.

"Well, I'm a seafood girl so I love their gumbo."

"Miranda, the lady has spoken. I'd like to try the gumbo and can I have a Heineken with that as well?"

"Great choice sir. I'll take your menus now."

As Miranda reached for our menus, I couldn't help but notice how handsome Law looked. There was a quiet confidence about him that I admired. He was dressed casually but with a tailored look to him. He was wearing a light blue and white striped collar shirt with a pair of fitted, but not skinny jeans that were of an indigo color.

His brown leather belt matched his oxford shoes and he was wearing a gray cardigan. He definitely had style and great taste and I was flattered that he liked my style as well. He looked like he recently shaved and of course, he smelled so good.

"Would you like a drink as well? Oh, I'm sorry I forgot this is your lunch break. You probably don't want to drink during work hours."

"It's fine. I'm actually taking the rest of the day off to relax and just have some *me* time so with that being said, I think I'll definitely have a lemon drop martini."

"I'll be sure to put that martini in for you. The lemon drop martinis here are very popular." Miranda was definitely a nice and attentive waitress.

"Aww, look at you. I like that in you. It's important to rejuvenate and take care of yourself. Work is important but trust me, it'll always be there. And you have little ones so you definitely need to have the energy for them, I'm sure."

Oh my God, a man that was encouraging me to take care of myself? And he made reference to my kids and knowing that I even needed a break from them sometimes? Who was this guy?

"So, do you have any children?" I said anxiously awaited his response.

"I sure do. I have two beautiful daughters but they're grown now of course. I'm also a grandad, and a proud one at that."

"Wow, I never would've thought you had grandchildren. If you don't mind my asking, how old are you?"

"I don't mind at all. You can ask me anything. But to answer your question, I'm fifty eight. I have a thirty-five year old daughter and my youngest daughter is thirty-two. I have four grandchildren. Does my age turn you off by any chance?"

"No, not at all. I'm actually very impressed!" Maybe I sounded a little too eager when I said that.

"Now why is that? You didn't expect an almost sixty year old to look like me huh?" Law said with a touch of arrogance but it was cute.

"Well, it's just that your youngest daughter and myself are the same age and yes, you look hot for an almost sixty year old. I'm sorry, did that make you uncomfortable?"

"No, not at all. I'm flattered and many times people don't think I'm the age that I am. But getting back to you. You definitely seem very mature for your age and you seem like you've accomplished a lot with regards to your career all while having children as well. So *I'm* impressed!"

I was definitely enjoying our conversation and I was loving the attention I was getting from Law. It was that feeling of an exciting first date and the butterflies that accompany the new stages of a relationship. The only thing is, I was married and immediately that changed my mood.

"So, how long have you been married?"

Wow, that was left field and kind of spooky considering I was just thinking about.

"Well, I didn't expect that question. But I've been married for ten years." This conversation seemed to take an uncomfortable turn.

"I didn't mean to catch you off guard. I just know that has kind of been the elephant in the room since we got here and I wanted to go ahead and talk about it because clearly, it's no secret that I'm very attracted to you. But I want you to be comfortable with us going to lunch like this. I don't want you to feel on guard with me. I understand the situation and I respect it."

I found Law's forwardness refreshing but what was he insinuating when he said "situation?"

"What do you mean?"

"Well, when we met at the bookstore, your beauty captivated me right away so when you stated to me that you thought I was attractive, it kind of made me feel at ease knowing that you were attracted to me too. But then you reminded me at the bar the other night you were married so I thought maybe you had a change of heart but now we're here."

I didn't know how to interpret this whole conversation. I had never been in a situation like this before. This was all pretty new to me but was he trying to say he was married too and he himself had a "situation?"

"So are you married too?"

"No, I'm divorced. I've been married twice. The first time I was married for about thirteen years and the second time I was married for five."

"Well, I don't have a "situation", I'm just———"

"It's okay and I apologize if I made you uncomfortable. You do not have to explain anything to me. Just know that I understand. This can be what you want it to be. If you just want to have lunch for now and it not be too heavy, I'm totally fine with that. We don't have to do anything you don't want to do."

This was such an interesting conversation to me. I loved how attentive Law was being but he seemed to be very casual about us possibly having an affair? Is this how a lot of married people are getting down these days for him to talk about this so casually?

"I'm just going through a lot. I love my job I do, but I need more. I know I can be successful at running my own business but my husband doesn't believe in me and he doesn't want to put the money behind it and so I'm considering taking this promotion because I'll be making so much more money and then I can fund it myself. And it's really sad that it has to be this way, together we make really good money. And I'm so embarrassed that I just told you all of this on our first time out. I'm so sorry."

"Like I said, no apologies necessary. I could sense you had some things on your mind."

"Wow, was it that obvious?"

"No, I wouldn't say it's that obvious to the everyday person but I'm in tune with you right now and I could feel there were some things going on. Look at it this way, from what you told me, you have a real knack for getting people to donate money to the nonprofit and that definitely takes a great deal of expertise and of course marketing, so clearly, you have that skill. But like you said, you do need money and maybe taking that promotion at work could be the best thing for you if your husband is not ready to fund it. For those that aren't entrepreneurs, it's kind of hard for them to see the vision like you do but you can't exert too much energy trying to convince someone of your dream. If you feel this business is the right step for you, then you need to do it and you *can* do it, Lita."

"I really needed to hear that right now because it's been hard. I'm always trying to consider how this affects everyone else except for me and I just finally want to do what I want for once."

"Well, maybe this is your time. So just breathe, you got this. And if there's anything I can help you with, please don't hesitate to ask. Since this is your first business, I would love to help you get started and hopefully help you avoid some of the pitfalls I experienced when I first started."

"I really like the sound of that and thank you, that means a lot."

"Let's cheers to your new business because you will succeed. I'm hoping this is the beginning of a beautiful friendship."

We couldn't help but laugh at the *Casablanca* reference. And for the first time in a long time, I felt very relaxed. This was really nice.

CHAPTER

4

Today was the big day, The Leadership Gala. The decor of the banquet hall was just how I imagined it. Everything from the twenty foot ceilings to the window treatments and decorative lighting made the entire space come alive. The seating and centerpieces provided a certain *je na sais quoi* that only my favorite planners could pull off. Mandy and Jim were a dynamic duo who planned some of the most prestigious events in the Chicagoland area and they always made themselves available for my events.

There were some very important people in the room; making connections, networking, laughing and schmoozing. The vibe was amazing as the live band provided the sounds of contemporary and traditional jazz music as the backdrop for the evening. We also had some surprise entertainment, including The Roots who were the official house band on The Tonight Show, starring Jimmy Fallon and Jazmine Sullivan who was scheduled to grace the audience with her soul singing vocals. Oh, yes, Lita is the truth, honey. I came so correct with this gala this year. I have to admit, I was impressed with what I pulled off and as I continued to walk through the crowd, I could actually see how much money was being generated from this one night alone. This had certainly been one of my biggest accomplishments to date.

"Everything looks beautiful, baby," Mike said to me while kissing my cheek.

"Thanks, hun." I smiled as I decided to remain in a state of gratitude as Mike being here really meant a lot to me. He seemed thoroughly impressed by my work. Mike totally fits in with this crowd. This environment is always his cup of tea. He loved wearing suits and talking business with others. He loves to feel important and rarely does he not associate with movers and shakers.

Yes, Mike was indeed a bit of a snob but he couldn't help it. He was practically taught from birth the difference between a salad fork and a dinner fork, he owned a pair of cufflinks at the age of ten and he graduated from Yale. This was most certainly his crowd. I was not always accustomed to this way of life. I had to learn on the job so to speak but I didn't mind. It helped me become more well-rounded and maneuver any crowd.

"I see some golfing buddies here so I'm going to talk to them. Baby, you look so beautiful tonight and you really did your thing this year. I'm really proud of you."

I appreciated Mike's kind words but I got the sense that when he said he was proud of me, the energy behind it felt more like he was talking to one of our kids instead of a grown woman who is well versed in her craft. Oh well, maybe I'm reading too much into this and maybe I'm just still feeling the hurt from Mike not supporting my dream in opening up my own marketing firm. I tried to not let it upset me and destroy my night.

As I looked out of the beautiful, large bay windows of the banquet hall, I couldn't help but notice how exotic the landscape looked covered with a small sheet of freshly fallen white snow and ground solar lights. It was the early part of December, just in time for the holidays and for a split second, my mind wandered to Law. The music being played made me think of him and his style. He was so handsome, mature, stylish, professional and just fucking hot. But he had a side to him that seemed like he grew up like I did. He appeared to have a street edge but because of growth, he doesn't let that get the better part of him and that intrigued me so much. I just wanted to see him, dance with him and feel him. I felt my phone vibrate in my hand. I looked down and I couldn't believe it. It was a text from Law. Oh my God, did I literally just manifest this man? I forgot that I had actually given him my number when we were out to lunch.

"Lita, I don't mean to interrupt. I know you mentioned your gala was tonight but I ran into one of my clients who was invited. He said he could no longer attend and wanted to gift me with a ticket. I stared at that ticket for some time as I was considering attending but I didn't want to put you in an uncomfortable position."

I wanted to see him so badly. What harm would it do if he attended? I'm pretty sure he would probably see a lot of people he knew and would camouflage within the crowd as Mike would not suspect a thing. It would be really nice to see him. I texted him back before I changed my mind:

"Of course, I would love for you to attend. The jazz band is playing right now and the guests are talking but the program will be starting in about thirty minutes."

Law's iPhone indicated he received my text and he began responding right away. I was so excited, anxious, and nervous at the same time.

"Great, I'm really looking forward to seeing you, and by the way you talked about your work, I can tell tonight is going to be a beautiful evening. I'm really happy for all of your accomplishments and if at all possible, maybe I can even steal a dance if the evening permits."

God, this man just had a way with words. Everything about him made me want to learn so much more. I could only imagine what he would look like once he walked through the door.

"I would like that as well. See you soon."

I started to walk around the room and speak to the guests trying to occupy myself so that I wasn't constantly looking at the clock or the door for Law to show up. My event planners had everything under control so there wasn't much left for me to do but enjoy myself. When I first began this job, I remember being so inexperienced as I was doing so much work by myself and running around with my hair on fire. Though, with time, I definitely morphed into a pretty damn good fundraising coordinator and tonight was the night I would tell Don I would be accepting the position as Senior Fundraising Coordinator.

"Lita, you did that shit." A whisper from behind me, could only be my girl, Val.

"Thank you, mama!" Me and Val hugged and laughed. Val always had my back and was so supportive of me.

"So, you are absolutely working the room like you're working that dress! I see you got the girls peeping out tonight. Now you know these stuffy people up in here are having a heart attack with you showing all your thickaliciousness!"

Val and I made up words all the time, we created our own little language.

"Girl, I'm just glad I can fit a dress like this. I've been really staying on my grind when it comes to working out and keeping my figure tight you know? Things ain't quite snapping back like they used to now that I'm in my thirties so I'm just trying to make sure I work at it."

"Well, you doing it! That red is hot on you and I'm loving your hair. You know with me being mixed, I get this stringy mess on my head but you can do so much with your hair, I love it!"

Val was really making a sista feel good which made me smile, but I also had Law on the brain.

"Uum, why you smiling like that? I mean I know I gave you a compliment and all but it seems like you got something else on your mind like some dick or something."

"Girl, you a trip. You don't hold nothing back." I couldn't help but laugh.

"Well, you know I calls it like I sees it. What? Mike did hit you with a little something before ya'll got here right? I saw him over there smiling too with them corny ass white dudes. Ya'll must be getting it in."

"Girl, please. Mike is happy right now because this is what Mike does, he kisses up to folks. He likes all his golf talk, pretentious ass fake talk."

"Damn, tell me how you really feel?"

"I didn't mean it to come off that way, it's just—"

"You still upset about the business?"

"Hell yeah, I am. I know I can do it, Val. I just want him to believe in me and support me."

"Well, I ain't gonna tell you not to be upset because those are your feelings. But tonight is your night, and you shining baby. Worry about that tomorrow. See, all they serving up in here is wine and champagne and shit. We need to get you a shot of something like for real."

I loved my girl, Val. This is what makes starting a business kind of hard for me because then I would be leaving her. As we were laughing, Don walked up to us and he greeted me with a hug and even though he reached for Val, she stepped back as it was quite apparent she was still hurt by him.

"You ladies look absolutely beautiful tonight. And again, Lita, I can't say it enough, you have outdone yourself with the gala this year. Just when I think it couldn't get any better, she strikes again."

We all smiled even though I knew Val was faking her way through our conversation. I just didn't like seeing her hurt like this.

"Before the night is over, let's be sure to discuss that opportunity we talked about earlier this week."

"Sure thing, Don, and again thank you for the vote of confidence."

"It's my pleasure, you deserve it. And Val, when you get a free moment, can you meet me by the bar?"

"Don, I'm trying to support Lita tonight so—" Val said hesitantly as I never see her get weak in the knees for any man.

"Val, just meet me by the bar in five." Don was stern but he said that in a bit of a sexy tone and then walked off with a stride in his walk like he knew he was the shit.

Val and I both looked at each other with a "well damn" look.

"See, Don gets on my last damn nerve but now he got me all wet and shit. I know that look. He knows I ain't wearing no panties up under this gown. He ain't trying to talk, he trying to fuck and dammit, I'm trying to let him."

"Ha! You two are a mess."

"Well, before I go letting Don get this pussy before this gala starts, seriously what were you thinking about earlier when you were smiling and shit?"

"Girl, nothing, I'm just glad everything is turning out like I envisioned it."

"Yeah, okay, you know I can read you like a damn good Terry McMillan novel."

"Okay, Val," I said sarcastically.

"Ha! Let me go find me some Don and see what the fuck he wants."

"Uum huh, you know what he wants."

"Yeah, I know. I just like playing dumb sometimes with him. It makes the sex that much more exciting."

I just laughed to myself while sipping my champagne. I continued to be in awe of what I had accomplished as I looked around the room. I noticed the time and it had already been thirty minutes since I'd texted Law back.

I wondered where he was and before I could wonder any longer, I could see a tall frame walking towards me in my peripheral view. As soon as I turned around, I felt my stomach drop as Law approached me smiling. He looked so damn good! He was wearing a slim fit two piece black tailcoat. He looked amazing.

"Lita, it's so great to see you." As Law reached for me, I thought to myself should I hug him or not? Will anyone suspect anything? And then I just had too many questions for my damn self and said fuck it and I hugged him. His embrace was always so comforting and strong. He probably hugged me longer than he should have but I didn't care, I just loved being in his arms.

"So did you just get here?" I said with excitement.

"Actually, I've been in the room for about five minutes. I spoke to a few people I knew but I spotted you right away. I couldn't help watching you interact and smile with your guests. You look absolutely amazing. And this gala! You have truly put together something special here tonight. I've been to quite a few galas and fundraisers and I can definitely tell you've got it!"

I felt so overjoyed to hear those words from Law and I appreciated how he could spot my talent. It made me feel so much more beautiful tonight.

"Thank you, that means so much! A sista trying."

"A sista is doing more than trying. You killing that shit, excuse my language."

I didn't give a damn about his language and honestly it turned me on.

"Ha! I like that. Can I get you some champagne?"

"How about I get you some champagne. A woman that looks as beautiful as you should not be serving anything, you should be getting served."

Law said that as if he wanted to rip my clothes off and by the way my body was feeling, I was definitely looking forward to getting served.

I was smiling at Law as he was walking to the bar and when I looked to my left, I noticed Mike was standing next to some guys he was talking to but he had his eyes locked on me as if he noticed me talking to Law. Did he see me smiling at him like I had a school girl crush? Why was he walking over here? Law would be coming back over to me with my champagne in a little bit.

"Lita Baby, you good? How's everything going?" I was nervous Mike noticed something.

"Oh I'm fine, I've just been talking to the guests and of course, Val always has me cracking up." I was hoping one of Mike's golfing buddies would come over to steal him away but they didn't. Law had gotten our drinks from the bartender and was heading back this way. What was I going to do? Okay, Lita, be cool, don't start acting all suspicious and shit, just be cool.

"Here you go, Lita." Law handed me the champagne and when I looked up at my Mike's face, I could tell he noticed that Law was a dude he may have to find out more about so I beat him to it.

"Thank you, Lawrence," I said his full name as to not bring about too much attention.

"Mike, this is Lawrence Davis. He owns an investment firm here in Chicago and has a couple of offices in Atlanta and Vancouver. He's a potential donor of Global Connections." I tried to make Law sound like he was just another business associate and nothing more.

"Nice to meet you my man. I'm Mike, Lita's husband." Mike reached out to give Law a firm, yet you know this is my wife handshake. Usually when I introduce Mike to my business associates, he typically goes into his spiel about being the Senior Vice President of Chase Construction and who he's affiliated with, blah, blah, blah but that was not the vibe I was picking up this time. I guess he noticed another good looking man in the room was talking to me because there damn sure weren't many.

"Nice to meet you. I was just telling Lita how impressed I was with her gala this year." Law said respectfully.

"Oh, so you've been to some of the previous galas?" Mike asked as if he was trying to gather information.

"No, this is actually the first one I've attended for Global Connections, but I have a few friends and clients who are here tonight and they've spoken only great things in reference to Lita's work." Law spoke so confidently and didn't appear to be phased by what Mike was dishing out.

"Most definitely, my wife rocks when it comes to fundraising." Mike grabbed me by my waist and pulled me close and then kissed me on my cheek. He was definitely laying it on thick and trying to mark his territory even though he always seemed to attend my galas to make his own connections instead of supporting me.

"Well, it was nice meeting you Mike and a pleasure to work with you, Lita. I'm going to find my seat before everything gets started." I was hoping Law wasn't put off by Mike's behavior and I really would've loved to sit by him before another woman in the room caught his eye. Law walked over to his table.

"So, I don't think you've mentioned him before," Mike asked with a concerned tone but also as if he was trying to trip me up.

"Well, this year, we had an abundance of donors especially right before the gala and I just really met him so it must've slipped my mind," I said very cool and calmly as to not raise any red flags.

"Oh okay," Mike said as if he was trying to figure me out.

"I see some more business associates I need to connect with. I'll catch up with you in a few."

"But the program is getting ready to start?" I was kind of surprised Mike was darting off yet again but obviously came over to me because he saw Law and wanted to stake his claim.

"I know baby, I'll be over in a few." And just like that, Mike took off. His focus definitely was not on me tonight. This was really starting to get to me and it definitely didn't make it any better that a man like Law wanted to spend time with me. I don't know, I guess I was just feeling a little confused. Maybe if I just sip this champagne I could enjoy the evening. There was a lot of great things on the horizon for me including accepting Don's offer and starting my own business.

* * *

"Girl that gala you put on last night was seriously your best work!" Val sounded so pumped on the phone. It was the morning after the gala and I was extremely tired from all the planning and the week leading up to it. I just wanted to stay in my comfy king size bed and enjoy every inch of it by myself. Mike was already out of the house for a business brunch with some entrepreneurs he connected with at *my* gala. But it was always a good feeling hearing from my girl, Val.

"Girl, thank you. You know the amount of work it took to pull it all together but it definitely went off without a hitch."

"Yes, hunny you did that! And you looked amazing on top of it all! Not a hair out of place, booty and breasts popping. I'm like, look at my chica!" Val always cracked me up.

"So Lita, who was that fiiiinnne handsome tall brotha you were talking to at the gala? I don't think I have ever seen him before? New donor?"

"Actually that was Law," I said while smiling.

"Seriously? Oh shit! He is so fucking hot! I see why you were stumbling all over your words last night when you were saying closing remarks."

"Now you know I wasn't stumbling. Quit trying to play me. But anyway, yes, that was Law."

"Wow! How did he end up there? You invited him?" Val sounded shocked.

"Well, not exactly. I did mention the gala to him but technically I didn't invite him. Actually a client of his was invited but couldn't attend at the last minute and gifted him with the ticket. Law actually made a sizable donation. I think his business check said $15,000."

"Well damn. What does he do?"

"He owns an investment firm here in Chicago. He has two other offices in Atlanta and Vancouver."

"Shit, you always hit the jackpot with these brothas."

"What do you mean?"

"Well, think about it. I know you have your hangups with Mike and all but he got his shit together. You know I'm right about that. And look at the life he's provided for you and the kids. And let's not forget every other man that wants to get with you and shower you with everything. And then here comes Law, he's sexy as hell and he's an entrepreneur cutting $15,000 checks and shit. And it's perfect because you want to start your own business. He's probably very knowledgeable and can help you with funding."

I was listening to Val but honestly, the only thing I could think about was when I would see Law again. I just really enjoyed his presence last night and I sensed he enjoyed being there as well. He seemed very impressed with my work.

It was refreshing how he encouraged and praised me. I wanted to get his take on the evening overall and just hear his views, learn from him and absorb him. I was deeply attracted to him. He was so subtle but his presence was so powerful. I felt like a lot of people were intrigued by him last night and he seemed to win the room over without even trying. He wasn't pushy or trying to impress anyone, he was just chilling and enjoying the atmosphere.

"Uum, hello are you there?" Val sounded frustrated.

"Oh huh? I'm sorry Val."

"Okay, where were you just now? Damn, that nigga got you twisted up already and you ain't even gave him your panties. Oh my bad, have you?"

"No, Val!" I said that with conviction as to reiterate the difference between her and I and that I don't go having affairs and having sex with every person I meet.

"Calm down, I just asked because the way you've been lately, this Law guy just seems to be consuming all your thoughts."

And Val was right. I couldn't deny that I was really into him.

"Anyway, let's focus on me for a second. You remember when Don walked up to us while we were talking?"

"Oh yeah, what happened with that? Did you punch him in the face?" I said while laughing.

"Girl, how about the complete opposite? He got me a drink at the bar and then he wanted to take me to one of those private offices he had access to, to "talk". All I remember is we walked in that office, he locked the door, didn't say a word and bent me over that desk. Shit, I'm having flashbacks just thinking about how good it was. You know, I swear Don has dated quite a few black women before because he fucks like a black dude. He handles ass like a black dude seriously. He got me there so quick and I was set for the entire night.

"Wow, I didn't realize it went down like that? I mean I could tell Don was on a little something when he asked you to meet him at the bar but I didn't know he was gonna just have you dip off with him like that."

"Look, we don't all have a husband and kids to come home to and have fancy dinners and talk about our day at work. This is how me and Don relate and I'm fine with that."

Val sounded a bit frustrated with me on the other end and I really didn't understand why she was coming for me like that.

"Val, you talking to me as if I was insinuating something. I wasn't. I just didn't realize it was going down like that because I know he hurt you pretty badly. That's the one time I've seen you heartbroken over a man and that hurt me. I just don't want him to take advantage of you."

"Well, like I said, everyone's romance is not your romance. Don and I are fine."

"Oh wow, so it's Don and I now?"

"Bitch, don't sound all confused and shit. I'm good, I can handle myself. I always got these men under control and Don ain't no exception. The sex with Don is good, that's it. I'm not in love with him anymore. I'm just getting what I can get since he raked me over the coals. I shouldn't turn down good sex with Don just because we're not a couple. That shit is simple. All that lovey- dovey shit is not the world I live in and I accept that. I'm just having fun and living my life."

I knew Val was hurt, I could hear it in her voice. But trying to tell her she's playing with fire would just set her off and I definitely wasn't in the mood for that this morning. I just hope Don doesn't hurt her again.

"So, changing the subject Lita, did you accept the Senior Fundraising Coordinator position?"

"I sure did, I told Don last night at the gala."

"Nice! I knew you would. That's too good of an offer. Well, I know your traveling schedule will pick up and I know Don may be on quite a few of those trips so keep an eye on his ass for me."

"And this is coming from a bitch that got it all under control and ain't in love, huh?"

"Oh okay, I see you trying to use my words against me. Imma give you half a point for effort. That was cute though, I'll give you that." Val laughed.

I knew how to reach Val. The preachy stance never worked with her but that real, raw and with a touch of hood always helped me get through to her. I just hope she takes heed to what I'm saying.

"Well, I gotta get off this phone. I booked a spa day for myself since my mother-in-law is coming over to take the boys to their piano lesson and Sheree to her friend's house while Mike is out doing what Mike does, trying to impress folks. I need this time to unwind. As a matter of fact, I hear this spa is top of the line. The reviews say the merlot is amazing, the music and ambiance is magical and the staff are extremely accommodating."

"Hmm, sounds like that usual bougie shit you're into. But imma pass. I'm actually meeting up with Don today before he heads out to Canada for a business trip. He said he wants to grab lunch but honestly, that's translation for he wants to grab my ass."

"You are something else. Well, have fun and I'll talk to you later."

"Okay, mama, love you."

"Love you too."

As I hung up from Val, I started thinking it would be nice to meet up with Law today too but it was last minute. Well, I could at least call him right quick to thank him for coming to the gala last night. Since everyone was asleep in my house, I thought I'd give Law a call. I got up to quietly close my bedroom door and for extra precaution, I walked into the bathroom of my bedroom and closed that door as well.

"Well, good morning beautiful."

"Now, how did you know it was me calling?"

"No surprise there, I locked your number in my phone once you actually felt comfortable sharing it with me."

"Funny. I guess I deserved that. Well, I just wanted to thank you again for coming out to the gala last night and for that amazing donation!"

"Well, it's a tax right off," Law said while laughing. "But seriously, it was my pleasure. I truly enjoyed myself and I had actually been talking to my accountants lately about wanting to make more charitable contributions and your gala had me sold. It was nice to hear about Global Connections and how much the company has contributed to the lives of so many including the many students you all support from Zambia. My mom's side of the family is actually from there. I wasn't born there as my family had already moved to the States but I still maintain very close ties with them and I still visit every 2-3 years. So I was truly impressed with your company's work and especially you."

"Wow, that's amazing and thank you so much for the great feedback."

"Oh, no doubt, you really did your thing last night. It was well put together from the ambiance to the entertainment and of course the guests that filled the room. I was definitely happy to be associated with someone like you last night. And you know I cannot leave out the fact that you looked absolutely breathtaking. I hope it's okay to say this, but you are one extremely sexy woman. Your hair, your smile and your curves all work together so perfectly to create you."

Law was making me blush and I loved the effect he had on me. His voice always did it for me when he talked. I could hear a subtle accent now that he mentioned his family was from Zambia.

"You definitely know how to make a lady feel special you know that?"

"Well, women were designed to be treated like queens in my opinion. It's just nice when you come across a woman that you want to talk to like that and you want to get to know and treat a certain way."

"Well, that is really nice, and it means a lot."

"You certainly make it easy."

"So…"

"What's up?"

"I'm heading to the spa today and I was wondering if you'd maybe like to meet afterwards for some lunch?"

"That sounds really nice."

"I mean, only if you don't have any plans."

"One thing you will learn about me is I don't let plans dictate my life. The only things I don't cancel on are my kids and grandkids. But everything else can take a backseat because life is for living and right now, seeing you is at the top of my priority list today. Just let me know where and when and I'll be there."

I loved how Law talked to me. It's as if he truly valued me like a rare diamond or something. I loved his thought process and how he chose to navigate life. He didn't try so hard to impress others or put everything before his loved ones. He lived life and he didn't let life dictate his every move.

"I'll be sure to text you the info as soon as I get out of the shower." I kind of said that on purpose so that he would begin visualizing what I looked like.

"Okay, imma pretend you didn't just say that because I want to show you respect at all times but just know that the mental picture I just got from that statement just did it for me." We both laughed.

"I'll see you soon Mr. Davis."

"Looking forward to it Mrs. Payne."

After I hung up the phone, I started panicking a little because it was already 9:15 and my appointment was at 10:30.

Thankfully the spa was right around the corner but typically I didn't wear makeup when I'd go to the spa so I didn't have to worry about that but I would just have to bring my kit and put it on after my manicure, pedicure and massage. I wanted to always look my best when I saw Law. I couldn't wait and the butterflies in my stomach were a clear indication of that.

* * *

"How can I help you?" The friendly receptionist greeted me as the soft sounds of nature played in the background and the aromatherapy filled the air.

"Yes, my name is Lita and I have a 10:30 appointment with Valencia."

"Yes, I see your appointment. Are you new to our spa?"

"Yes, and I've heard great things so I'm really excited."

"Well, thank you, Mrs. Payne. I noticed you didn't complete your online registration profile and we want to make sure we gather as much information about you as possible before Valencia comes to service you."

"Oh yes, I completely forgot about that."

"Not a problem Mrs. Payne. Everything here is done digitally so I'll give you this iPad to complete your profile. In the meantime, please enjoy some cucumber water in our lobby while completing your new member registration."

"Thank you so much." I loved cucumber water and I loved going to the spa. I would always feel an instant ease come over me; from the aroma to the gentle, yet relaxing music, the attentive staff and just having time to myself. At times, I would try to recreate the same experience at home but it just wasn't the same. The kids were either always bugging me about something, or the volume from the TV was sky high from Mike watching sports or me being distracted by the million and one things I always felt I had to do that lingered in my mind. The only thing that seemed to relax me these days was touching myself during a long hot bath or using my vibrator. I've just been feeling like I don't really get what I want sexually from Mike so I take care of it myself. And most of the time, I don't mind doing that but it would be nice to be touched by someone who is really in tune with my body and willing to explore all parts of me. I seriously craved that.

"Mrs. Payne, our sincerest apologies, your massage therapist, Valencia had an unexpected emergency and has to leave and will not be able to perform your massage today. Again, this is not something that typically happens and we want to accommodate you anyway we can. We can either reschedule your appointment with Valencia, provide you with another massage therapist who's available during your scheduled time, or offer you with a substitute service that was not originally included in your spa package today."

I was a little disappointed as Valencia received rave reviews about her work online but I still needed my massage today so I decided to keep my appointment and go with another masseuse.

"I understand things come up. I would still like to keep my appointment today if that's possible?"

"Yes, it certainly is Mrs. Payne. Would you prefer light, medium or deep pressure?"

"Is it possible to have a combination of medium and deep pressure?"

"It sure is. Would you like that for your appointment today?"

"Yes, that would be perfect."

"Okay, our only massage therapist that's available during your time that provides a mix of medium and deep pressure is Eduardo. Are you comfortable with a male massage therapist?"

"That's fine." I had never had a male massage therapist before but hey, there's a first time for everything.

"Okay great, Eduardo will be out shortly to greet you and take you to your room."

"Sounds great, thank you."

I was still slightly disappointed but I was just happy to be having this time to myself. My phone vibrated as I was receiving a text. I checked my phone and it was Law. As usual, my face lit up when I saw a text from him.

Hey beautiful. I'm really looking forward to seeing you this afternoon. I know you're getting pampered right now, which you deserve so take your time and enjoy. Just send me a text of the location when you're ready.

Not only was I excited about receiving Law's text, but I loved the fact that he sent intelligent texts that included complete sentences with the proper punctuation marks. I know, I'm such a nerd when it comes to that but I hate receiving texts that I can barely understand or are spelled wrong. It's just frustrating.

One more thing that made me excited about Law.

I haven't met with my massage therapist yet, but I will be heading in shortly. But I'd love to try that cafe that's about 10 minutes from here. I think it's called Daisy's?

Oh yeah, I've been there plenty of times. My buddy Jerome owns that place. Their tacos and wraps are really good. You'll like it plus they always have some kind of live music playing and I know you like live music seeing that you were at the Jazz Bar that night.

That sounds perfect. Let's meet there at 2pm. I should be done with my massage, manicure and pedicure by then. Sounds great. Looking forward to seeing you.

Same here.

I was so excited but immediately reality hit me yet again as I started thinking about what I was doing? I'm basically planning another date with this man, in a public place, at a restaurant in the South Loop? I'd be sure to run into someone I knew. Okay, that's me worrying again. I meet with people all the time for work, how is this any different? *Uum, Lita, this is different because you actually think he is hot that's why.* Okay, I don't want to change my mind. I really want this. If for some reason, I get a weird feeling about all of this, I won't go. But right now, I'm going to enjoy this massage.

"Mrs. Payne, hi my name is Eduardo and I'll be your massage therapist for today."

Well hello, Mr. Eduardo I thought to myself. He came out looking like a mix between Lisa Bonet's husband, Jason Momoa and the actor William Levy. Like seriously, how is that even possible? Hell, I don't know but one thing I did know, was that I was going to enjoy this massage today.

"Hi Eduardo, it's nice to meet you."

"The pleasure is mine Mrs. Payne, you can follow me."

As Eduardo walked in front of me, I noticed how fitted his white uniform was as it showed his slightly ripped arms and you could tell by the looks of his back and his butt that he worked out. Even the way he walked, you could tell he lifts weights but he wasn't bulky, he was just right. He didn't look any older than twenty- five.

"Here's room ten, we'll be in here today."

"Thank you." I walked into my dimly lit room and as I inhaled the eucalyptus in the air, immediately my body relaxed and it seemed like the tension started melting away.

"You can have a seat here Mrs. Payne. I just want to start off with a few things. So you mentioned in your profile that you prefer a mix of medium and deep pressure for your massage. Do you have any problem areas that you would like me to focus on today?"

Hmmm, besides my va jay-jay screaming for attention? I thought to myself but of course, I didn't say that out loud.

"Not really, I just tend to hold more tension in my shoulders and lower back."

"That's very common for many people. I can definitely take care of that for you. Are you comfortable with a scalp massage as well?"

"No, I don't really like the scalp massage."

"Okay, what about the gluteus maximus region?"

Oh, I was definitely okay with that especially since he was going to be doing it.

"Yes, that's fine." I tried to sound cool about it.

"Okay great. Are there any other areas you need direct focus on or just those specifically stated incorporated into your full body massage?"

"Those are fine."

"Okay great. I will give you some privacy to undress to your comfort level and I'll be sure to knock on the door prior to entering."

"Thanks, Eduardo, I appreciate it." I gave a slight flirtatious smile without being too obvious so I'm not sure if he even picked up on it. I wasn't really interested in Eduardo as I knew nothing about him but a little flirting is always fun and he was fine.

Once Eduardo closed the door, I began to undress and I looked at myself in the mirror. Even though the room was dim, I began to admire my chocolate skin and the way my curves looked. And I would just imagine all the things Law would probably do to me. I wondered often what it would be like to be with him. Was he a slow and sensuous lover? Or was he the fast pounding lover as if his life depended on it? Did he like to give oral? Did he like to receive oral because even though I've never been involved with anyone who didn't like it, I've heard that it does exist. Did he like to kiss slow or at all? Did he have quick orgasms or was he able to control his urge to "cum" and focus on pleasing a woman as well? I know I shouldn't be thinking about this but so many guys don't even have a clue that women *do* think about these things and yes, some of us are married. I just wish I had someone to really talk to about these things. Even though I had Val, she was single and pretty much fucking everybody she came in contact with. But I often wondered how many married women were unfaithful and did they find that it totally destroyed their life or did it actually enhance their marriage? I just believe Mike is a good man but we're just in different places right now and there's a certain kind of attention and affection I crave that he just doesn't provide. I think at times, he's willing but many times he's not which is so frustrating. Okay, this is starting to make my brain hurt. As I slipped under the covers on the heated massage bed, I immediately allowed the thoughts to dissipate from my mind.

There was a knock on the door and I heard Eduardo say, "Are you ready?"

"Yes."

"Okay great, before I get started, is the temperature of the bed comfortable for you?"

"It sure is, thank you so much for that."

"No problem at all. I know it's a bit of a winter wonderland outside so I just wanted to make sure everything was to your liking. Now take a few deep breaths, inhale and exhale."

I loved this part of the massage as I was preparing for an amazing hour filled with total relaxation. Eduardo's hands felt so good moving up and down my back and my shoulders. When he touched the small of my back, there was a sensation between my legs as that was an erogenous zone of mine. He later moved to my butt and began massaging it, in a professional way of course but it still felt so good. I was most ticklish on my feet so I always had to have a talk with myself before any massage therapist would massage me there so that I could fully enjoy the experience and not burst out into giggles. The strength of Eduardo's hands felt amazing and all the while I'm thinking to myself, why haven't I requested a male massage therapist sooner? I began to relax and enjoy my massage and try to release the sexual tension by focusing only on the massage. I knew I was going to be meeting Law later and I definitely didn't want to start acting like I was in heat around him.

* * *

"How was your massage, mani and pedi today Mrs. Payne?" The receptionist asked.

"It was amazing," I said while feeling totally relaxed and pampered.

"That's so great to hear. Would you like to go ahead and schedule your next appointment?"

"I would love that. As a matter of fact, I would like to sign up for the membership program if that's okay?"

"That would be wonderful and I can certainly assist you with that." The receptionist was inputting my information online.

"Lita, is that you?" I turned around to see Natalia who used to be the Senior Fundraising Coordinator before I accepted the position due to her having to resign abruptly because of some health concerns. But from where I was standing, Natalia still looked to be in tip top shape. Her hair was full and healthy looking. She appeared to have just stepped out of the sauna as her skin was extremely dewy and very youthful looking, her eyes were bright and clear and even though she still had a towel wrapped around her, it looked like she still had that banging body.

"Oh hey, Natalia! I didn't expect to run into you here." I was unsure of what to say seeing that I was her replacement and I didn't know how bad her health was so I wanted to be respectful, and not pry into her business.

"Yeah, I've actually been coming here since they've opened. This has become one of my favorite spas."

"Yes, this is my first time and I will definitely be frequenting this place more often. I'm actually signing up for a membership now."

"Oh that's great, well hopefully we'll be running into each other more often," Natalia said with a smile and also appeared to seem as if nothing was wrong which puzzled me.

"So, Natalia, uuumm, how have you been feeling?" I asked with a concerned tone.

"I've been great, never better!" Natalia said with a perky voice.

"Well, that's great considering your health concerns. I'm really sorry to hear that you had to resign. I was hoping to talk to you before you actually left the office."

"Health concerns? Oh is that what Don decided to tell everyone about me leaving? Oh okay, well I left it to him to figure that out, so…"

Now I was really confused, what the hell was Natalia talking about? This was starting to feel like there was so much more to this story.

"Don asked me to come to his office the week before the gala and he offered me your old position. I was confused but he stated to me that he thought I would be a great fit seeing that you had to leave due to health concerns. He didn't tell me what those concerns were which I thought was out of respect for your privacy so I left it at that. But I really wanted to talk to you about it before I accepted the position."

"You have always been such a class act, someone that has decency and morals. I always admired how you carried yourself at the workplace. You've always been laid back, yet professional and you were never shady you know? I really appreciate you for actually thinking of me like that. But please know, I am not having any health concerns unless you call the recent abortion I got a health concern."

"Oh wow, I didn't know you were pregnant."

"No one knew, and actually no one was supposed to ever know but I really respect and like you, Lita. I always have. The only reason I didn't come to you about this sooner was because I know you and Val are best friends and I didn't want it to be a conflict of interest for you."

Now what did Val have to do with this and why was I feeling like this was about to go south really quickly?

"Why did you mention Val?" When I asked that question, I felt like I already knew the answer. My heart was pounding because I just had a funny feeling I knew exactly what Natalia was about to say.

"Honestly, Don is no good. He's an opportunist, a chauvinist and an egotistical jerk who feels like he can do whatever the fuck he wants to people and they shouldn't say a damn thing about it. But I beat him at his own game. The difference between Val and I is that I was never in love with him. I always thought Don was hot and I can't lie, I wanted him. I was not looking for anything too serious and for a while it worked out because due to him being married, he didn't want anything too serious from me either. We're both professionals just trying to make our mark in our careers, we both enjoy the good life and hell we both enjoy really good sex. I was on the pill but there was this time I was taking antibiotics which made my birth control ineffective and I got pregnant. Don had an entire fit and threatened my job. He wanted to make me out to be a gold digger and tried to even dig up some past relationships I was involved in to make me look like I had an agenda which I did not. But hey, I accept my part in sleeping with my boss but I refused to go down as this cold calculated bitch. So I found plenty of dirt on Don and told him he either had to pay me or I would expose him. He played a little hardball but he said he would pay me double if I would get an abortion and leave the company all together so that's what I did."

I couldn't believe what I was hearing. I was getting the feeling that Natalia was involved with Don when she started talking but nothing to this magnitude. Seriously? I mean, I knew Don was cheating on his wife with Val but Natalia too? Did Val know? No, Val couldn't know or she would've beaten Don *and* Natalia's ass. But seriously? Is this how the game is really played as you move more and more towards the top? Do I really want to be bothered with all of this? All I wanted to do was make more money to start my own business and do my own thing. But this right here takes trifling to a whole other level. But look at me! Am I becoming that person? I mean seriously, I'm married myself and I'm going to meet up with another man right after I leave here. I'm honestly not any better than them. I just can't deal with all of this right now.

"I can tell by your face that this is a lot to take in. And I really didn't want to put you in an awkward position regarding your friend Val. I mean I know Val and I weren't exactly the best of friends but I respected her. I actually stopped seeing Don by the time him and Val hooked up but while Don and I were away on a few business trips this year, we messed around a few times but it didn't really matter to me because I knew I wasn't in love with him so I knew I could end it at any time. I really enjoyed my position as the Senior Fundraising Coordinator. It came with a lot of perks but all I can say is, Lita be careful. I'm not saying that you would fall for Don. Hell, you have no reason to, you have a beautiful family and you're very level headed. But still, keep an eye out on what the lifestyle can do to you. You're going to come across all kinds of people. You're going to have way more at your disposal than you would've had in your previous position and you're going to meet many more "Dons" that will talk a good game but will try to crush you on the way to the top without even blinking an eye." Natalia said in her Panamanian accent.

"I still can't believe all of this. But I'm glad I ran into you. And most importantly, I'm glad you're really okay in spite of it all. You didn't deserve that."

"And that's why I respect you, Lita. I appreciate that. I can't say I didn't deserve some things. Like I said, I have a responsibility in all of this too but I was not going to be ambushed. I'm just glad that I still got mines. But I'm good. I have a few projects I'm working on, I'm going to do some traveling and just move on. This was a learning lesson for me."

By the looks of it, Natalia seemed to be in a good place with everything but I can't imagine how Val is going to react. I just didn't want to see her experience more hurt at the hands of Don but Val was my friend, my sister, and my confidant. I had to tell her.

"It was great seeing you Lita and I wish you the best. I truly feel you are going to do great thing in your new position and I believe you can handle those snakes like Don and the rest of those motherfuckers. You really have a knack for working with people and also creating those boundaries which I struggled with a little. But please don't be a stranger. I hope we can still workout together sometime and maybe get together here at the spa."

"That sounds good to me Natalia." We hugged and I signed my paperwork for my membership and headed out the door.

CHAPTER

5

As I was walking over to Daisy's, I wondered why I didn't just drive. The snow was steadily falling and the wind was blowing which only increased my anxiety about what I was doing. Seeing that I was in the South Loop, it didn't make sense for me to pay for parking as I lived within 10 minutes of this place. What was I doing and why was I meeting with Law in the first place? I really had no business doing this. I couldn't help but think about the conversation I had with Natalia. Let me not even start with the hurt Don's wife had probably experienced over and over again due to his lies. I just know I don't want to be that person. And whatever Law may have thought was developing between him and I, I would have to shut that down today.

"Hey beautiful, it's great to see you," Law said as he gave me the most warming hug.

"It's great seeing you too, Law," I said with a bit of uncertainty in my voice.

The atmosphere at Daisy's was nice with its wide open floor plan and skylight windows. The natural light gave it an airy feel. Even though we were in the dead of winter with snow everywhere, this place was giving me California vibes.

"Are you okay? You seem a little uneasy." Law said with a concerned tone.

"It's just———" and before I could get the words out, I began to feel overwhelmed with my life, the things I wanted to accomplish and not feeling like I had Mike's support. Also, the info I had access to could really hurt Val and the fact that I was extremely attracted to Law but knowing I couldn't indulge myself, engulfed me and then...a tear fell from my eye and as much as I tried to stop it, I couldn't. I felt the warmth of that one tear on my cheek and my vulnerability made me feel so exposed.

"Hey, come here." Law held me and I allowed him to console me. "Do you want to go somewhere more private to talk?"

As much as I wanted to, I knew I couldn't. I barely knew Law, but for some reason, I felt like he knew *me* so well.

"It's probably best that we don't."

"You seem really distraught. I would be lying if I said that didn't concern me. As a man, it's kind of in my nature to want to fix whatever you're going through but one thing I've learned about women over the years is that you really just need a listening ear so I'm here for you in that way if you want."

"Oh my God, this is why I can't be here right now!" I said in a strong tone of voice.

"Excuse me, you lost me now." Law looked a little offended.

"Look, I'm sorry, I didn't mean to come at you like that. I just can't do this."

"Do what?" Law looked at me very sternly with a look that screamed I needed to grow the fuck up and truly express what was on my mind and not hide it. In the short amount of time I had known Law, I'd always caught the vibe that he could possibly know more about me than I knew about myself and I couldn't get away with just brushing things off with him. He quietly demanded my truth which made him even more sexy because I felt like I was unfolding right in front of him.

"I just want to be happy. And based off of my life and what I possess, everyone feels that I already am."

"Listen, you are truly an amazing and phenomenal woman. Yes, you have the external qualities that many are seeking; the marriage, the kids, the education, the career, the money, the lifestyle, and let's not forget the beauty, you have it all. But your heart yearns for something more. You have a passion burning inside of you that is itching to get out and a lot of times, that cannot be tamed for too long. Your passion seems to be hiding behind all those external factors. But you are in your prime right now. You can't allow anyone to dictate how you should live your life. One way or another you will have to come to terms with that and be honest with yourself."

Law's words hit me like a ton of bricks. In these past five minutes, he'd summed up my life and even though we hadn't known each other long, I knew he was right but it also scared me.

"And when you said you can't do this, were you referring to not seeing me anymore?"

"Well, it's just—"

"Lita, you don't have to say the quote on quote right thing to me. You don't have to craft your words to sound eloquent or politically correct. I want you to give me your raw and unabashed truth. I know you have that boldness in you because it's present in your work but when it comes to matters of the heart, it seems like you retreat. So just tell me exactly how you feel."

How could I be so emotional yet turned on at the same damn time! The way Law talked to me made me want to further expose myself to him. I needed this. It just seemed like I was always open minded and respectful of everyone else's opinions and thoughts, but when it came to mine, I never really allowed myself to be vulnerable.

"I have a lot going on in my life right now and sometimes I look up and think how did I get here? But it's been a culmination of years of just adding more and more to my plate and never really taking inventory of what I really want for my life. Or should I say, I have wanted certain things for my life but I put them on hold for others whether it be for my husband, my kids, work, my sister, my dad or whoever at the time. I've always had to be the responsible one, even when I had my oldest child at 19, I worked and scraped to build myself up. I sacrificed clubbing and doing dumb shit when I was young to make sure me and my daughter had a good life.

My child's father was dead ass broke and couldn't pay for shit but I kept going, I didn't bug him or try to get him for child support. I only focused on what I could do within my power. Fast forward to today, I've supported my husband's dreams, I've financially helped my sister open her salon, I've supported my dad and helped him pay his bills while he's been on disability,

I've brought in top of the line donors for my job and I'm tired. I'm just really tired." I couldn't believe I said all of that but it felt so good to release.

Law grabbed my hands and looked at me intensely.

"You have been through a lot which makes you a fighter and it's okay to take care of yourself. But answer this, why do you want to stop seeing me? Because that's what you said before you shared all those things about yourself."

Did I really have to spell this out for him? But maybe I just needed to be honest for once.

"Look, I am extremely attracted to you. I have met many good looking men but when I saw you at the bookstore, I knew that I wanted to know you. I can't exactly put my finger on why but I felt a strong attraction to you. I feel that's a dangerous place to be right now considering where I am currently in my life. I don't want to confuse you or complicate our lives. I just think it's best that we stop before things get out of hand."

"First, I want to say I sincerely appreciate your honesty because I'm extremely attracted to you as well. You are a grown woman that can definitely make her own decisions so I'm not here to tell you what to do. If you feel that it's best we part ways, I will respect that because I respect you. If at any given moment you decide you want to continue a friendship with me, I can honestly say, I am here to listen to you, challenge you if you'd like, comfort you, spend quality time with you and give you the things you've been desiring for a long time and trust me, I can provide ALL of that and more. I'm almost sixty years old, Lita. I've lived a bit and I understand where you're at. With that being said, you can decide the terms of this friendship and I'm open to making it work with you. You are not obligated to me. I just want you to enjoy what I have to offer and I want you to bask in every minute of it because I feel you deserve it."

Law lifted my hands to his mouth and kissed them. I felt appreciated and paid attention to. Was it really that simple? Could he be the man that I could be my true self with and he would still accept and embrace me for who I was? I'd felt like I was always trying to smooth things over with Mike to make *him* feel comfortable and more like a man but with Law, I felt like there was no need to do that because he was so confident in who he was that he didn't need that ongoing validation from me. Just seeing me happy and flourishing was enough for him.

"Wow, I really don't know what to say."

"You really don't have to say anything, because your facial expression says it all. I think deep down inside you know what you want to do. You just have to be the one to make that decision."

"I've really enjoyed this time with you but I probably should be heading back home," I said with hesitation.

"You haven't even ordered any food. And the food here is really good. I also wanted you to meet my buddy Jerome who owns the place before you leave."

"I would've liked that, but I really should head home. It's the weekend and that's kind of our family time you know? It's best that I take off."

"Okay, well if you insist? Can I at least walk you to your car?"

"I actually walked because I live less than 10 minutes away."

"I don't want to pressure you but can I at least drive you around the corner? It's snowing like crazy outside and I just don't feel comfortable with you walking in this weather."

I knew Law meant well and I really liked that about him but I really needed to get home and process some things.

"Thank you so much. I promise, I'm not trying to be stubborn but that's probably not the best idea. I'll be okay."

"Okay, well if you're able to call me when you get home, can you please do that? Or text me if that works better for you?"

"I'll be sure to do that," I said with a disappointed half smile.

Law pulled out my chair and helped me with my coat. Everything about him was so endearing and I loved how he displayed his chivalry so naturally.

"Okay, well be careful walking home and I look forward to your text or call. Now give me some love."

Law reached for me and hugged me. I let the scent from his NYU sweater fill my lungs as I knew it would eventually linger onto my clothes but I didn't care. I was mesmerized by him but I was fighting it at every turn. I wanted to gaze upon him just a little longer but I knew that I couldn't. I had already crossed some major boundaries just by being here with him in public let alone a place so close to my home.

"Thanks again for listening to me today. I actually really needed that."

"You know it's my pleasure."

I could tell we both didn't want our time together to end. The way he looked at me, I could tell he wanted to say more but was holding back out of respect. He looked like he wanted to lean in and kiss me but I quickly hurried out the door.

* * *

The fresh scent of laundry detergent and snickerdoodle cookies in the oven greeted me as I walked into my home. I really loved when my mother-in-law, Diane came over to watch the kids. Whenever she saw a need in my home, she just quietly stepped in and helped. I never had mother-in-law horror stories like some of my friends talked about. Diane was amazing. She kind of looked like Phylicia Rashad and exhibited the same style and grace. Many of the women in Mike's family were like that. My family was the complete opposite; country hood is what typically came to mind when I thought about them. But I ain't never the one to down my family because they raised me. They taught me about the streets and groomed me for real life and when I was pregnant with Sheree, I was able to hold my own because I learned how to be strong at a young age. But I still really loved being around Diane.

Even though she was extremely smart, eloquent, classy and refined, she was definitely a boss in her own right. She was a homemaker all throughout Mike and his brother's school-aged years, but when they entered high school, Diane decided to go back to school. She received both her Bachelor's and Master's Degree in Business Administration.

Diane later opened her own bakery and named it Annie's Sweets after her mother. When I decided I wanted to start my own marketing firm, she was the first person I told because I knew I would receive her support. I really liked talking to Diane but I always refrained from talking about Mike in a negative light in front of her. I typically kept our issues private because as much as I loved Diane, I just assumed she would always take Mike's side and that would've hurt me so I never talked to her about it. There were many times I wanted to though.

I never really had a mother figure except for Diane, seeing that my mom left when I was only thirteen. That was truly when I needed my mom the most. I needed that reassurance and someone to talk to about relationships and how I was becoming a woman. I don't ever take for granted how much my dad loved me, spoiled me, taught me how to play sports, how to shoot a gun and how to recognize deadbeat dudes, but I still craved that woman's touch in my life. And Diane was that for me.

"Hey, beautiful. How was your massage?" Diane asked with a pleasant smile on her face.

"It was amazing," I said with a sigh of relief.

"I can tell," Diane said while making another batch of snickerdoodle cookies.

"Mom, have you ever tried that new cafe Daisy's about 10 minutes from here?"

"Oh, yes I know the owner, Jerome! Great guy and the food is really good! Did you get a chance to check it out today?"

"Wow, does everyone know the owner except for me?"

"What do you mean?" Diane said with a confused laugh.

"Oh, I just meant that one of the donors from the gala mentioned that place to me and I thought I'd check it out seeing that he knows the owner as well, that's all." I stuttered a little hoping Diane didn't pick up on a vibe from me as if I was hiding something.

"I'm in the pastry business and Jerome runs a cafe. Even though Chicago is so big, it's yet so small. A lot of the black business owners know one another and try to support each other. But speaking of business, have you started strategizing yours? You know I'm here if you need anything."

Immediately, my mood changed and I started thinking about Mike's lack of support.

"Well, I would love to start creating a business plan but I have so much on my plate now that I've accepted the Senior Fundraising Coordinator position at my job."

"Oh, that's right. Mike told me you were offered that job. I was wondering if you were going to take it after our last conversation. I didn't mention anything to Mike because I kind of figured that needed to be a conversation between the two of you."

And this is why I loved Diane. I felt like we thought a lot alike. She was able to just sense things and not interject because she felt like she could.

"And I really appreciate that mom, I really do."

"Lita, is there something going on?"

"Well, I really want to start my marketing firm. I'm extremely passionate about it and I honestly know I would be damn good at it."

"You know you don't have to convince me. The way you run those galas and all the support and money you bring in for that non-profit is nothing short of amazing. You know your father- in-law and I would've been at the last one if it wasn't for us being out of town for our anniversary."

"Don't worry. I know I always have your support."

"You got that right. You're the only daughter I have and I value that honey."

I loved when Diane showed her sassy side but more importantly, I loved receiving her support.

"But something else is going on, I can feel it."

"Well, Mike is not interested in helping me start this business financially."

"Okay, and why not?" Diane put her hand on her hip.

"Well, Mike seems to feel that we would be throwing money away because he doesn't know if the business will thrive. He feels I would be taking a gamble starting this firm. Mom, you know Mike makes almost $200,000 a year and of course I'm not making as much as he is but together, we're doing really well for ourselves. We don't have a lot of debt. Our cars are paid for and we don't have much left on this condo." I was getting emotional and even feeling my eyes watering a little.

"So, Lita Baby did you take the job because you're trying to fund your business?"

"Yes," I stated while looking away so that Diane wouldn't see the tears in my eyes.

"You don't have to turn your head. I know you're pretty upset about this. It's okay if you need to cry it out for a minute. It seems like you've been holding in a lot."

Diane's words just allowed the floodgates to open while we were sitting at the kitchen island. Diane came over and hugged me for some time as I needed that so badly but I didn't know how to tell her. She started to slowly rock me back and forth and my heart began to race so fast because it was the first time I had really shared how sad I was about Mike and I. I always made things seem like they were so great between us in front of her. I wondered if she knew all along I was not exactly happy.

"I could tell some things had been going on with you and Mike, not so much about the business but I've noticed. Don't ever get it twisted. I may not be your biological mother but I've known you for a *long* time so I could tell there were some things on your mind.

"You're going to have some struggles in your marriage from time to time. It's just a part of life. I'm not excusing Mike's behavior at all on this one because I feel that he should support you. You are an amazing woman, wife, mother, daughter, friend, businesswoman and everything in between. I feel like you would do a phenomenal job as an entrepreneur but between you and I, Mike is so much like his dad. Your father-in-law had a serious fit when I decided to go back to school. He felt that if I "needed something to do" or a "hobby", I should've just volunteered more at the boys' school or at church and excuse my language but I thought to myself; *hell naw, I have so much more to offer than that.* I wanted more for my life and I felt that I had given a big portion of it raising our family so it was time for me. Your father-in-law and I argued, we didn't speak to each other some days, he didn't value my education and work and we just totally distanced ourselves from each other. But you know what? He was scared. He felt that I was changing and it freaked him out. Well hell, I *was* changing but I felt it was for the best but he didn't see it that way. And honestly, Mike has always been the same way. Growing up, he always struggled with change and it looks like he's experiencing that right now."

"Yes, mom! It's like every time I mention something new I want to try or even if I have new ideas about the decor for the house or if I allow the kids to try a new hobby, he always has something to say about it. We just don't see eye to eye on anything these days and honestly, I just took the job to keep the peace because I'm tired and I don't want to argue."

"Well, all I can say, is it's only so long you can keep sweeping problems under the rug. I did that for years and there were a lot of things that were said and done that I'm not proud of but you have to eventually confront those issues even if Mike gets upset. You have to be willing to take that risk or you'll regret not doing the things you truly enjoy and living up to your full potential. Girl, I knew some things were going on but I said to myself, *Diane, don't meddle, she'll come and talk to you when she's ready.*

"Mom, I love you so much. I was just nervous talking to you about Mike. I didn't want it to seem like I was complaining and throwing him under the bus. I thought you would just take his side."

"Girl, look at me. I am your mother just as much as I am his. You both mean the world to me. I love my son, but I also know about that married life. I know how things can come up and cause friction in a marriage. I'm definitely not naive when it comes to my son either. You've been married ten years and you're bound to experience some things but they need to be addressed.

You can ALWAYS talk to me, you hear me? I don't care what it is. Don't try doing this alone because believe you me, it can get really hard sometimes and you'll look up one day wondering; *how did I get myself into this mess?* Trust me, honey, don't let the class fool you. I have stories. But that's all the more reason you can talk to me. I will never pressure you but I'm always here."

"Thank you." And just like that, I cried in Diane's arms again. Wow, I really have been keeping a lot bottled in these days.

And then Diane said in a soft voice, "Have you thought about finding your mom?"

Whoa, that caught me off guard. My birth mother was a very sensitive subject for me and quite frankly it annoys the hell out me.

"Diane, why would you bring her up?" I asked with utter disgust.

"I know you're serious right now because you called me Diane."

"I'm sorry mom, no disrespect at all."

"None taken whatsoever. I know that's a very complicated question for me to ask and I know you usually don't like talking about her."

"No, I do not," I said very sternly.

"Listen, coming from a woman who had a very poor relationship with her mother, try and find her."

"Okay, Diane with all due respect, my so-called biological mother left when I was only thirteen. And you know what? I was left to raise my baby sister on my own because my dad had to work all the time just to keep food on the table. He didn't know the first thing about doing hair, menstrual cycles, and other shit that girls have to think about. No, my dad wasn't perfect as I'm very aware of that. He could barely keep the money he earned because he always gambled it away. He was always tired when he got off work. He barely attended any functions or activities we were involved in and honestly, being a parent myself now, I can understand how hard it could've been to juggle it all. But that woman literally pushed me out of her vagina and then said fuck you and left. I don't owe her shit. Even when she was living with us, she wouldn't even ask us about our day, help us with homework let alone make time to wash her own ass. She could never keep a job and I'll never forget that one time she slapped my baby sister so hard her tooth fell out prematurely just because she spilled her cereal on the floor. My dad had to literally wrestle a knife out of my hand because I was about to stab her ass. So please Diane don't tell me about finding my mother. The only mother I've ever known is you and I'd rather keep it that way."

"That reaction I just got from you, is a clear indication that you need to try to find your mother and talk to her honestly about your feelings. My relationship with my mother was pure hell which is sad because none of my girlfriends grew up with an alcoholic mom like mine but that was the hand I was dealt and I didn't deal with the issues and make peace with my past until my mother was on her deathbed. It's not worth it, Lita.

There were so many dynamics to our relationship I'd learned from those last encounters I had with her. If I had reached out earlier, maybe I could've dealt with the healing process a long time ago and possibly avoid some of the pitfalls. I do believe there are things that happen out of our control, but we also have the ability to change the trajectory of our lives if we're willing to master that ship. I'm saying this to you now because I've watched you over the years and I know this has been weighing on you. You have a lot going on but you have to always make time for self-care. And yes, me watching the kids and you going to get a massage once or twice a month is good. Keep doing that. But you need to go deeper and deal with your past or things will spiral out of control and you'll wonder, how did I end up here? Now, I've said enough and I definitely don't want to upset you anymore. But take some time and think about it and I won't bring this topic up again."

Even though I was extremely upset at the thought of talking with my mom, Diane made a good point. It's been almost twenty years since I've seen my mother and ten years since I've heard from her. Somehow, she got my number from somebody and called me right before Sheree's first birthday but that's the last time I've spoken with her. Last I heard, she moved to New York to stay with some of her family but I just never really cared enough to try to keep in touch. My life is very good right now, and just hearing her voice would upset me.

"Mama, you look like you been crying." Tariq said while nearing the foot of the stairs.

"Hey Tariq, I'm fine. Where's Sheree?" I totally brushed Tariq off as I just didn't want to go into all of that with him right now.

"Upstairs on her phone."

"Umm huh, she's still on that phone? Well, I see you finally came up for air from those video games."

"Ha, yeah I'm killing it on *Call of Duty*, Rashad is mad because I'm beating him."

I still have yet to see what the fascination is with those video games, but the boys are limited to only playing on the weekends after their rooms have been cleaned and their chores are done.

"I bet you can't beat me." I said jokingly.

"Mama, you're not serious, are you? You know I'm the reigning champ in this house."

"Yeah, I know, I'm just messing with you. You know I can't stand those games. So how was your piano lesson this morning?"

"It was fine, you know grandma dropped us off and went shopping like she normally does. She said she needed a new fur?"

I couldn't help but laugh because that was so Diane.

"That's right baby, your grandma likes to shop but that's because I can. I have worked very hard over the years and it's very important that I treat myself every once in a while." Diane said while smothering Tariq with kisses.

"Grandma, you said every once in a while but it looks like you treat yourself more than that." Tariq said in his precocious nine year old way.

"Don't get cute, Tariq."

"Grandma, you know I'm already cute." Tariq said while pretending to pop his collar.

"You and your brother are too much, looking just like your daddy." Diane chuckled and gave Tariq a big hug.

"Well, Lita Baby, I'm going to head out of here and check on some things at the bakery."

I smiled at Diane.

"Well, it's nice to see that smile on your face."

"I was just thinking about how Mike calls me Lita Baby because he gets that from you."

"He sure does, because you are my Lita Baby and don't forget what we talked about earlier."

"I won't mom, I'm serious."

"I know you are. Now give me a hug so I can get out of here. I love you." Diane kissed me on my cheek.

"I love you too. Be careful, it's still snowing pretty hard out there."

"Okay hun, I will and tell my son I love him too."

"Okay mom.

CHAPTER

6

Clearly *you* were hungry." It looked like Val seriously swallowed her turkey burger in less than 2.5 seconds while I was still waiting on my food because the waiter got my order wrong.

"Uum, yes, that's why I asked you if we could go out to eat first before we headed to the "Old Skool vs. New Skool" Hip Hop Jam.

"You know we gonna have so much fun tonight. Sheree was so jealous that I wasn't taking her to the concert with us."

"Aww, you could've brought my baby girl Sheree with her little hot self. You betta watch out for that one."

"Girl, you know Mike is already on that. Sheree can't go two feet without Mike saying something to her about what she's wearing, who she's hanging out with and who the knucklehead boys are that want to take her to school dances. But I really appreciate that he stays on top of her like that. Especially, since I had her when *I* was nineteen. I knew what I was starting to get into at her age."

"Oh okay, so yo ass was fast too huh?" Val said with a mouthful of fries.

"No, I wasn't fast, I just wasn't being monitored."

"Like I said, fast ass."

"Anyway, we ain't gone even talk about you, Val."

"I ain't got no shame in my game. I know I was fast. The first time I had sex was in eighth grade with Tyrone Miller. Girl, he was a junior in high school and he asked me to come over to his house when his mama wasn't home and before I knew it, he was pulling out the condoms. He didn't have too much of a package down there but he knew what the hell he was doing I can tell you that."

"How the hell would you know? It was your first time."

"Girl, let me tell you something. That Tyrone taught me a thing or two. The first time hurt a bit but he kept on hitting it, and I kept on learning. I'll never forget him." Val started to go deep in thought again.

"You still keep in contact with him, don't you?

"Why you gotta say it like that? Like I'm just out here fucking everybody? Well, I know that's what it looks like at times but I really ain't, Lita."

"I know you're not Val, I'm just fucking with you."

"But on the real, we *are* Facebook friends and we follow each other on Instagram. That's about as much social media I can take. But girl, he's married now and his wife just had a baby so you know he been a little low key since the wife came on the scene.

You know how niggas get. They act like they can't even look up to see which way they're going cause they gonna get bitch slapped just for having a conversation or something and I ain't got time for that. I ain't on a leash so I don't need anybody around me that need me to be talking in codes and shit. Girl, but he still fine though."

"But you said he ain't have much of a package."

"Girl, it ain't like it was small, it just wasn't huge. But if he had those skills in high school, I can only imagine what he's like now, damn!"

"Girl, you keep me laughing."

"And you keep looking at me like you don't know what the hell I'm talking about. Why you trying to act like you ain't no freak Lita?"

"I'm not acting like that. You're just more expressive than I am."

"That's right goddammit!" Val said while putting another handful of fries in her mouth.

"It's about time they brought my food. I could kill these wings."

"Yeah, those do look good. Let me get one."

I really wasn't trying to share my wings with Val's hungry ass today but I really needed to talk to her about my conversation with Natalia and I needed her to be good and full once I dropped this bomb on her. "Soooo—"

"So what?"

"I ran into Natalia at the spa the other day."

"Okay? And?"

"Well, we had a nice little conversation." I was really procrastinating.

"You seem to be really tiptoeing around something. So you ran into Natalia? And what? Did she gain some weight or something? Did she finally get some thickness like the rest of us motherfuckas? What?"

"No. She's still shaped like a cute little Barbie doll with Kardashian curves. But that's not why I brought her up. She told me something that really disturbed me and I think you need to know."

"Okay? Why the suspense?"

"Well, her and I finally got a chance to talk about how I accepted her old position. She seemed really cool about it and all—"

"Well, why wouldn't she be? She's the one that felt it was best to resign. Plus, she really likes you. Unlike me, she gets all twisted in the face when I come around. Not sure what that's about but she doesn't want none of this. I would snap her little ass in two."

I was becoming really hesitant about telling Val about me and Natalia's conversation but I knew she needed to hear this and she needed to hear it from me.

"So, Natalia left Global Connections because her and Don were fucking at one point in time. She got pregnant. Don wanted her to get an abortion but she said to Don she wasn't doing it without a price. He basically paid her off so that she would get an abortion and leave Global Connections. Don telling everyone that Natalia was having health concerns was just a cover up." Whew, that was a mouthful but I was glad I got that off of my chest.

"So, you mean to tell me this skinny bitch gets pregnant by Don and he pays her? How much did he give her?"

Val was making me nervous as I could see her getting really upset.

"Now *that* I don't know, she never said."

"Clearly it was enough money for her to leave her cushy ass job on the fucking nineteen floor!" Val's voice was becoming more elevated and she even stood up from her chair.

"Listen, don't let all this get to you. Natalia wasn't trying to dig into you like that. She just wanted me to know because she knows you and I are friends."

"Please don't take her side. I'm pretty sure this shit was going down while Don and I were sleeping together and I'm pretty sure she knew about it. Why the hell should I be mad though? I was fucking him while he was married so it ain't like I had any rights to him. I thought I felt stupid before but I really feel stupid now. He had the nerve to actually pay her? And here is my stupid ass still giving Don the pussy for free when he calls. I've just been his black bitch. He always tried to come off to others like he was so high class with his privileged ass life and his privileged ass wife but he was blowing my back out every chance he got. But he didn't just keep me hidden because he was married or because we worked together, he was ashamed of me. But now that I think about it, Don would flirt with Natalia a little more openly and when I called him out on it one time, he said, *You know how I am? I'm personable like that and yes, I do tend to flirt with a lot of women but I have to be really careful with you in public, Val because everyone would be able to tell right away we're having sex.* But here comes the exotic Panamanian chick and she gets money for fucking with yo lame ass? And what the hell did I get?"

Val was so angry, I could see it in her eyes as they began to water. I really felt sorry for Val because out of all her sexual conquests, she really loved Don but the circumstances were definitely not in her favor. And as much as she tried to hide it, she couldn't. I wanted to reach for her and hug her but Val really wasn't the affectionate type and I didn't want her to feel any worse than she already had.

Val quickly wiped her eyes and shrugged it off.

"Okay, I'm ready for this concert and maybe we'll be able to get backstage and meet Method Man. Now that's one rapper I would be a groupie for."

And just like that, Val decided to switch gears and bury her feelings once again.

* * *

The crowd was so hyped and I loved singing along to so many of the old school hip hop jams. The air was filled with the heavy scent of weed and cigarettes even though smoking wasn't allowed in the concert hall. The energy of the crowd was amazing. The women were dressed to the nine in their thigh-high boots, skinny jeans, and tight Bodycon dresses. The long weaves, braids, dreadlocks and natural fros were definitely highlighted tonight as the ladies were representing from head to toe. The men were extremely sexy too with their Timberland boots, leather jackets and fitted caps and chains. It took me back to the 90s when hip hop reigned supreme.

It was always refreshing hanging out in the city like this because my typical conversations were with plenty of people who didn't look like me and who were scrutinizing me based off of how I looked. At work, I could be black, but not too black, passionate, but not too passionate and talented but not too talented as to not show anyone up. It was really exhausting at times but being here allowed me to let my hair down and truly be comfortable in my own skin.

"Be livin' in the fucking lap of luxury, I'm realizing that cha didn't have to fuck with me, but cha did, now I'm going all out kid, And I got mad love to give, you my nigga".

Val and I, along with the rest of the crowd were rapping the verse to "All I Need" by Method Man and before we knew it, Mary J. Blige made a guest appearance and showed out! She was rocking a red skin tight catsuit, with a thick black waist belt along with some patent leather thigh high boots to match, oversized sunglasses and long blonde tresses. Mary started doing her signature dance across the stage and the crowd went wild, myself included. We all had liquor in our cups, just having a good fucking time and it felt fantastic.

"Lita, this place is lit! I'm so glad you told me about this concert, we needed this honey." Val was screaming over the music and the crowd.

"I know! I can't lie. I don't want this night to end."

"Well, it doesn't really have to. Let's stay out all night like we're in our 20s or some shit." Val was moving in closer to talk to me so that I could hear her over the music but all I could focus on was the smell of Hennessy on her breath.

"Okay after we leave here, I'll call Mike and see what's good."

"Ha, that's right. Gotta check in with the husband. But it's cool, I definitely understand. Tell Mike he can hold it down for one night." Val's words were starting to slur.

"Yeah, it's a good thing I drove because it looks like you may need me to drive you back to your house anyway."

"Yeah, you're right 'cause I'm so fucked up right now."

After the concert was over, we slowly made our way through the large crowds of people making an effort not to bump into anyone too hard. We definitely didn't want to be involved in a fight because that could very well happen in crowds like these. Once we left the concert hall, it was so cold outside as we were still in the middle of winter. Couples were huddled up waiting for their Ubers and chicks with skin tight dresses and five inch stiletto heels were freezing their asses off as they were reminded that no man was worth this much effort to look good.

"Hey, Lita!" Someone screamed my name from a distance. Both Val and I looked at each other and then looked around trying to figure out who was calling me. Wow, it was Sheree's dad, Lamont! I hadn't seen him in a little over a year since he'd moved to Atlanta.

Lamont never really had much to give to Sheree financially since she was born as he always struggled to find a good paying job. Lamont dropped out of high school when I got pregnant. He never returned as he started working at the grocery store full time.

As he was running closer to me, I couldn't help but notice how good he looked. I mean really good like he came up on some serious money.

"Oh my God, Lamont how are you?" We gave each other a big hug and Lamont kissed me on my cheek as we always remained friends.

"Man, Lita, I'm doing really, really good!" Lamont said while rocking back and forth trying to create some warmth.

"Hey, Lamont. You *do* look good, damn. What you been slanging?" Val said sarcastically.

"Val, you still crazy as hell. Come here and give me some love." Lamont grabbed Val and hugged her as well.

"Lamont, you smell good too? Shiiiitttt, somebody on their grind." Val said as if she was giving Lamont his props.

"Well, you know. I've been doing a little bit of this and a little bit of that. No slanging though. I ain't on that. I'm somebody's father and I'm about to be a father again." Lamont said proudly.

"Wow, congrats!" I said a little surprisingly. "Who's the lucky lady?"

"Well, it ain't like no wedding bells in the near future or nothing. We good. We kind of got a situation, but we're good." Lamont was being a little cryptic in his description of his supposed relationship but clearly, this wasn't a serious thing.

"Well, no matter what the situation is, congrats. I haven't been trying to avoid you or anything. I know you and Sheree have been keeping in contact which always makes me happy that you continue to make an effort to be in her life."

"Oh no doubt, that's my baby girl and you've always allowed me to be there for her in the only way that I could and I'm always appreciative of that. You made sure our baby girl was good and well taken care of even when I didn't have anything else to give but my time so I'll always love you for that, for real Ma."

Lamont was originally from Staten Island, New York but moved to Chicago when we were in ninth grade. His place of origin was always so prevalent when he talked. His accent, his slang and mannerisms were all the things that attracted me to him when we were kids.

"Well, your time has always been much more valuable. So I appreciate you too."

"Well, look Ma, this cold is straight bananas. I ain't used to this no more since I've been living in Atlanta."

"Lamont, you ain't been out there but a year. You getting soft on me already?"

"Ma, you know I never go soft. C'mon girl you know me too well for that." Lamont winked at me but I just laughed it off. We were always cool but Lamont ain't had a whiff of this in years so I just let him do his little flirting thing.

"But on the real Lita, I love you and I love Sheree with everything in me. I just flew out here earlier today and I was going to call her to surprise her. But after seeing you, can you set something up for me? I have some gifts for her?"

"Gifts?"

"Yeah, Ma. I've been out there doing my thang in Atlanta. I know we haven't talked much about it but before I left Chicago, I got my G.E.D. It was right on time because I was doing my music thing trying to break out into producing and what not and literally the day after I got my G.E.D., I got a call from a guy out in Atlanta who had heard about me making some music for some local rappers here in the Chi and said he wanted to fuck with me. His crew flew me out to Atlanta and introduced me to 9th Wonder and man the rest is history. I've been working with some sick producers, rappers, and DJs. It's been a real blessing. Money is starting to flow a lot smoother and I just wanna give my baby girl the world. I haven't been able to really spoil her like that but I got it now Lita, so it's my turn you know?"

"Wow, I'm so happy for you! Now you know Sheree is already a spoiled little something but I totally understand you wanting to do that for her."

"Yeah, she be sending me little texts of her fly ass clothes and J's so I know she been well taken care of. But I wanna take my princess out on a date. I wanna do it in style and take her to a luxury restaurant and maybe take her to a concert of one of her favorite rappers or singers. You know? I just wanna make up for that."

"Well, you know I'm definitely not gonna stand in your way of that. I love ya'll bond so yeah, I'll definitely get on that right away."

"Thanks, 'cause I gotta head back to Atlanta in a couple of days."

"Okay cool. I'll see about getting you two together tomorrow. She'll be so excited."

"Thank you thank you, Ma. Hey, maybe you and I can kind of link up too before I head out. Just you and I. We haven't really had any time to just sit down and chop it up."

Okay so as much as I appreciated Lamont's gesture, he was pushing it a little bit. I know we co-parent and everything but Lamont was looking like he wanted something a little more intimate and I definitely wasn't on that.

"Now Lamont, c'mon. I've been married for ten years. You know it ain't that type of party."

"Well, can't blame a brotha for trying. You looking a little thick these days, Ma. I can't help it. You always been right, I mean... that's how we had shorty, but damn, Lita is all I have to say."

"Well, I'm pretty sure there are plenty of women and I use the term women loosely that wouldn't mind entertaining a top producer like yourself."

"Ha! You know you always had faith in me, Lita. Even when I was dead ass broke you said I was gonna be alright and I knew you meant that shit. Even now, you already speaking that top producer title into existence." Lamont was getting a little emotional, New York style of course.

"Well, you know we've always been friends and that'll never change. But let me get out of here. I guess Val was like forget this, I'm going back inside. It's too cold to be out here." We both laughed.

"Okay cool. I love you Ma and I look forward to seeing my baby girl tomorrow."

"Okay, I love you too Lamont." Lamont gave me another hug, a little longer and tighter this time then he leaned in and kissed me on my neck.

"Damn, you tasting all good and shit. Listen, my flight doesn't leave until—"

"Naw nigga, I'll holla at you tomorrow."

"Aight Ma," Lamont said with a sly and seductive grin.

Lamont ran across the street to meet up with some guys.

I tried calling Mike to let him know I was going to hang out a little while longer with Val and possibly spend the night at her house seeing that we were going to hit up the club scene and probably drink some more. Mike didn't answer. He had probably fallen asleep so I left a message. I even sent him a text to cover all bases. It's been a long time since I've been out in these streets at this hour but I just really needed my time for once. I really hoped Mike would understand. In the meantime, I pulled Val from the concert hall and we headed to the nearest club.

Val and I were dancing with so many young guys who were trying to hit on us but we just kept taking pics and drinking. Even though we both were on social media, we didn't live on it like many of the twenty-somethings that filled the bar that night. It seemed like most of the women were too busy "Snap Chatting" like my daughter does all the time, so a lot of the guys just kept dancing with us. I looked across the room and I thought I saw a man who resembled Law but that was just wishful thinking on my part. For a minute, I visualized myself being single and hooking up with him. Clearly, that wasn't going to happen. As angry and frustrated as I would get with Mike sometimes, we had so much history and of course, we have beautiful children. And I would be lying if I said I really wanted to give up the lifestyle that Mike has afforded us for so long.

I hadn't talked to Law since Daisy's and it appeared as though he was respecting my wishes by not reaching out to me. On one hand, I was happy that I had been able to move on with my life and not be distracted by Law but on the other hand, I really loved being pursued by him. And the more I drank, the more I thought about him. Should I or shouldn't I text him?

"Lita, girl why is Greg here? What the entire fuck? I really don't need him fucking up my vibe tonight."

"Well, maybe he won't, it looks like he's with that Latin chick over there and she looks like she's barely twenty-five."

"Good. Cause he ain't good for nothing else. I definitely don't wanna be bothered. And on that note, let's go say hi." Val grabbed my arm so quickly that I didn't get a chance to decline as I could feel her inner petty rising up.

"Hey, Greg how are you, hun?" Val said while poking out her 36 DDD's in Greg's and his date's face.

"Oh hey Val?" Greg said as if to look confused at Val's grand introduction.

"Hi, I'm Camila." Greg's date reached for Val's hand but as soon as I recognized Val's uninterested body language, I reached for Camila's hand.

"Hey Camila, I'm Lita and this is Val. We both work with Greg." I said trying to smooth things over.

"So Camila and I have been to this club before but we've never seen you ladies, here." Greg awkwardly tried to make conversation while Val clearly looked pissed.

"Well, we just came from the Old Skool vs. New Skool Hip Hop concert and we thought we'd just hang out a little longer. We typically don't come to this club." I said while trying to hurry the conversation along.

"Yeah, honestly, this is not our scene. Most of the time we're dining with executives and the like. This club is always filled with teeny boppers in Fashion Nova dresses." Val said with major attitude and quite frankly a whole lot of shade.

"Well, hmmm it was great seeing you both." Greg took Camila by the hand and escorted her to the other side of the club as he probably didn't want to feel Val's wrath.

"Uum Val, what the hell was that?"

"What you mean what the hell was that?"

"Oh, so you gone stand there and play dumb like you ain't just throw all kinds of shade towards Greg's girl?"

"First of all, that ain't Greg's girl. She's just some little bitch he fucking. Trust me I can tell."

"But why does that matter to you? C'mon now? Greg ain't even your man and you've said plenty of times you didn't want him to be. Look we're just out here having some fun. Leave him and that girl alone."

"You know what Lita, fuck you!"

"Wait one goddamn minute! Who the fuck do you think you're talking too?"

"You, Lita! I'm tired of you always acting so high and mighty. Sometimes, I like to be petty, shit. You know that about me. I ain't mean no harm but I'm tired of these dudes thinking they can just fuck me over and then bring their little tramps around me like I ain't supposed to say one goddamn word!"

I could tell Val was getting heated and I knew she was drunk but I really didn't want to go there with her tonight.

"Val, look, let's just get outta here. Let's not make a scene. We can just chill at your house." I said calmly and with a level head.

"See, there you go again always trying to make it seem like I'm the one that's crazy. Just because your life is set up so perfectly don't mean you gotta judge me."

"What the hell? I am not judging you! What are you even talking about?"

"You out here with your rich husband, cute little catalog looking kids, now a six-figure salary, witcha thick-fit ass while I'm just fat, and even your baby daddy got the fucking nerve to be on the come up. And I'm out here forty fucking years old, no man, no family, an abortion from the one man that I ever loved and now I gotta watch Greg's no dancing-ass feel on this little Mexican chick's titties."

"Val, she's Cuban."

"Lita, I don't give a fuck!!! And how the hell do you know that?"

"Okay, Val, I'm taking you home now," I said with a sense of urgency.

"I ain't going nowhere with you bitch. I'm tired of living in your shadow. Did you know that my ex Arab husband got a damn attorney and asked for the money back? I knew I should've spent that shit." Val was really losing it now and she was crying in the middle of the club and could barely walk because she was so drunk. I grabbed Val's arm and even though she was trying to pull away from me, I started treating her like one of my kids. I acted as if she was having a tantrum in the grocery store and grabbed her ass out of there and pulled her into my car.

The ride to Val's house was silent, mainly because Val was completely knocked out in the back seat and I didn't even bother to turn on any music in my car. I was just alone with my thoughts and even though I knew Val was drunk, some of the things she said really hurt me. I knew those were her true feelings too. I could tell sometimes by the things Val would say to me that she was a bit jealous. I had always been a genuine friend to her so it bothered me that she felt that way. But I had to remind myself that was Val's problem, not mine. Those were issues she had to deal with. But when was the last time someone took my feelings into consideration? I felt like I was always saving everyone, making the best decisions for everyone and quite frankly I was tired of it.

"Bitch where you taking me?" I just ignored Val as she was mumbling in the back seat. I was just praying she didn't throw up in my truck especially since I had just gotten it detailed a couple of days ago. As I was pulling up in front of Val's house, I wondered how the hell was I going to get her drunk, heavy ass out of my car.

Thankfully, Val's neighbor Bob was walking out of his house and saw me trying to get Val out of the car.

"Hey young lady, wait let me help you," Bob yelled from his front door.

"Bob right? Val speaks very highly of you." I honestly didn't know what to say seeing that the only thing I remembered Val mentioning about Bob was that supposedly he has an Italian- bred dick he'd love to fuck her with.

"Oh, you don't have to make small talk young lady. Just let me help you with Val right quick. It's so cold out here."

Surprisingly for a seventy-two year old man, Bob was rather strong. He lifted Val as if he had done this before. I started to wonder how many drunk nights had Bob encountered with Val. The thought made me a little sad because maybe Val had been drinking more so to cope as opposed to just having fun. Bob and I walked Val into her bedroom and laid her down on the bed.

"Thanks so much, Bob, I'll take it from here. I really appreciate your help."

"It's no problem at all. You're Lita, right?"

"Yes, I am." I was trying to smile even though Val totally upset me.

"Now she *really* speaks highly of you, unlike that lie you told me earlier." We both laughed.

"I'm sorry about that. It was just an awkward first encounter."

"Look, you don't have to explain. Try not to hold this against your friend though. I could tell by the way you were helping Val out of your car that you were upset with her about something as opposed to just helping out a drunk friend. Hey, some of us have a lot of things going on in our lives. I'm not saying it's okay, but we all deal with it differently you know?"

I felt like Bob knew so much more about Val than most people. I could see why she said she just sits and talks to Bob for hours sometimes.

"Well, I'm really glad she has a neighbor like you. It's nice to know someone is looking out for my girl like that."

"It's my pleasure. Well, I'm going to go because Val always thinks I'm trying to take her to bed which I'm not but if she found out I was actually in her bedroom, she would have a fit."

"Are we talking about the same Val?" We laughed again. "Thanks, Bob, again I really appreciate it."

"It's no problem at all." Bob walked to the door and let himself out. I pulled the covers over Val and I slept in her guest bedroom for the night because I didn't want to leave her alone.

* * *

"What are you doing here?" Val's morning greeting was anything but welcoming.

"You were pretty out of it last night. I didn't want to leave you alone." I said while stretching and wiping the cold from my eyes. I was thinking to myself, *is she really going to start this first thing in the morning, damn!*

"Well, I don't need a babysitter, Lita. I'm a grown ass woman."

"All I wanted to do was make sure you got home safely and keep you company, that's it. Excuse me for trying to be here for you."

"Why do you feel that I need you? You act like it's a crime to have fun and get drunk."

"No, I do not. But there's a difference between getting drunk and then getting drunk and insulting me and crying in the middle of the club at the same damn time."

"I ain't got time for yo stuck up ass this morning."

"Wow, so that's how we're doing this now Val? All I did and all I've ever done is be a friend to you. I was just looking out for you but you're acting as if you'd rather I left your drunk ass at the club."

"Maybe, you should've then I could've snatched that bitch up that Greg was with with her young ass, get on my damn nerves. Or maybe find *me* one of them young boys to take me home last night."

I couldn't believe how nonchalant Val was reacting to everything that happened but it was a clear indication that I needed to leave.

"Val, I know you don't want to hear this but——"

"Well, bitch don't speak then."

"You know what? It's taking my all not to slap the shit outta you right now Val. You had the muthafuckin' nerve to practically call me an insensitive, bougie bitch in the club, even though I've done nothing but be a real friend to you! I'm sick of this shit. Your attitude sucks and you need to quit lying to yourself and get some damn help. I never judged you for fuckin every nigga that practically said hello to you, or getting sloppy ass drunk with yo old ass, or even telling you that's what the fuck you get for messing around with Don."

"Get—the—fuck—outta—my—goddamn—house—Lita!"

I was so angry as I was walking to Val's front door. I could feel the tears swelling in my eyes because I literally felt like I was losing my best friend. The things we said to each other were enough to destroy any friendship. All I wanted to do was get as far away from Val as I could. It was like someone literally kicked me in my back and the pain wouldn't stop.

* * *

My house was in view. I tried to get myself together before entering. I checked my eyes and clearly it looked like I had been crying seeing that I couldn't turn off the waterworks as I drove home. I just kept thinking about some of the things Val said to me.

I couldn't believe how mean she was. I knew she could be sarcastic at times, but she was pure evil last night. I really think she's been having some issues with abusing alcohol the way she was throwing back those shots last night. All I wanted to do was take a shower and lie down. It was about nine-thirty a.m. when I entered my house. Typically, everyone was asleep at this time on Sunday mornings so I slowly unlocked the front door and crept in as if I was a teenager trying to dodge her parents because she missed curfew.

"Well, good morning to you." Mike entered the living room from the kitchen to greet me as if he was disappointed in me for not coming home last night.

"Oh, hey Mike. Did you get my messages?"

"Yep. I fell asleep around eleven o'clock so I didn't listen to your messages until I rolled over to hold you at three a.m. and noticed you weren't in the bed."

"Yeah, it was quite an interesting night."

"Clearly. You look like you barely got any rest." Mike said with an accusatory tone.

"Well, Val and I got into a fight."

"What? Like physical?"

"No, but with the way she was acting, it could have easily led to that."

"Wait a minute, what the hell happened?"

"Well, in a nutshell, Val called me a bougie ass bitch and said she's tired of living in my shadow. She was drunk as hell and she really hurt my feelings, especially seeing that I drove her drunk ass home early this morning. I also stayed with her even though she made me so angry but I didn't want her to be alone. We started arguing again this morning and she kicked me out of her house! Can you believe that?"

"I hate to say this but she's always been jealous of you and quite frankly I think you're too good to be hanging around her anyway."

"What? What would make you say that?" Mike's comment was really starting to bother me.

"C'mon now. Val may have a pretty good job but she really doesn't fit into the caliber of people she supposedly surrounds herself with."

"Well, this is news to me. I wouldn't say I fit into that category either."

"Trust me, you do. All of those businessmen I play golf and poker with give me the inside scoop and everyone speaks very highly of you. Val's name gets dragged through the mud quite often. Basically, she's synonymous with the company hoe, their words not mine."

"Mike, I really need you to stop talking about my friend like that."

"Oh, the same friend that called you bougie? The same friend that's extremely jealous of you? Or maybe you're talking about the friend that kicked you out of her house just because you tried to help her? Or better yet, maybe you're talking about the friend that fucked your married boss and got pregnant by him?"

"Who told you about that?"

"Trust me, more people know about that than you think. My question is, why didn't you think to tell me?"

"I shouldn't have to tell you. That's Val's personal business."

"Oh, so you didn't think it was okay for me to know you were spending time with someone who could basically tarnish your reputation? I had a meeting the other day with one of your regular donors. He's married to the woman who heads the Public Relations department at Global Connections, I think her name is Nancy. Well, somehow Nancy found out about Val's relationship with Don and told her husband. He conveniently brought it up to me after our meeting. I basically shut that down really quickly and made it seem like you and Val were just colleagues, nothing more. We've worked too damn hard to get where we are now. I'm actually glad the truth is coming out and maybe you can disassociate yourself from her."

"Wow, so tell me how you really feel? I get that impressing people is like a full time job to you, but in my world, I look out for the people I love. I don't throw them away just because they're going through things."

"Dammit, Lita! Val is a functional drunk who practically slept her way to where she is right now. I know you don't wanna hear that, but I'm in many circles who know Val extremely well if you know what I mean. I've been real cool about all this until she had the nerve to treat you like she did last night. I don't want you hanging with her. It's not cool. We don't need the Paynes affiliated with that bullshit!"

"So it's about the Paynes now, not just me? Oh, that's right because all you care about is your precious name, your precious reputation. Fuck what Lita wants! It's all about Mike!"

"Damn, why are you being so dramatic right now? If you would get out of your feelings for a minute, you would see what I'm saying is true. Listen, I know you're not trying to hear me but in due time you will see."

"Don't talk to me like I'm one of the kids! I'm going to give Val some time to cool down and get her head straight but I will not turn my back on my friend."

"Oh, so you can turn your back on me but you can't turn your back on your "friend?""

"First of all, what the hell are *you* talking about? And who's being dramatic now?"

"I know I've been coming home late the past few weeks but when was the last time you left a plate for me after dinner? You don't call me on your way home from work anymore. And let's not get started on the last time you gave me some. Got me over here hanging out with this bottle of lotion in the bathroom all the damn time. This shit is for the birds. I should not be getting myself off when I have a wife. This is some bullshit!"

"You know what? I'm not going to even begin to talk about how you're not meeting my needs because we'll be up all damn day and night talking about *that* shit."

"It's amazing how we get into an argument because of some shit Val did."

"You know goddamn well this conversation is not about Val. We've been having problems for a long time. We've tried the counseling thing, we've tried "date nights", we've tried going away on trips together, we've tried everything. I'm just tired."

"So what are you trying to say?"

"All I can tell you is that I'm tired and I don't have it in me to even get upset anymore." I started to walk up the stairs so that I could finally take off my clothes from last night and take a nice, long, hot bath.

"Maybe *I* should stay out tonight," Mike said as if he was trying desperately to retaliate.

"If that's what you want to do, then do it. I'm tired." And I slowly kept walking up the stairs. As soon as I reached the bedroom, my phone began to vibrate with a text message. It was Law.

"Hey, I hope I didn't catch you at a bad time. I will continue to respect your wishes and give you space. You were just on my mind and I wanted you to know I was thinking about you."

And just like that, I knew I wanted to start seeing Law again.

CHAPTER

7

Spring had finally made its appearance but everyone knows there are only two real seasons in Chicago; Winter and Summer. At least winter was finally gone as it was about seventy degrees outside and sunny.

The Lakefront was extremely crowded with joggers, stay at home moms power walking with their babies in tow, and millennials eagerly awaiting to break out their string bikinis and shorts. We were on the cusp of "Summertime Chi" which was more so a state of mind rather than a legitimate season. This was the time when outdoor festivals and concerts began, food trucks and pop up shops appeared, and day parties and bar crawls became regular scheduled events following our winter hibernation.

I was excited for my future. I had been in my new position as Senior Fundraising Coordinator for five months now and I was really enjoying my new responsibilities. I was making some major power moves and connections. I had already been out to Atlanta three times to organize their fundraising committee. I also had an opportunity to travel to Sedona, Arizona for a Fundraising Conference as well. While I was there, I even treated myself to a spa and meditation retreat. I was finally doing things that made me happy. Of course, I checked in with the kids but Mike and I were extremely distant. We barely talked unless it was about Sheree and the boys or finances. We hadn't made love in almost three months and I even began wondering if Mike had started seeing someone else considering he wasn't even trying to get me into bed anymore.

I had seen Law a few times since he'd sent me that text message the night Mike and I had that big argument. The times we were together were all in public places. Law had invited me to a networking event at the Willis Tower to help me gain some exposure to some of the people he networked with. The whole time we were there, we tried focusing on business but we continued to flirt with one another and make intense eye contact from across the room. Afterwards, he took me out for a drink and we just talked.

I started telling him more about my life and he shared more about himself as well. I was experiencing a level of intimacy that I had never felt before even with Mike. I enjoyed every minute of it. We met up two other times to begin working on my business plan and goals. I convinced myself that if I was attending networking events and having "business strategy" meetings with Law, then it wasn't considered cheating. But I wasn't kidding anyone, definitely not myself.

We had not become physical but the feelings were so strong between the both of us. One night after meeting up with Law, I was so damn horny that I came home and fucked Mike's brains out.

That was the last time we'd made love. Mike enjoyed it but he didn't really get his hopes up that time. I guess he could feel how distant we were too and didn't want to make too much of it. I also realized I couldn't keep this up too much longer as I was completely mesmerized by Law.

I was enjoying my new career and working on my new business goals and Law was definitely keeping a smile on my face as I always felt like I was learning something new from him. That's always been a huge turn on for me when a man could actually teach me something. Law was exposing me to things I was not quite accustomed to in the entrepreneurial world.

Val and I still weren't on the best of terms even though I wished we were so I could tell her what had been going on in my life. With my office being on the nineteenth floor now, we barely saw each other unless we made a special effort and that was few and far between.

"Lita, I have to take a quick business trip this weekend to Los Angeles." Mike called me while I was taking a walk along the beach. I was making more of a habit to enjoy the outdoors this year. When I saw Mike's name appear on my phone, I debated whether or not to answer because lately, our conversations were either extremely dry or we would began arguing. Either way, I didn't want anything to upset me and take away from this carefree mood I had adopted these days.

"Oh okay."

"Would you like to come with me?"

"Hmmm, that's interesting. You rarely ask me to come along on your business trips."

"Well, this time is different."

"But why?

"Do you want to come or not?" Mike sounded like he was getting irritated.

"Well, not exactly with that attitude."

"Damn, Lita! All I did was ask if you wanted to come to L.A. with me. It requires a "yes" or "no" response. Why is that so hard?"

"We haven't exactly been on the same wavelength these past few months."

"And can't you tell that I'm trying to change that? Usually, I don't ask you to come on my business trips because they're typically so jam packed with meetings that we really wouldn't get a chance to spend any quality time together. I know I could just send you to the spa or shopping while I'm working but I know you. You're going to want to explore the city and I usually don't have time to. But this time, the itinerary for this trip is not as hectic and I thought it would be great for us to get away together."

"I just don't think this is the time for us to be traveling together."

"Alright. Just forget I asked." Mike hung up the phone before I could say bye.

Was I being that harsh? I just felt that no amount of getaways was going to help us. If I had gone on that trip with Mike, he would've gotten a false sense of everything being okay. I needed for Mike to understand that I needed more from him than just putting a band-aid on the problem.

"I'm sorry. I didn't mean to upset you." I decided to call Mike back even though I was worried that it would just turn into another argument.

"I just don't know what you want anymore. I get that we haven't been connecting but I'm trying to change that. Lately, it just feels like you're purposely shutting me out. I mean, just keep it real with me. Do you still want to be married?"

"Of course I do! Just because I don't think a trip is going to magically heal our marriage doesn't mean I want a divorce."

"Lately, I've just felt like I'm the one who still wants this but you act like you can just take it or leave it."

"We're just responding to the situation differently. I still want our marriage but I don't want a temporary fix."

"And you're saying that's what I want?"

"Please don't put words in my mouth."

"Anyway, I don't wanna go back and forth about that. When will you be home? Are you still downtown?"

"I'm actually over by the Lake right now. I'll probably be home in another hour or so. I'm not really in the mood to cook so I'll probably just pick us up something to eat."

"While you're out, do you mind picking up my dry cleaning on your way home?"

"Well, that's not exactly on my way home but——"

"Don't even worry about it. I forgot we're not on the same wavelength so I'll just pick it up myself. And honestly, you don't have to pick up any food for me either. I don't want you to be inconvenienced." Mike hung up again. I could definitely tell Mike was pretty upset but that was precisely the problem.

I'm constantly giving, making his life easier and he's not thinking about what makes me happy and what my needs are. I've decided I'm not falling into this trap again of doing for everyone else and not myself. Seeing that Mike was going out of town this weekend, I was going to make it all about me. I was going to call my mother- in-law and ask her to watch the kids. Maybe I would get a hotel downtown and just relax. The more responsible thing to do would be to probably work on my business. Maybe there was a way to could incorporate the two.

* * *

As I watched Mike pack his bag for his business trip, part of me felt a sense of sadness as I could feel our marriage unraveling. I had made a conscious decision not to pick up Mike's dry cleaning for his trip this time, or make sure he didn't forget anything that belonged in his luggage. I didn't review his schedule with him either or tell him how much I was going to miss him like I normally did. I was actually looking forward to Mike leaving town. Even the times I had traveled to Atlanta for work, I was still checking in to make sure everything was on point with the kids and their schedules. It gets exhausting being the gatekeeper of everyone. Enough is enough. I needed *me* back and I was determined to get it.

"Mama, can I spend the night over Tasha's house this weekend?" Sheree barged into our room like she normally does.

"I'm not sure yet. Your grandma Diane will be coming over this weekend so we'll have to see."

"Oh, she is?" Mike sounded surprised.

"Yes, she is."

"Is there a particular reason?"

"Well, there shouldn't be a specific reason for your mom to come over and spend time with the kids."

"So are you not going to be here?" Mike sounded concerned.

"As a matter of fact, I will not. I asked Diane to come over and watch the kids this weekend as I was thinking about booking a room downtown and just having some me time."

"Hmmm…"

"Is there something you want to say?"

"Nope, we can talk about it another time."

"Sheree, can you excuse yourself for a minute?"

"Mama, are you all like about to argue or something?"

"Sheree, just excuse yourself," I said to Sheree in a very serious tone.

"Okay, mama." Sheree left the room as she seemed more concerned about us than hanging out with her friends for once.

I closed our bedroom door so that the kids wouldn't be privy to our conversation.

"Mike, are you upset that I'm taking time for myself?"

"Let me get this straight. You don't want to go to L.A. with me because you feel that a trip right now is just putting a band-aid on the situation. But you want your alone time and I get that. You say you don't want a divorce but it just baffles me that you keep pushing me away."

"Mike, I just need this time. I'm always doing everything for everyone else even carrying our marriage emotionally and I just can't do that anymore."

"Look, you don't have to explain it anymore. I really don't even wanna argue. I just want to make sure I pack everything I need. I don't want to forget anything because I have such an early flight tomorrow morning."

Getting Mike prepared for his business trips was always something I had done. I had felt kind of bad that I'd stopped doing that but I knew how the situation would play out. The minute I stepped in and began taking on that role of the Stepford Wife again is when Mike would expect it all the time. He would no longer put any effort towards making our marriage work. I think I'm beyond that now.

* * *

Mike left this morning without even saying goodbye. I definitely wasn't trying to hurt him but I was really fed up with how our marriage was unfolding. I just expected so much more for us. When we were dating and even when we first married, Mike continuously made an effort to surprise me, listen to me, and please me. These days, Mike just seems so content with how things are that he doesn't even try anymore. I couldn't even remember the last time Mike really looked deeply into my eyes or kissed me passionately or just rubbed my back or my feet just because. So many of these relationship books tell you to be very straightforward with your partner and say exactly how you feel and what you want, but the times that I've done that, Mike would get so upset and just shut down emotionally. And quite frankly, some things I don't want to have to say directly. I would've hoped after ten years of marriage, he would just know.

"Is this a good time to talk? I received a text from Law.

Usually, when Law texted me on the weekends, he would message me in the morning because I told him everyone was typically still asleep as I was the early riser in my house. Instead of texting him back, I decided to call because I'd much rather hear his voice. As soon as I typed the letter "L" on my phone, his name appeared and immediately I became excited.

"Hey, beautiful," Law answered when I called. His voice was so deep which always turned me on.

"Hi, Law. How are you feeling this morning?"

"I'm feeling really good especially now that I'm speaking to you. So what's on your agenda today?"

I decided not to even beat around the bush. "I was thinking we could get together maybe early this evening?"

"No doubt, it's always a pleasure seeing you. Were you looking to brainstorm some business ideas? Or did you make some progress towards meeting some of your business goals?" Law was completely clueless that I wanted to spend more intimate time with him.

"Well, I was thinking maybe we could do dinner?"

"Oh, this sounds like it's not exactly business related?"

"You can say that." I was smiling on the phone.

"Well, you know I'm always up for that. What place did you have in mind?"

"I was thinking maybe you could decide." It's very rare that I just sit back and allow someone to take control but for some reason, I trusted Law. I was really interested in him taking the lead.

"Hmm, are you sure?"

"Yes, I am. I trust you."

"Again, I'm trying to remain appropriate with you, but the way you said you trusted me kind of did something to me just now."

I was smiling again, I could tell a man like Law enjoyed taking the lead on things and actually took pride in it so I could see how that was a turn on for him. I craved that from a man and Law was excited to do it. "Am I turning you on?" I said playfully and flirtatiously.

"Uum, yes you are?" Law laughed.

"So where should we go?"

"So I was thinking, how about I cook for you? I hired a personal chef for a gathering at my home about a year ago. The food was so delicious that I hired the chef again for cooking lessons. I've always known how to cook but I just wanted to switch things up a bit and add some new dishes to the repertoire. If you're not quite comfortable coming over to my house, I completely understand."

"I'd love to." Wow, that was extremely easy on my part. I didn't hesitate or contemplate it for a second.

"Great! Now you know you got a brotha smiling from ear to ear. I'm looking forward to having such a beautiful guest at my home this evening."

"Well, I don't want to intrude especially if you have a few earrings or panties stashed away somewhere," I said jokingly.

"Trust me, things have been pretty chill in that department for a while but remember I asked *you* over so you're not intruding at all."

"I was just joking, I'm looking forward to it. Would you like me to bring some wine or anything else?"

"You are more than enough. I just look forward to seeing your beautiful self."

There was something about Law that I yearned for. I liked how he wasn't afraid to share how he felt about me, but he was never crass about it. His maturity was sexy as hell. When he spoke, I hung on to every word. He said things in a way that I knew if given the opportunity, he would please me to no end. That made me excited but also scared. Was I really about to go over Law's house tonight? I wasn't exactly going to plan to have sex with him but I would definitely shave and wear some of my sexiest underwear just in case. Who the hell was I kidding? I was feeling him and there was no turning back now.

"Well, thank you for the invitation. How does seven o'clock sound?"

"That's perfect. That gives me enough time to do a little shopping and start preparing."

"So what's on the menu Chef Davis?"

"How about I surprise you? You did tell me you liked seafood so that will definitely be on the menu."

"Oh, you're trying to get me excited for real!" I said joyfully as if I was a kid who just found out they were getting the gift they've always wanted for Christmas.

"Well, just bring your fine self over here tonight and I'll be sure to have a delicious meal waiting for you."

"Hmm, I like the sounds of that."

"I'm glad you do Ms. Lita. I'd better head over to the store and pick up a few things. I'm really looking forward to seeing you this evening."

"Okay, I look forward to seeing you too, Law."

"I've never told you this but I love the way you say my name."

"Well, I like saying your name."

"Okay, well I'd better let you go before I say hell let's just skip dinner and make some other plans." We both laughed. I knew what Law was insinuating and I was loving every minute of it.

"I'll see you tonight."

"Okay baby, I'll see you later." After I hung up the phone, I asked myself if I was really going through with this? I mean, I couldn't possibly go over to another man's house thinking he's not going to want to get physical. For the past ten years, it's only been Mike. But I was so enticed by Law and I wanted him to explore every inch of me.

* * *

As I walked out of the door of my South Loop Condo, my stomach was in knots but this is what I wanted. No, *needed.* No longer was I interested in waiting on Mike to "show up" for me; for us. The moral compass in which I used to guide my marriage was now obsolete. Even though I had never done anything like this before, I knew it was going down tonight. I was hurting from Mike's disengagement, his lack of concern regarding my goals and dreams, how he spent so much time at work, and his unwillingness to please me in certain ways sexually. I justified this at every angle.

As I admired the beautiful evening and the fresh scent of spring rain filling the air, flowers and trees were finally beginning to bloom after a long, brutal winter. I admired couples walking alongside each other sharing an umbrella as the rain progressively began to fall. I reminisced about Mike and I and how we once had that same love that said we would conquer the world together. It's crazy because in the midst of the hustle and bustle of building our careers, caring for our children and just mainly navigating the different stages of life, we lost our connection and the passion for each other. Nothing really excited me anymore about us. Seriously, is this what most long-term marriages resulted in? Is marriage even feasible anymore? If I could be honest with myself for a minute, what did I really need Mike for? Yes, I enjoyed the perks of a dual income but it's not like I couldn't support myself and our children. My own income had increased significantly and I had very healthy savings and investment accounts all on my own. I was starting to question the reality of marriage in the 21st century and its overall benefits for women.

I began to grow nervous as I approached Law's neighborhood. I didn't even realize I was so close as I was lost in my thoughts while driving. Hyde Park presented itself as well established with its impeccable manicured lawns and smiling neighbors. The area boasted about its top-notch schools and its easy access to all things city life related. I always loved Hyde Park for that reason. When Law told me he lived there, it didn't even surprise me because he represented the beauty and essence of the urban professional in Chicago. His demeanor, his intellect, his confidence, his stance and his perspective on life drew me into a trance and as much as I liked being in control, I was very willing to let him be my tour guide. I wanted him to show me so much more to make up for the areas I was deficient in. I felt myself falling for him more and more each day.

I stepped out of my car and approached the steps to his townhome which appeared massive from the outside. My heart was racing but I liked the feeling of anticipating his appearance. I felt like I was in a movie. I could smell the aroma of herbs and spices from his home on the outside as well as hearing neo-soul music playing in the background. Oh my God! Was he listening to "Girl" by The Internet? Seriously? What did his old ass know about The Internet? I chuckled to myself. It was a given, I knew I wanted to be here.

"Hey you." Law opened the door and smiled at me exposing his pearly whites.

"Hey." I said happily.

"C'mon in. I can't have you standing out in the rain. Your sexy chocolate self would melt.

"Ha, you're silly."

"Just trying to make you smile. Let me take your jacket." After hanging up my black leather biker jacket, Law, reached for me and hugged me tight.

"You are really impressing me right now. You're playing one of my favorite songs. How do you know about The Internet?"

"Lita, please. I may be almost sixty but I'm well-versed in all kinds of music." I heard what Law was saying but I was extremely distracted by his bulging arms in his fitted black t-shirt and his jeans fit his ass to perfection. He had a long dish towel hanging over his shoulder as if he was really throwing down in the kitchen. And by the smell, I think it was safe to assume that he was.

"Well, I won't ever assume anything about you again." I smiled.

"Please don't 'cause a brotha has many hidden talents." Law winked at me.

"You have got to take me into your kitchen because it smells like you're doing some damage in there, in a good way of course."

"Oh yes, yes. C'mon over here." Law grabbed my hand and guided me into his kitchen. "You have to taste the roux I made for the étouffée. It's divine." Law slowly lifted the warm spoon to my mouth after he blew on it first. It tasted so good!

"Wow! This is amazing!"

"Why thank you. And that's definitely a compliment coming from you seeing that seafood is your favorite dish."

"I am extremely impressed, I can't wait to eat."

"Well, we have a little more time. But while we're waiting, I'd love to show you the rest of my house."

"Oh, most definitely."

Law's home was beautiful. I thought I had an idea what his home would look like but it was more than I expected. The walls were graced with beautiful African art. Pops of color were present in each room and exposed brick and hardwood floors seemed to be a common theme. The pictures of people who I'd assumed were his family made his home very warm and inviting. Of course his home smelled like sandalwood as I knew I caught a whiff of incense on him a few times. Law was so eclectic. I loved it.

"Here's few pictures of my daughters and my grandchildren when we were in Zambia."

"Your family is so beautiful! I've never been to Zambia before. Actually, I've never traveled to Africa but I'd sure love to go."

"Well, in time I'm pretty sure you will. It truly is a beautiful place but I guess I'm impartial due to my family being from there. Come with me, let me show you the rest of my house."

I loved how excited Law was to share with me the different aspects of his home. I felt like I was learning so much more about him just by being there.

"So how long have you been living here?"

"Actually, I moved to Hyde Park about eight years ago but I just bought this townhome six months ago. I'm really digging it so far."

"Yeah, Hyde Park is really nice. I'm in the South Loop you know?"

"Right, I remember you were telling me that. How long have you been there and how do you like it?"

"It's cool, I definitely can't complain. We've been there for almost five years now." I felt kind of weird saying "we" because that included Mike and I didn't want to talk about him too much around Law.

"Well, owning a condo in the South Loop is definitely nothing to sneeze at. I think that's pretty cool. My apologies, I didn't even offer you a drink. Are you a red or white wine drinker?"

"I like red, preferably Merlot if you have it?"

"I sure do. I will get you a glass." Law went downstairs to get us some wine. I just continued to admire his home and how it spoke volumes about his style and who he was as a person.

"Here you go babe. Let's make a toast." We both held up our glasses. "I just want to toast to the beginning of something new, and the amazing friendship we are building."

"I like that." We both sipped our wine. "Law, you have made me feel so welcomed in your home and I feel like I've learned so much more about you."

"Well, that's good because I want you to know more about me."

"And I want you to know more about me too."

"Are you sure about that because I want you to feel comfortable sharing whatever you like."

"Thank you, I appreciate that." We sipped some more.

"How about we continue our conversation over dinner?"

"Sounds good."

I was really enjoying our conversation and meal. We laughed and of course we gazed at each other. I felt like I had known Law longer than I really did. Everything felt so effortless as our connection seemed so easy.

"So how did you enjoy dinner?"

"Oh my God, it was amazing! The shrimp, the spices, the roux was perfection. Those cooking lessons are definitely paying off."

"Well they should. I definitely paid a grip for it. But let me take your plate. I'm going to fill the dishwasher right quick and then we can talk more on the couch."

Law seemed genuinely excited to have me at his home. He was so attentive. I kind of questioned why was he still single?

"Lita, do you mind if I dim the lights a little?"

"By all means, do your thing."

Law walked me over to the couch.

"So, I know I tell you this every time I see you but you are extremely beautiful. And you smell so good. Is that the Jimmy Choo scent you were talking about when we met?"

"You know, for someone who says they have a bad memory, you sure remember a lot about me."

"Well, believe it or not, you motivate me to remember and that's what I like about you so much. You have a way about you that requires no effort. You have a quiet and subtle confidence that I really like. When I saw you at the bookstore, I thought to myself, I see beautiful women all the time but you were so exquisite to me. I love everything from your beautiful chocolate skin, to your smile and the way you wear your hair in its natural state. It reminds me so much of the women of the Black Panther movement. But you just carry yourself with such style."

"I'm extremely flattered but I can curse like a sailor at times."

"Hey, no one is perfect and yeah just like you said, at times. It's not all the time. But I can respect that because you're being yourself."

"I just feel like you're the first person that really appreciates my true self. I always feel like people are more into my image, or what I have to offer on paper, or what I can do for them. I just feel like no one truly knows the real Lita."

"But have you invited them into that space?"

"Hmm, that's a good question."

"It's definitely something to think about. I take it that you don't just walk up to random guys and tell them how handsome they are and ask them for their number. They may do that to you, but you don't strike me as the person that typically does that. And here comes little 'ole me and you just let yourself be free for a moment and started talking to me. I think that was the true Lita coming out."

"I don't know how you do that, but you hit the nail on the head with me every time."

"Well, like I said, I'm into you, probably more than you know."

"I must admit, this is still a little awkward for me. I mean, I know my husband and I haven't been on the best of terms and he's even out of town right now as we speak and he hasn't called me like he normally does."

"Does that bother you?"

"Not really, I think it just speaks to where we are in our marriage right now."

"And where is that?"

"Distant, non-communicative."

"How does that make you feel?"

"I guess a bit disappointed considering all the time and effort that I put into my marriage."

"Well, those are definitely natural feelings especially for a woman. I've been married twice so I truly understand the range of emotions that can come with that."

"Is it weird or uncomfortable for you when I talk about my marriage?"

"No, not at all. Here's the thing. I really like you. I like every facet of you and that includes this vulnerable side of you right now. It just seems like you don't allow yourself to really open up to others. You're always there for everyone else but you need that sometimes too. I'd like to be that for you."

"The only thing is, you're a man that I'm extremely attracted to."

"I get that because I'm extremely attracted to you too. Like I said before, this can be whatever you want it to be. There's so much I want to spoil you with but you have to be in a space to be ready to receive it."

"I just——"

"What is it? You know you can be completely free with me."

"It's just, my husband and I lost our connection a long time ago and I'm hanging on by a thread these days. I don't feel fulfilled like I should. We don't spend much quality time together and he just doesn't please me——" I tried to take back what I said but it was too late. I didn't want to talk about my sex life with Law.

"So, if I can be frank, you are feeling depleted emotionally and you really need more in the bedroom as well. Does that sound about right?"

"I'm embarrassed to say, but yes."

"You don't have to be embarrassed about that. That is something we humans desire."

"But it's just hard saying that I like—"

"Good sex, I know. I'm a fan of quality sex myself." Law smiled at me and then he took my hand.

"Lita, for tonight, I want you to relax. I don't want you to think about work, starting your business, your problems with your husband, your kids or anything else that is weighing you down right now. I would like to see you unwind a bit and I would like to be the one to help you get there."

"And how do you plan on doing that?"

"Well, I can start by just listening to you talk? I can rub your feet and your back if that's something you like? I can kiss you in areas that you liked being kissed. I can touch you in the areas you like to be touched. I can caress you just like you need to be caressed and I would love the opportunity to explore in between your legs with my tongue—"

"Wow, you're definitely exciting me right now."

"That's the whole purpose. Tonight is all about pleasuring you. I want you to reach a level that you've never reached before. You deserve that kind of satisfaction and I'm more than willing to provide you with that if you'd let me."

"Damn Law!"

"Ha! That's that sailor coming out of you right now isn't? I like that. Here, come with me."

"Where are we going?"

"I'm taking you to my bedroom."

"Well, lead the way."

"Now that you've seen all of my home, I'd like for *you* to lead the way. I just want to admire you from the back for a minute."

Dammit! Once these panties come off, Law is going to think I peed on myself, they're so wet right now. How could he have this effect on me? He hadn't even kissed me yet, let alone even really touch me. When we got to the top of the stairs and I turned around to look at Law, he picked me up and I wrapped my legs around his waist. He kissed me with so much passion. It didn't feel rushed or too timid, it was just right. I just loved how strong he was.

Law gently placed me on his bed and undressed me. He didn't take off any of his clothes yet as he said he wanted to give me a full body massage which was divine. He laid me on my stomach and when he kissed me behind my ears, I got goosebumps. When he kissed me behind my knees, I trembled. But when he licked the small of my back, I almost climaxed. His touch was everything. Law was playing Anita Baker in the background and it truly set the mood. I was really enjoying how he was taking his time with me and the foreplay was absolutely amazing.

"How are you feeling?"

"Oh, I'm doing very well."

"That's what I like to hear."

Law continued to rub my body and when he gently turned me over on my back, I knew how it was about to go down. Law kissed my lips and made his way down to my neck and then my breast and my nipples. He kissed my stomach and licked my navel and when he touched the inner parts of my thighs, he spread them apart. He looked at my pussy and then looked up at me and smiled.

"All I can say is damn. You are so beautiful right now. The smell of you is seriously turning me on. You have such a beautiful pussy."

And before I knew it, Law was licking every part of me, exactly how I liked it. He started off slow and then progressed and when he felt me shake a little bit, he slowed down. His tongue was definitely the star of the show and I couldn't take it anymore, I felt my legs starting to tremble and I locked his head in between my thighs because I could no longer control what was happening. Thankfully Law was patient with my reaction and once I loosened my legs, and he lifted his head up, I could see all of my natural juices dripping from his lips. It was such a beautiful sight and then he kissed me, wet mouth and all and I loved it.

"I'd love to return the favor Law."

"Trust me, as much as I want you to, I'm making it my mission to making pleasuring you my top priority tonight."

Law got on top of me and I moaned and moaned some more as he talked dirty to me. When he turned me over, he entered me from behind and the hardness of his dick had me making foreign sounds that sounded as if I was going into a convulsion. I hadn't experienced multiple orgasms like that in a long time. And shortly after, Law climaxed as well. I couldn't believe how wonderful it felt to be with him but the guilt started to creep in. I tried to push it down at least until I left his house.

"You were amazing you know that?" Law said while he held me.

"No, *you* were."

"Well, let's just agree we both pleasured each other. What I enjoyed the most, is how free you were with me and the sounds you made were the most beautiful thing. You are truly an amazing woman."

"Thank you. Being with you tonight made me feel so sexy and alive."

"I'm glad that I could do that for you. But you know, in my eyes, I already saw you as beautiful and alive. I just think you forget that at times."

"Well, there's just so much going on in my life—"

"And you don't have to explain a word of that to me. I know you have a lot going on which is why I only want to pour into you and not just take. You really deserve that."

Law was so much more than I imagined. The sex being phenomenal was just the icing on the cake. But I felt torn because the connection I was experiencing right now was something I'd always desired with someone. It just hurt that I wasn't experiencing that with Mike.

"You are truly something special."

"Well, I try." Law chuckled. "Hey are you okay? You seem a little indifferent all of a sudden."

It was amazing how Law could literally pick up my mood without me saying a word.

"I'm okay. What made you ask that?"

"Now Lita, I know we haven't known each other a long time but I think you know by now how much I'm into you and how I can feel your energy. Are you having second thoughts about what just happened between us?"

"I know my marriage to Mike has been over for a long time, but I would be lying if I said I didn't feel somewhat bad about being unfaithful to him."

"And believe it or not, I truly respect you for that. I believe we met at a time when we both were seeking something more with regards to relationships. I know that timing plays a huge factor in all of this. I know that you have a lot to sort out and you won't get any friction from me. Remember I'm here to bring a sense of calmness to your life, not chaos. I want you to make the best decision for you."

"See, when you talk like that, I ask myself what did I do to deserve this kind of affection and attention?"

"You don't believe you do?"

"Yes, I believe I really do! It's just been such a long time since I've felt that way in my marriage."

"Well, take it from a man who's been married twice. Marriages can be pretty complex and both people are always growing and evolving. It can be really hard to balance at times. Men don't always express themselves in a way that women understand and vice versa. And depending on the man, it takes certain experiences to help him evolve into the man his woman is desiring him to be."

"I'm listening to you talk and you're so calm about all of this."

"Well, how am I supposed to be?"

"I don't know, I guess I didn't expect the response I'm getting from you seeing that we just made love and I'm talking about my marriage."

"Well, I'm definitely a grown ass man that understands a lot about life and relationships. Now, I'm no expert, but I understand there can be a lot of gray areas and things aren't always so cut and dry. What's important is being able to share how you feel about things that are on your mind without being judged."

"And I definitely appreciate you being that person that I can share my true feelings."

Law kissed my forehead and held me some more. Was Law really this genuine or was there an ulterior motive? I wasn't sure but I was definitely enjoying the moment. I just didn't want to think about any consequences or repercussions of what happened between us. I just wanted to enjoy the night. But as I laid there, I knew I would not return home the same and that scared me.

CHAPTER

────────

8

"Lele!" I gotta talk to you! Where the fuck have you been?"

Niecey said with a sense of urgency. But again, everything was urgent with Niecey which is why I wasn't answering any of her calls.

"What is it Niecey?" I said dryly.

"I was over Daddy's house earlier today and he started having difficulty breathing."

"What? Oh my God! Did you take him to the hospital? What the hell is going on?"

"No, he said he didn't want me to."

"Dammit, Niecey! You know how stubborn Daddy is! You just left him there?"

"Umm, no? I stayed with him all damn day! Where was yo' ass? I had been trying to call you!"

"You didn't leave a message!"

"It doesn't matter, Lita! If you see me constantly calling you, you should've picked up the damn phone! I ain't got time for this shit."

"Whatever, where is Daddy now?"

"He's still at the house. I'm on my way back from the grocery store. He didn't have a damn thing in his fridge."

"I'm on my way over there now!" I immediately hung up the phone. I told Diane my Dad was having an emergency and that I would be back soon. She instructed me to go and see my Dad and that she would be praying for him. And like any concerned mom, she told me to be careful.

I got in my car and sped off. What the hell was going on with my dad? Of all times I decide to avoid Niecey, why did it have to be an emergency? I felt horrible. Anything could have happened to Daddy and I wouldn't have been there. I had to call Mike. He wasn't expected to be back from L.A. until tomorrow.

"Hey." Thank God Mike answered the phone.

"Hey." I said frantically.

"What's wrong? You sound out of it. What's going on?"

"Daddy had shortness of breath today. I'm on my way over to his house now."

"Oh, wow. Let me go ahead and book a flight home. I'm just wrapping up my last meeting."

"You don't have to do that, I was just keeping you in the loop."

"Seriously Lita? I get that we're practically separated these days but I'm still your husband and I need to be there with you just in case—"

"Just in case what?"

"I'm just saying that your dad has had his moments."

"What are you talking about? Do you know something I don't?"

"I'm just saying when Frank called me a while back, I think it was that night you went to the bookstore, he said he tried calling you but you didn't answer so he called me. He said he was cool but from time to time he gets shortness of breath."

"And why the hell didn't you tell me?"

"He said he didn't want to worry you and honestly I can understand where he's coming from."

"I can't believe this right now."

"You know how us men can be. If he says everything is under control, why don't you trust him?"

"I'm not doing this with you right now. See, this is what I'm talking about. We just can't get on the same page for shit and I'm tired of it. This is my daddy we're talking about and you're being nonchalant about a major health concern. Look, I just need to be with him and Niecey right now. Honestly, you don't have to rearrange your flight to come home early. I'll just see you tomorrow."

"You know what Lita?"

"What?" I said with major attitude.

"Don't even worry about it. I'll see you tomorrow and please send Frank my love."

"Fine." I hung up the phone. Everything Mike said and did these days irritated me. I knew I could probably be more loving and understanding towards him but it was hard. And ever since I had sex with Law last night, I felt even more distant from Mike. It was like Mike couldn't do anything right in my eyes anymore. I wondered, if Law was my husband, what would he have done? I just think he would've understood me enough to tell me about my daddy. What the hell was I saying? I slept with this man one time and I'm already imagining him being my husband? Now I know I'm out of it. I just need to be with my daddy right now.

* * *

As soon as I approached my dad's street, I saw the ambulance and immediately my heart sank because I knew they were there for him. I pulled up in front of his house and jumped out of my car.

"Niecey!" I screamed from outside of the house. Niecey came running out of the door crying. "Niecey! What is going on? I just talked to you like twenty minutes ago! Where's Daddy?"

"He's in the house. They're trying to resuscitate him. I can't watch this right now. I just can't." Niecey could barely get the words out of her mouth without sobbing.

"Wait, what?" I ran into the house to see Daddy lying on the floor as the paramedic continued trying to resuscitate him. At that moment, everything looked like it was happening in slow motion. I heard their voices but the sounds seemed jumbled. I was in a fog as I watched the jolt to my daddy's lifeless body bounce him up and down. I couldn't believe just a few hours ago, Daddy seemed fine and then this was happening. But like a miracle, he opened his eyes and immediately the paramedics hooked him up to an oxygen machine and rushed him to the hospital.

"Niecey get in my car now!" I ordered.

"I can't believe this, I just can't fucking believe this!" Niecey was screaming uncontrollably.

"Niecey calm down and tell me what happened?" I tried to remain calm which was typically my role as the older, sensible sister but also because I didn't need to be in a heightened state while I was driving.

"When I got off the phone with you, I had just pulled back up to Daddy's house. As I was bringing his groceries in, I saw him on the floor trying to breathe but he was really struggling. I didn't have time to call you Lele, I'm so sorry! I had to call 911!"

"Okay, okay, I understand and I'm glad you did. Otherwise, it would probably be a different story right now. We just need to get to the hospital to find out what is going on with Daddy."

"Fuck this! Why is this happening?" Niecey continued to scream at the top of her lungs. I too felt her frustration and pain but

I was just reacting differently. I knew I had to be the strong one like I had always been.

"Hey, Niecey, Daddy's gonna be fine. I really need you to know that."

"How the fuck do you know that? We can't lose him.

He's all we have. I just can't lose my Daddy!"

All of a sudden, the pain I saw on Niecey's face reminded me of the many times she cried for our mother who just wasn't there for us. I was always Niecey's protector and I just wanted to make sure she was okay.

"Niecey, he's gonna be fine, he has to be." As much as I wanted to convince Niecey that Daddy was going to be okay, I didn't know if I quite believed it myself. Everything was happening so fast and other than Daddy getting injured on his job, I knew of no other health concerns.

Daddy died that night upon arriving at the hospital. For some reason, I thought I would've at least had a chance to tell him I loved him but I didn't. There were so many unanswered questions. So many things that left me feeling empty. After talking to Diane that day, I had told myself I would tell Daddy I was ready to talk about my mother. But I never got that chance. The doctors said Daddy had lung cancer and was diagnosed about six months ago. He never told us. The doctor said Daddy refused all kinds of treatment and told his doctor he didn't want anyone's focus to be on his sickness. I just felt cheated. My mother, who was never really a mother at all left me when I was only a teenager and now Daddy was gone. Life sure had taken an unexpected turn. And the first person I thought to call was Law.

"Hey beautiful, how are you?" Law was clearly happy to hear from me. We had just been together last night and other than a few quick texts this morning, this was our first time speaking since then.

"Not good, not good at all," I said trying to fight back the tears.

"Baby, what's wrong?"

I couldn't hold in the overwhelming sadness. I could barely speak clearly and for some reason, I felt like he was the only person I could be totally vulnerable with. "My daddy died tonight."

"Wait a minute Lita! Where are you? I will come to you, just tell me where you are."

"I'm at the hospital right now but you can't come. I'm here with my sister and we're about to start calling my daddy's family in Arkansas. I just needed to cry this out really quickly. I can't do this in front of my baby sis right now. Oh God, this hurts so bad!" I continued to cry uncontrollably.

"Okay. I'll respect that you want me to stay behind but I'm worried about you. This is very awkward for me because I care about you and I want to be there for you but I understand due to the situation, I can't. Can you please keep me posted? I'll wait up all night for you. I'm here if you need me."

"Thank you Law, thank you." I hung up the phone and I dropped to the floor. I couldn't believe Daddy was gone. I knew I needed to call Mike but I couldn't help but be upset with him for not telling me Daddy was sick. If he had told me about Daddy's health, maybe I would've been able to convince him to go to the doctor to see about his shortness of breath and maybe even convince him to get treatment when he found out about the cancer.

I called Diane first as she was still at my house with the kids. She tried to console me but I was just too hurt. I was in no condition to talk to the kids so I decided to wait until I got home. They would be devastated to hear the news as they loved their "Paw Paw" as they affectionately called him. I got up enough nerve to call Mike but surprisingly there was no answer so I left a message.

* * *

Early the next morning, Mike had returned home from his business trip and I finally told him what happened to Daddy. I held my frustration towards him as I did not want the focus of Daddy's death to be on him. We told the kids together which felt like I had lost Daddy all over again by their reaction. Sheree took it the hardest as her cry resembled that of a strong piercing sound that could've cracked all of the windows in my home. She locked herself in her room and the agony of her sobbing hurt me to the core.

I couldn't believe how fast the whole process went. I had to literally discuss insurance policies, funeral arrangements, burial and tombstone preferences all in a matter of a day. I was overwhelmed but I was Daddy's primary beneficiary and power of attorney so I had to handle all of the specifics. Niecey had checked out. All week she acted like everything was normal as if Daddy was still alive and nothing ever happened. She was not in a space to really help me plan Daddy's service, let alone pick out the suit in which we would bury him in. And again, I felt the weight of the world was on my shoulders.

The only thing that was keeping me sane was sporadically talking to Law. He had helped me so much. He even convinced me to come over his house so that he could cook a meal for me. I never knew what it felt like to make love to someone while grieving but I experienced it that week. I needed some kind of outlet and even though Law did not want to make love to me under those conditions, I looked him in the eye and told him I needed to be comforted and I wanted it in that way. He made love to me and as he held me afterwards I just cried and cried in his arms. In my mind, I knew no one would understand why I kept running towards Law because a lot of times *I* didn't know. One thing was for sure; he filled so many voids in my life at the present moment that it was almost toxic.

"As much as I would love for you to stay here with me all day and I just take care of you, I don't want your family worrying. You're finally so relaxed but I can tell you might fall asleep and I don't want you to lose track of time. Are you going to be okay driving home? "

"Yeah, I guess." I said not looking forward to getting back to the reality that Daddy's service was in two days.

"I really wish I could be at your dad's service with you.

"I really wish you could too, but it just wouldn't be the best decision."

"Trust me, I know. Again, I'm here for you in any way you need me to be."

"Thank you." I kissed Law on the lips passionately and he gave me a long hug before I started getting dressed. "I will definitely try to connect with you when I get home.

"Try your best not to wreck your brain trying to figure out everything right now. Allow yourself time to grieve and also be with your family. You know I love seeing you and spending time with you but please don't feel obligated to call or text me right now. I understand situations like these so don't worry yourself thinking my feelings will be hurt if I don't hear from you. And don't try to analyze what you and I have and what's going on in your marriage. Just allow me to be someone that makes your life easier. I hope you can do that."

I was truly in one interesting situation. Morally, this affair with Law was wrong on so many levels but he was such an amazing and understanding man that didn't focus on our unconventional relationship. He just wanted to see a smile on my face and I really appreciated that in my life right now.

* * *

It was the morning of Daddy's service and I cried pools of tears last night so that I could keep it together today. As I put on my black empire waisted dress and cream pearls, I couldn't help but think back to the time Daddy gave me those very same pearls to wear at my wedding. He said it belonged to his mom and said I always reminded him of her. I never had the chance to meet her as she died before I was born but he talked about her so much I thought I knew her. Everyone always said I was the spitting image of her and I could definitely see the resemblance from the pictures Daddy kept of her at his home. In my own way, I was honoring both of today by wearing the pearls. I put on my large Hollywood shades as Daddy used to call them to avoid direct eye contact with anyone and I walked out of the door.

There was something about black funerals. The display of fashion and pomp and circumstance was like no other and we were able to send Daddy off in a grand way. My family and I arrived in a stretched luxury limousine as we were all dressed in black while the women wore off white pearls and roses pinned to our dresses to match per my suggestion. Daddy loved bowling so all the men wore his bowling league pins on their suit jackets.

The church was filled to capacity. Daddy didn't have a lot of family in Chicago but they all arrived from Arkansas to pay their respects. Daddy moved to Chicago forty years ago when he was only twenty years old so he made a lot of friends during the time he lived here. His old co-workers, stepping crew and bowling league buddies were there. So many people from our old neighborhood that I hadn't seen in years were there as well. There were so many fond memories triggered by those faces and for a minute, my sadness was put on hold while I basked in those memories. So many elders hugged and kissed me saying they knew my Daddy was smiling on all of us right now. They also kept saying Daddy raised some beautiful girls and that he would be proud of how I put everything together for his service.

We hired a professional band for the service as Daddy was always a fan of blues and jazz music. He was actually good friends with Nancy Wilson, the jazz singer, so I was extremely grateful when she agreed to sing at his service. Daddy's casket was immaculate and I chose a Hugo Boss Herringbone Three-Piece Suit for him to wear. He always had that Chi-Town style about him and whenever his cousins used to visit from Arkansas, they would always say he was so "sharp". I still laugh when I think about that.

So many great stories were shared, beautiful songs were sang, laughter was had and tears were shed. Even though it was a sad occasion, I couldn't help but be filled with so much joy seeing all the people who loved and cared for Daddy. As I sat on the front pew with Mike and the kids, I started thinking about how precious life was. I started thinking about how Daddy used to say Mike was a really good man and he respected him so much for taking care of me and the kids the way that he did. Daddy said Mike wasn't a street dude but he was a real dude in his eyes. Daddy used to tell me not to get hung up on unnecessary shit but look at how a man takes care of his family. He would say, "Yeah Lita, you gonna meet some good looking brothas because you're fine but pay attention to the one that comes home to you every night, makes his money the legit way and never raises a hand to you and your kids 'cause that's all that matters." I kind of lost sight of that over the years and I felt like sitting next to Mike and the kids was where I needed to be and not running into the arms of another man.

I was extremely emotional and so many thoughts were running through my mind. I just couldn't believe this lifeless body lying in front of me right now was Daddy. I just wished he was here, alive and well. I hadn't even really talked to him about my issues with Mike because I knew he would just say, "Baby girl, you got a good one, figure it out."

Daddy decided to never remarry because he said he didn't feel like many women were really about loyalty these days so he just dated from time to time. I always wondered why he stuck with my mother all those years with the way she treated us. He said she had a rough life and that I should try not to fault her but I always felt like that was a wack excuse. She was evil and he was loyal and even though Mike was far from evil, we just didn't mesh anymore and I didn't feel the need to pretend like this is what I wanted for my life.

I don't know, Daddy came from an era when couples were loyal to each other to a fault. This was a new day and I just wasn't feeling it.

As the service was coming to an end and the eulogist was reading Psalms twenty three from the King James version of the Bible, Mike pulled me close as he saw me tearing up again. Mike, the kids and I followed behind Daddy's casket being carried by the pallbearers, walking slowly outside of the church towards the funeral cars.

"Lita! Lita!" Who was calling me so loudly I thought? I turned around. "Mom?"

CHAPTER

9

It had been a month since Daddy's death. I returned back to work about a week after his service just to get my mind off of things. Everyone was so thoughtful, as many of them attended Daddy's service. Don was even there with his soon-to-be ex-wife which took me by surprise. Daddy had come to my job and my galas over the years so my co-workers knew of him and spoke very highly of him.

Val called me the day before Daddy's service to send her condolences but stated she wouldn't be able to make it because she would be heading out of town early that morning. I knew things were still very different between us because knowing Val, she would've rescheduled her flight to attend the service but hey things were different. Maybe she knew Don and others from the office would be there and just didn't want to be bothered. Either way, I felt some kind of way about her not attending.

I hadn't really talked to Law much as I was kind of avoiding him. When I was at my daddy's service, I started feeling an overwhelming sense of guilt about having cheated on Mike and thought maybe I should just stay away. Law said he understood that I may need some space due to my daddy's death so I used that as a way to avoid him. I missed him though. I really wanted to see him but I kept telling myself to try and work things out with Mike. I kept thinking about what Daddy would say about marriage and maybe I didn't have that same loyalty in me like he did. I mean hell, I don't think I was cut out to stick by Mike the way Daddy did with my mom. That was just too much.

Law activated something in me that I hadn't felt with any man. The way he looked at me, held me, made love to me, understood me, talked to me; I was hooked and I couldn't replicate that same feeling with Mike. At times, it made me sad and other times it made me angry. Mike just always seemed so complacent in our marriage. He never abused me or cheated on me to my knowledge but he was rarely at home and when he was home, he would be working. He didn't spend much quality time with the kids, especially the boys, we rarely went out on dates and I just never felt appreciated on days like Valentine's Day, Mother's Day, my birthday and even our anniversary. I was always the one organizing everything and it was getting old. I wanted to know what it felt like to be sexy with a man again and Law gave me that feeling and I was addicted to it.

"Mama." Sheree walked into my room.

"Yes baby, how are you feeling?"

"Could be better. Missing Paw Paw, that's all."

"I definitely understand honey, come here." Sheree sat down next to me on the bed and she cried as I held her in my arms.

"It's just that Paw Paw said he was gonna take us to the Taste of Chicago this year and now that ain't happening."

"I know baby. It still hurts to think about all the things him and I said we were going to do together too."

"Mama?"

"Yes, baby?"

"Can we go visit my daddy in Atlanta?"

"Okay?" That was an unexpected switch in conversation. "You wanna do something like a family trip?"

"Naw, just me and you. I just want to go on a girls trip with you mama. I miss *my* daddy and I want to start seeing him more."

"Okay, that's understandable. That'll give Daddy and the boys a chance to have some guy time. I can understand with Paw Paw being gone it's probably made you want to be even closer to him."

"Yeah, I just wanna spend more time with him. And it just seems like Mike——"

"Umm, wait a minute, Mike? You don't call him Mike, that's your daddy too and has been for the past ten years. Where is that coming from?"

"Mama, don't get all extra on me right now, it's just that Mike, I mean Daddy and I haven't really been that close lately or should I say, I just haven't really felt close to him lately."

"Why is that?" I asked with a concerned tone.

"I don't know mama, he's just never really here and when he is here, he doesn't really do much with us. I talk to my real daddy like every day and he lives in Atlanta! We crack jokes on each other, he's been buying me nice things and that time he came to Chicago, we spent the whole day together! We just have so much fun." Sheree seemed genuinely hurt.

"Well, your daddy, and I'm speaking in reference to Mike, is a good father you know? He has been in your life since you were two years old and has always stepped up to the plate when it came to taking care of you. He may not always buy you Jordan's when you want, but he can. He just wants you to earn it Sheree. Lamont couldn't always afford those nice things but he's in a different place now and he's doing much better financially so he wants to give you more. But they've both been very good dads to you."

"And I get that mama. You always told me the truth about both of my dads. But it just seems like Daddy treats me differently because I'm not his real child."

"Wow, Sheree, you really think that?"

"I can't explain it, it's just the way Daddy looks at me and then how he looks at Tariq and Rashad. It's just not the same.

When my daddy, Lamont was here and we spent the day together, I could tell he really, really missed me and that he was proud of me. I just wanna see him that's all."

"Okay, honey no need to explain anymore. If that's how you feel, I will honor that. I'll call Lamont and see what his schedule is like. You'll be getting out of school in a couple of weeks for summer break so that would be a good time to go. I could definitely go out there and do some networking too for my business."

"Mama, you are so cool for starting your marketing business. I be telling my friends you know celebrities and stuff and you're able to get backstage at concerts and in VIP and everything!"

"You're so funny Sheree. I don't have it like that yet."

"Mama, what are you talking about? You do! Those galas you do for work be lit and filled with celebrities. And even though the pics be posted on Facebook and Twitter which are for old people, we still be seeing it on SnapChat."

"First of all, we ain't old but I'm so glad you're hyped about what I do. I'm excited too because I'm definitely laying the groundwork for my own business and a trip to Atlanta would definitely be good for me right now."

"Okay, bet mama! We gone have so much fun!"

"Yes, but let me call Lamont first."

"Mama, can I ask you something?"

"Yep, anything."

"Why didn't you and my real daddy stay together?"

"Well, to be honest, we were so young when we started dating and really too young when we had you. We both weren't ready for anything serious. Lamont had a hard time finding work and I told you he chose to sell drugs to make ends meet and to help his mom with the bills. I just didn't want to get caught up in that lifestyle. I really debated how much contact he should have with you because of the kind of lifestyle he was living but I didn't want to keep you all apart so most of the time, he would come over to Paw Paw's house and visit you while I was at work. That made me feel more secure you know?"

"I get it. You and Daddy just seem like you get along so well and you all laugh together."

"Well, that's because we've always been friends. That'll never change."

"I hear you. I just think it's cool that ya'll don't have all those crazy baby mama and baby daddy stories." Sheree laughed.

"Nah, that's never been us. I will always respect Lamont for simply being there for you. He wasn't really in a position to provide for you financially and accepting his drug money definitely wasn't an option for me but he always made his presence known in your life."

"That's real cool mama."

"Yeah, it is." Sheree kissed me on the cheek and gave me a hug.

* * *

"Lita, we need to talk."

"Yes?"

"I noticed ten thousand dollars withdrawn from our joint account. What's going on?"

"When did you start checking our bank accounts? Usually, I take care of all our financials but if you must know, it was an initial investment in my business."

"So, I know you said you were going to start your business anyway, but typically we discuss big purchases like these ahead of time."

"Well, you made it painfully clear that you wanted no parts of my entrepreneurship endeavors so I used my increase in pay to fund my business goals." I really didn't understand how Mike had the nerve to be getting so worked up over this.

"Wow."

"Wow, nothing? You said you didn't want to fund my little "hobby" and since I believe in my damn self, I made a business decision on my own with MY money."

"First, I didn't call your business a hobby. I just said I didn't think financially it was the smartest decision for our family right now."

"Okay, whatever, try to smooth it over and make it sound like you were really being that tactful. As I recall, you said you didn't want to put YOUR money into it so I got my own and did it myself dammit."

"Look, I know you're still very emotional right now with Frank's death so—"

"Don't you say a goddamn word about Daddy's death seeing that you didn't think it was necessary to tell me he was sick."

"You know what? Fuck it. No one knew he had cancer at that time. He didn't even know. He said he had some shortness of breath but that he was cool. He asked me man to man not to tell you because he knew you would worry and he didn't want to put the added stress on you. I was just respecting him like he's always respected me. So don't throw that in my face, Lita. That's triflin' as hell."

"Oh, so now *I'm* triflin'?

"Damn, calm your ass down! You get all worked up every time I say anything to you these days. It's like you trying to find something to argue about. I don't get it. You act like you don't even like the sight of me or some shit. If you don't want this anymore Lita, just say the goddamn word!"

"Oh, so you forcing my hand?"

"Well, it sounds like you got your whole life planned out and it doesn't include me?"

"Well, maybe that is what I want. This shit ain't serving me no purpose no way. I mean, let's keep it real. I'm the one keeping this family together. I take care of the kids, I take care of all our financial affairs, I run this household and it ain't like I'm half stepping in making money too. Hell, I don't even remember the last time I had a real orgasm with you."

"You know what Lita, fuck you! I'm done with this shit. Imma stay at my brother's house tonight."

"Yeah, you do that."

And just like that, Mike packed a quick overnight bag and walked out the door. He didn't even say bye to the kids. How did I let my emotions get the best of me like that? How did I even allow myself to utter those words to Mike? Grant it, it's how I felt but I probably shouldn't have said it like that. But I was angry and I was tired of always having to be the "bigger person." Why couldn't Mike realize that not supporting me with my business was a huge slap in my face considering I always supported him? Why was that so hard for him to understand? Why was it so hard for him to be like okay Lita, you want some good head? I got you. Or why couldn't he say "Lita, your dad doesn't really want you to know this and I don't want to worry you but I feel it's important that you know your dad hasn't been feeling too well. You may want to check on him." I mean seriously, damn! Why did this shit have to be so hard?

I wished I could talk to Val. I missed my friend and I missed being able to say what the fuck I felt. But after that big fight we had, who knows? Her jealousy was starting to get the best of her and maybe she wanted my life to eventually end up like hers. Maybe she secretly wanted me to be miserable too. I don't know. This shit sucks though.

I looked down at my phone. I scrolled past Law's number a few times before eventually calling him.

"This is a pleasant surprise. How are you?" Law kind of sounded formal with me on the phone.

"Well, all things considered, I'm doing okay." I lied but I didn't want to sound pitiful.

"Well, it's definitely good to hear your voice. It's been a while."

"Yeah, well I knew you would understand considering the circumstances."

"Of course, you know I understand. I definitely told you to take your time and I meant that."

"I was wondering if you were free this evening. Maybe I can stop by in about an hour or two. I was going to see if my mother-in-law could come to my house to watch the kids."

"Hmmm, can we shoot for another time?"

Wow, was Law dismissing me after he told me anytime I wanted to talk to him or see him, I could? And why was he being so formal on the phone with me this time? Was he seeing another woman?

Would that bother me? It sure felt like it was bothering me. "Umm, okay?" I said perplexed.

"Are you okay?" Law asked confusingly.

"Well considering my dad just died, hmm, I could be better?" I responded sarcastically on purpose to see if he would change his tune.

"I know this is a hard time for you. I really do. I would have loved for you to come over this evening but my daughter just dropped my grandsons off to spend the night. If you'd still like to come over, I wouldn't mind at all. Now my grandsons are preteens so they'll probably be smiling at you, and having some not so innocent thoughts because you are so beautiful." Law laughed and he sounded like his normal self again. But he was right. I didn't feel comfortable meeting his grandsons considering I was having sex with their granddad and I was married.

"Aww, thanks so much for wanting me to come over even though your grandsons are there but we can take a raincheck."

"Are you sure? I can have some chamomile tea waiting for you when you get here?"

"Your grandsons won't think it's awkward meeting their granddad's very young, friend who he happens to be sleeping with and who is also married?"

"First, I love my grandsons, but there's a level of respect that is shown over here. Yes, they're young impressionable boys that might sense something but I will not be disclosing to them that much detail about my personal life. They do not need to know who I'm sleeping with."

"So, since we're on the topic of sleeping with people, are you?"

"Now, how long have you been wanting to ask me that question?" Law chuckled even though I didn't find it funny.

"Not long, you just brought it up so I thought I'd ask." I said seriously.

"Well, I didn't bring up anything, but I'm only making love to you. I have not had *sex* in a long time because that's just not my forte at this point in my life."

"So what is your forte?"

"Would it sound cliché' if I said, *you?*"

"Yes." I was demanding answers at this point.

"Lita, I'm fifty-eight years old. I would be lying to you if I said I haven't slept with a lot of women. I have and I've also been married twice. I'm not necessarily proud of this, but I've also cheated in my marriages and I know things are not as black and white as we would like them to be. But through my experiences and where I'm at in a lot of areas in my life right now, I'm just not interested in bringing a lot of women into my home. I'm not interested in just having sex. I'm not interested if there's no connection. So with that being said, I am only making love, and I stress that making love part, to you. And I'm so okay with that. As a matter of fact, I'm more than okay."

"So what about me? I'm married?"

"Now are you asking me if I want to know if you and your husband are having sex? Umm hell no! But I don't question you about that because I understand the situation. I've been there and like I said before, it's not that black and white. I understand there are a variety of gray areas and there are children involved as well. Plus, I don't like to put demands on people. I want you to make the best decision for you and I will do the same."

"So are you saying if, given the opportunity, you would sleep with someone else if you felt connected to them?"

"I know you may not believe this, but I am *really* into you. You keep me extremely engaged with your mind and aura alone. You being beautiful was an added bonus and the sex is just a by-product of everything we've shared anyway. I have met and been involved with a lot of women in my life but the connection I have with you does not happen often. So with that being said, I honestly don't think a connection stronger than this with another woman would happen right now. And I believe that because I choose to focus my energy solely on you."

Well damn. Did my nipples get hard just by listening to Law? I swear I could've just had an orgasm right then and there. That was kind of some hot shit and no one has ever told me anything like that before. He just reminded me why I'm so drawn to him.

"If it wasn't for your grandsons being at your house right now..." I said seductively.

"Hmmm, what would you do to me?" Law sounded intrigued and excited at the same time.

"Well, I would walk you to your sofa pretending to make you take a seat but then I would tell you, I would rather you stand up. I would unbuckle your belt and slowly unzip your pants. I would place my hand on your dick and give you a nice hand job. And then I would put my entire mouth around that big dick of yours and slowly guide my tongue up and down all the while creating some serious wetness in my mouth. I would lick your balls and suck some more until you came and I would take it all in."

"Ha! I can't lie, I love that freak in you. By the way you described what you would do to me, I can tell you've been waiting to do that for a long time to me huh?"

"Well, you can say that. The times we've been together, you have always spoiled me rotten in the bedroom and you never asked or insinuated that in return."

"And that's because I want you to do whatever you're comfortable doing. I want us to always focus on pleasuring each other. When that is a priority, the love making will be good every single time. But now that a brotha knows you like to get down like that!"

We both started laughing and I wanted him so badly right now, that I was feigning for him.

"So do you think we can probably make that happen tomorrow?"

"I would love that Lita."

"Great, I'll wear something very, very sexy for you."

"Hmm, and what might that be?"

"Well, it's a surprise."

"Well, if I can offer a quick tip, I love the color blue, preferably royal blue."

"You got it, Mr. Davis. Blue it is."

"Now you got me too excited and my dick is over here hard as a rock."

"Hmmm, just like I like it."

"Imma let your fine ass go for now. Let me get back to my boys and I can't wait to see you tomorrow."

Sounds good. Talk to you soon."

"Okay baby."

That conversation put me in a totally different place from before. I swear Law was such a drug to me. Whenever I talked to him and when I was with him, I would get so caught up in him. I knew on the surface, no one would even know that I had this going on.

Everything about Law was so fucking sexy and goddamn, the sex was through the roof! I swear people be sleeping on these older dudes. I was having fun getting caught up in my thoughts until I got an incoming call. It was my mother!

She had heard of my father's death from a family friend and I didn't even know she was at Daddy's service until she caught me afterwards walking to the funeral car. In one way, I was thinking "Who the fuck do you think you are showing up at Daddy's funeral?" But then in another way, I was thinking, "I definitely got some shit to say to you". When she handed me her number she said she was going to be heading back to New York soon but wanted to pay her respects and she wanted to catch me before the burial. I asked her if that was her cell number and she said yes. I told her I would text her soon. I really wanted her to know she may have to wait before getting a phone call from me because she's been gone practically my whole life.

I texted my mother about two weeks ago saying that I hadn't forgotten about her but I needed some time before I reached out. She texted me back stating she understood. But one thing that was visibly different about her that day at Daddy's service was she looked extremely good. I would go as far as to say, she looked like she was in a really good space and healthy. My mother was extremely skinny when I was a kid but she had gained some weight and she looked really nice. Her hair and makeup was immaculate, she was dressed very classy and she spoke so well, nothing like her stressed out, disheveled appearance from back in the day.

"Hello?"

"Hey Lita, is this you?"

"Hey, it is." I didn't know what to call her. I couldn't exactly imagine calling her mom, but I didn't want to sound too disrespectful by calling her by her first name, Lorraine even though that's what I had in my phone.

"Did I catch you at a bad time?"

"Umm no, just trying to relax." I said with sort of a tone.

"Oh, well I won't keep you. I know that you said you would reach out to me but I just wanted to let you know I was going to be visiting Chicago again in a few days and I would love to get together with you and your sister for lunch?"

Why was my mother talking to me like she had been in our lives all this time, but then moved when we were adults or something and now she's visiting her girls for a little bonding time?

"Umm okay? Well, I'll have to talk to Niecey to see what her schedule is like. She owns a salon over on 119th."

"Oh, yes, she told me?"

"She did?" I sounded surprised.

"Yes. I actually gave her my number as well at your dad's service and we've been talking ever since."

Oh wow, so Niecey has been talking to our mother and hadn't even mentioned it to me? This was interesting.

"Oh okay. So did you already talk to her about meeting for lunch when you come into town?"

"Yes, but I also wanted to include you so that's why I called."

Why was this woman talking to me as if she was doing me a favor by "including" me in any goddamn thing?

"Okay, well I guess everything is all planned out and the only thing left for me to do is show up." I said with a sort of sarcastic tone.

"Great! Thank you so much, Lita. I can't wait to see you! I've booked my flight and I just received my itinerary so I'll text you the info regarding when I'll be landing and when I check in to my suite so we can plan a time."

Who the hell was this woman? She was using words like itinerary and suites. My mother barely had a decent vocabulary when I was growing up so I didn't feel like I knew who this chick was on the other line. This person seemed like an imposter. I mean, I recognized the face but her whole demeanor was unusual as if she was a totally different person. I realized I didn't know *this* Lorraine and going to lunch with her would feel rather awkward.

"Okay, well, I'll see you in a few days."

"Okay hun, see you soon."

My mother hung up the phone. But seriously? Hun? We weren't close like that? I was starting to get angry all over again. I called Niecey.

"Hey trick." Niecey laughed when she picked up the phone.

"Umm Niecey, please don't call me that." I said seriously.

"I was just playing withcho bougie ass."

"Whatever. Anyway, so when were you going to tell me you talked to your mother?"

"And that's exactly why I haven't told you. Seriously, Lita? Your mother? Last time I checked she popped you right out of her coochie just like me."

"Niecey, why you gotta talk like that?"

"Oh, sorry I don't use words like vagina, or vulva or fimbriae. See you didn't know a bitch knew some shit."

"Here we go again Niecey. Anyway, what the hell did ya'll talk about?"

"Well, with the way you coming at me, I shouldn't tell you a goddamn thing but if you must know, mama said she heard about Daddy from Theresa, you know her friend from the old neighborhood. She sounded really sad about it but made a point to drop everything she was doing to come to Daddy's service."

"She dropped everything? Like what?"

"I swear you a piece of work but mama has a pretty different life now. She got remarried back in '05 or some shit to a doctor—"

"Wait a minute, a doctor?"

"You are so predictable. Yes, yo mama married a doctor. You ain't the only one in the family that got money now, ha!"

"You know what Niecey?"

"What? What you gonna do? Anyways, like I was saying, before you rudely interrupted me, yes mama married a doctor in '05 and had a baby like two years later."

"Are you serious?"

"Yep, she has a son and we have a brother that's like ten years old."

I couldn't believe my ears. The mother I knew as a kid was barely functioning and now she had a whole new life with a doctor at that! And she had another child? Like what the hell? I had a brother that was the same age as Tariq? I couldn't believe this!

"Please get over yourself. Everything ain't about you."

"What are you talking about?"

"Well, for starters, I know you just zoned out on me just now because you were thinking about how all of this affects you."

"Well, didn't you think the same thing?"

"Not really, I mean c'mon mama been gone since like '98. Did you really expect her to be exactly how she left?"

"Umm yeah? Or worse, maybe? How else could you explain her being gone for so long?"

"A lot of shit went down back in the day that you don't know about."

"Like what? And why are you so calm about all of this? Lorraine was a horrible mother who showed no connection to us whatsoever except for when she called herself trying to fight us. Then she just up and left!"

"When you see mama, she will explain everything to you. I would have loved to tell you what happened but she wanted to be the one to tell you so I'm just respecting her wishes."

"Oh, ain't this cute. So ya'll done kumbaya-ed up in this motherfucker and now you respecting *her* wishes?"

"See, when you get to cussing like that, I know we may exchange some words and I ain't really tryin' to go there with you right now. Trust me, when you talk to her, it's gone change how you see everything from the past."

"Oh, I highly doubt that shit."

"Aiight, whatever, be your bougie, non-forgiving self and pretend like you ain't got no skeletons. I'm out."

Is that really how people viewed me as bougie and non-forgiving? Or was that only how Niecey viewed me? Well, I knew what Val thought of me. Was Mike seeing me in this light as well? Well, he definitely wouldn't be able to call me bougie, his ass is probably where I got it from. I wanted to call Law so badly and ask him but I didn't want to sweat him. But this whole meeting up with my mother was really making me feel uneasy especially knowing she started a whole new life and didn't once think to fill us in over the years. Well, as much as I didn't want to go, I needed to find out what caused her to be such a raving lunatic when we were kids. Niecey made it seem like this shit was out of her control or something. I couldn't imagine that being a good enough excuse.

* * *

I decided to take an Uber over to the Hampton Social Restaurant where my mother wanted to meet. When you live downtown, in the South Loop, or the North Side, typically public transportation was the way to go due to limited parking unless you wanted to pay a hefty fee in parking garages or valet. And I definitely was not in the mood for all the interesting personalities on the train and the bus so I opted for the ride sharing option.

When my mother suggested we meet up at the Hampton Social, I was surprised. The Hampton Social is actually one of my favorite restaurants because of its light and airy feel. The Smash Burger is my fave and that Frosé drink was so delicious. I couldn't help but wonder how my mother was hip to this place. I couldn't exactly question how she could know about it now seeing that she was married to a doctor. For a brief minute, I wondered, where was this mother when I was growing up? If she only knew how I longed for that feminine influence in my life as a teen and young adult but hey, it was too late for that now.

"Lita, you look absolutely stunning."

My mother noticed me as soon as I walked through the front entrance. She hugged me and to say it felt awkward was an understatement.

"Thank you. You look very nice yourself. That's a beautiful Chloé Nile Shoulder Bag."

"Oh, thanks, honey! You know your handbags huh?"

I wanted to say of course I do. The question is how did you develop such exquisite taste?

"I guess you can say that." I know my mother had to pick up on how fake my smile was.

"Do you know if Niecey is on her way?"

"I'm not sure but I can send her a quick text?" I was really hoping Niecey would arrive soon so I wouldn't have to endure this encounter with my mother by myself.

"I tell you about you millennials, I guess no one actually calls anyone anymore," my mother said jokingly.

Wow, the nerve of this woman. I really need for her to stop acting like she knows us.

"So, Niecey just texted me saying that she got caught up with a client and that she wouldn't be here for another thirty or forty minutes but that we could go ahead and order without her."

I became even more uncomfortable being with Lorraine by myself..

"Oh, that's no problem. I kind of wanted to have some alone time with you anyway."

And what the absolute fuck does she need alone time with me for? I knew this was a bad idea. I was trying to figure out any and every way to get out of this lunch with my mother. What would be a good excuse?

"Lita, I know you're probably curious about a lot of things and have a lot of questions so I won't waste your time and I'll cut to the chase."

Oh, you think? Yes, why in the hell are we sitting here dining at my favorite restaurant like we've been close all these years? Where the hell have you been and what the fuck have you been doing?

"I can't lie, Lorraine; sorry if that bothers you but I honestly don't know how to address you. But yes, I'm very confused as to why we're sitting here together like you've been in my life all this time."

"You have every right to be upset, and first I want to start by saying, I'm so sorry for leaving the way that I did when you and your sister were kids and not exactly being the best mom I could be."

"Please Lorraine, don't make it seem like you just made a few mistakes here and there during our childhood. I could have dealt with mistakes but sitting around all day shooting the shit, or bitch slapping your own daughter because of some spilled cereal, or just leaving without any explanation is hardly a damn mistake." I hated how upset I was getting in front of Lorraine. I hated that she got the best of me. I wanted to be cool around her and act like she was a non-motherfucking factor but I couldn't because I was hella hurt and I ached for many years thinking she just didn't want us.

"I can explain a lot of what you're referring to and I'm definitely not trying to make any excuses. But there was a lot that happened to me during the years I was married to your dad."

"Oh, I know you're not going to tell me somehow this was Daddy's fault because——"

"No not at all, but something did happen during our marriage and it appears your dad never told you about it."

I was getting even more upset because I felt like she was trying to somehow drag Daddy into this especially since he was not alive to defend himself. All I know is that she was treading on thin ice at this point.

"What could you possibly tell me, almost twenty years later?"

"When your dad and I first got married, we partied a lot, like a LOT. We had a blast. We were always at someone's house drinking and smoking, we even did a little coke here and there but never anything too crazy. Hey, it was the late seventies and early eighties so we were just living life or at least that's what we thought we were doing. But shit did get out of control one particular night. Your dad and I were at a friend's house and he was ready to go, but I wasn't. One of my girlfriends was joking about how your daddy had me well trained because even though I wanted to stay, I could tell by the seriousness in his eyes that it was time to go so I hurried up and got my purse from one of the guest bedrooms. He didn't really give me an explanation he just said; *Lorraine, I'm just not feeling this place, something doesn't feel right.* Before we were about to go, my girlfriend offered me one last drink saying that maybe I would need a stiff one before going home with your dad. She was implying that he was acting uptight. I never remembered what happened after I took that drink. I just remember that I was not the same."

Lorraine began to stare out the window of the restaurant and I noticed a tear slowly gliding down her right cheek.

"Are you implying that someone slipped something in your drink?"

"I'm not implying anything, it really happened." Lorraine quickly wiped her eyes with her freshly manicured hands as if the shame of the entire incident was enough to have her flying back to New York and never returning again.

"So, if you don't remember anything, how did you know someone slipped something in your drink?"

"It was a chain of events but your dad said I fell asleep in the car but in actuality, I blacked out. He said it took several forceful nudges to wake me up. But even then, he didn't think anyone drugged me, he just thought I was severely drunk. I mean I acted as a typical drunk person would; slurred speech, stumbling while walking and passing out on the bed. He said the next day, he noticed I was acting weird and that it seemed like it was more than just a hangover. He said my mood literally changed within an instant and I became angry over every little thing that day. He said he started to take me to the hospital but he knew they would start asking questions and he didn't want them to find traces of cocaine in my system.

Your daddy was dealing at the time and he didn't want to risk going to jail. He said he could totally tell someone had slipped something in my drink. He eventually told me, the day after the party, he went back over to that same house and threatened everyone over there to tell him who could've slipped me the drugs. A guy named Rudy who was also dealing in that neighborhood was supposedly the guy who originally gave my girlfriend the drink but then she gave it to me.

I can say this now that your dad is no longer with us, but he shot and killed Rudy. Even with my messed up head, I always kept that secret. Needless to say, the drug had long term effects on me and your daddy never forgave himself for exposing me to that lifestyle. He said he never felt right about that house that night and should've went with his first mind. He said he knew we needed to leave and that's why he was so adamant about it that night. That's why your dad was always so patient with me because he knew my behavior was not my fault and it wasn't his either but he put that blame on himself.

Even though I wasn't always there mentally, deep down, I knew your dad was suffering and felt extreme guilt over what happened to me and how I turned out. I had to leave. I called my mom who I hadn't talked to in years and asked her if I could move in with her in her tiny apartment in New York and I never looked back.

Eventually, I found work and joined a local church that really helped me with my recovery. I started going to therapy and that's actually how I met my husband James. Believe it or not, he was my therapist but we didn't start dating until after I was no longer his patient."

"So once you started getting better, why didn't you reach out to us?"

"Honestly, so much time had passed and I really didn't know what to say or where to start. For the first few years, I didn't even tell your dad where I was because I knew he would come looking for me and try to bring me back home. At the time, I was in no condition to be a wife or a mom. I thought your lives would be so much better without me. Eventually, I made contact with your dad during the years I was trying to get better. He said that he would always be there for me and that he would fly out to New York and come get me but by that time, I had started a whole new life. I wasn't married or anything but I just no longer felt connected to anything or anyone in Chicago anymore. I asked your dad for a divorce and it devastated him. I just felt like I was no use to you all anymore. In my mind, I really thought I was doing the right thing."

I couldn't believe this is what kept my mom away from us all these years. For so long, I harbored so much anger and resentment towards her. I tried to deal with it by erasing her from my mind and just acting like she never existed. As far as I was concerned, I didn't have a mother and because of that void, I took on the role of caregiver to everyone else because I didn't want anyone to experience the loneliness I felt all my life.

"Lorraine, do you understand how many years my heart ached for you? I always wondered what it would have been like to have a mom that I could go shopping with, talk about boys with, or hell just a mom I could say I love you to. That was stolen from me!"

"I know baby——"

"Don't call me baby Lorraine! I'm not your fucking baby! I never was and I never will be!"

Some of the guests at the nearby table were staring at us but I couldn't help expressing myself. My hands were trembling and the tears were falling at a nonstop rate. Lorraine slowly got up and she began hugging me tightly.

"Lita." Lorraine said with a comforting voice.

"Get off of me!" I tried to jerk myself away from Lorraine but she gripped me tighter without even uttering a word. The comfort I began to feel from her overwhelmed me. I continued to cry uncontrollably in her arms and she continued to hold me in silence. For the first time, I felt a sense of safety and freedom from the pain I'd felt all those years. This is what Diane was talking about. Somehow, Diane knew this is what I needed all along but I fought it. The way Lorraine stroked my hair and the scent of her perfume that boasted citrus and rose notes calmed me. Oh God, I needed this. I needed my mother and even though it was almost twenty years later, she showed up for me in a way that I needed most.

"If you want, I can just grab you some lunch to go and we can head over to my hotel."

"Thanks but I just need some time to digest all of this."

"I know it's a lot to take in."

"I've kind of lost my appetite. Do you mind if we catch up another time?"

"Sure, honey whatever you like."

"How long will you be in town?"

"Well, I was going to head back tomorrow but I can stay a little longer if you want me to?"

"Can I call you and let you know?" I started getting emotional all over again because the way Lorraine looked at me and told me she would stay longer just for me made me feel like she really loved me. If she only knew how much I needed that from her. But again, maybe she really did know.

"That's absolutely fine, take your time. Are you heading home?"

"I'm not sure. I'm not really ready to see my family just yet and my kids can always sense when something is wrong with me."

"That's a beautiful relationship to have with your children. I saw them at your dad's funeral and they are gorgeous. And that husband of yours is quite a catch." Lorraine sounded a bit envious but not in a mean way. It just appeared she wished she could've had that relationship with us.

"Thanks, Lorraine. I'll definitely call you. Can you do me a favor?"

"Anything honey."

"Do you mind calling Niecey and letting her know I had to go? I don't feel like hearing her tell me everything revolves around me and everyone caters to me blah, blah, blah."

"Wow, after all these years, you all are still the same.

Niecey always used to say your Dad and I spoiled you more than her. Maybe we did. You *were* our first born so we may have been a little impartial." Lorraine smiled at me.

"Thanks for wanting to meet with me and thanks for being honest about what happened all those years ago."

"I wish I could've done more but all we have is now. But I'm glad you were willing to open me. That means the world to me."

Lorraine hugged me again before I left the restaurant. Wow, so many things were changing in my life lately, but never had I imagined reconnecting with my mother like this.

CHAPTER

10

I decided to go jogging and to try and get some perspective on things. I couldn't believe everything that had transpired over the past eight months. I met Law, I was offered a promotion at work, I was in the early stages of starting my business, the relationship between Val and I had significantly changed and not for the better, Mike and I were separated, but not legally, Daddy died and I reconnected with my mother after twenty years. I was overwhelmed. I really didn't know where my life was headed.

There were some things though I *was* quite sure of. I was sure of my beautiful children and how I loved being their mom and nurturing them. I was sure of the kind of employee I was at work and my accomplishments. I was sure that I wanted to eventually branch out on my own and start my own business. I was sure that my name was Lita Sheree Payne, a beautiful black woman with sun-kissed chocolate skin, a gorgeous afro, wide nose, and killer curves.

But even with all that certainty, I was still discovering myself. I was discovering the capacity of love that I had in my heart to give to my children even though I had never experienced that from my own mother. I was discovering that I had a belief in myself and my abilities that was monumental. Starting out as a young, single parent, whose mother left her at thirteen, the odds were stacked so high against me but I persevered. Somehow, I discovered what I was passionate about and good at and I pursued it as a career. I discovered that even though Mike and I had very different upbringings, we found each other and we made a choice to commit to one another. But I also discovered that I married Mike because he was "good" for me. Mike was a healthy contrast to what I had experienced. Being with him made me feel like I was making the "right" decision and that marrying a man like Mike was what I was supposed to do. Mike seemed like the perfect man to raise children with and share a life with so I went all in. But for many years, I felt like something was missing.

There was a burning passion inside of me that honestly had nothing to do with sex. It was an excitement for life, a yearning for growth and self-discovery. There was something I was searching for that I knew Mike couldn't provide and I often questioned if I was supposed to look to him for that missing piece, or another man or maybe no one except myself. I was discovering that marriage really had nothing to do with love and excitement per se, but really it was about making a choice. And I felt more often choosing the path of being single again these days. I was kind of confused by that at times though because Mike had all the "qualities" of a great husband or whatever that meant. He was fine as hell, he worked out so his body was in impeccable shape, not only did he work but he was wealthy, he could be funny at times, and he took care of me and the kids. But even though the next woman would probably argue with me, it just wasn't enough for me anymore.

I wanted to connect with Mike on a deeper level. I wanted to know how he was *really* feeling and not just the typical conversations about work, the kids or playing golf. I wanted to know his fears and his desires. I wanted to know what made him tick as well as what made his heart sing. I wanted us to risk more together in business and not always play it safe. I wanted more passionate sex from Mike and not lazy sex. I wanted his presence fully and I had been feeling like I wasn't getting that.

We weren't an overly religious couple, but we did the church thing for some years and sought counseling through a pastor. It just really wasn't our cup of tea. We had both gone to church as children and adolescents but we didn't live there Sunday to Sunday like some of our friends. We had gone on marriage retreats and tried various games and "homework" to work on our marriage but honestly, it still felt like we were trying to force a connection that maybe never really existed. So, we eventually succumbed to focusing on work and the kids and not really getting to know each other all over again.

Now when I met Law, it was like a fire lit up in me. He made me feel sexy and alive again. He reminded me of who I was in a sense. And when he looked at me, I could tell he was trying to look deeply into me which seemed so effortless on his part. He would tell me things about myself that I often wondered how he was able to read. But one thing I did discover after cheating on Mike with Law, was how easily it became for me to cheat on him again. There were times I felt guilty, but then there were times I felt justified by thinking it was okay because Mike did not fulfill my needs.

And I kind of surprised myself when I took Sheree to visit Lamont in Atlanta. He insisted on us staying with him at the house he had been renting as opposed to staying in a hotel. While Lamont and Sheree had their bonding time, I visited the Atlanta office of Global Connections, I did some networking, I went shopping, visited one of my college friends who lived there and even hit up a couple of day parties.

One evening, after Sheree had gone to bed, Lamont and I stayed up and talked for a while. It was a pleasant surprise to hear how good things were going for him in Atlanta with his producing. He seemed genuinely happy. He was getting ready to be a father again in a couple of months but he was no longer with his child's mother which he didn't seem too distraught over. He mentioned that she was a wardrobe stylist for T.I. and he honestly just wanted to "hit it". Lamont was always an honest person and never attempted to sugarcoat anything which I always liked about him. We were always friends, but some things changed between Lamont and I when I was in Atlanta. He started flirting with me and I just gave in. I was horny as hell.

I had been on again off again seeing Law, but I could tell Law's feelings were growing more and more deeply for me. He even asked me one night if I was trying to get a divorce any time soon. I'll be honest, I was very much into Law, but I wasn't exactly ready to end my marriage yet. I started feeling a tad bit of pressure from Law even though he said he wouldn't do that to me.

But when I was at Lamont's house we were just chilling, talking and drinking some wine, and having a really good time with no obligations. Lamont had a playlist that was out of this world that included, Tank, *H.E.R.*, SZA, Chris Brown, Rihanna and a whole bunch of other shit that was definitely setting the mood. Lamont didn't question me about Mike, the kids, work, nothing. He just wanted to know what was up with me and scoping me out to see if I was open for a night with him. He started giving me that look while I was talking. He started rubbing my thighs and kissing my neck and I got so excited. He went down on me and before I knew it, he had my legs spread cross country on the island in his kitchen. I knew we were taking a risk because Sheree could've awakened and walked in on us but we were so far gone at that point. Lamont was giving it to me like his life depended on it and I was taking it all in.

It was dark in the kitchen but the street light from outside was glaring into the window and I could see the sweat dripping from Lamont's forehead down to his chest. He said he always loved the way I climaxed because it excited him so much. After we had sex that night, I just felt like I couldn't go on this way. I had already slept with two other men who were not my husband and I knew I needed to make a decision.

My thoughts were interrupted by an incoming call. I couldn't believe it. It was Val!

"Hello?" I answered in a perplexing way.

"Hey, Lita."

"Hey, Val? I'm so sorry I sound surprised to hear from you but I *am* surprised to hear from you!"

"Look, I know a bitch been ghost on you but I miss the fuck outta you and we need to connect soon."

Val calling me and telling me she missed me was music to my ears. I craved the friendship we had and I would do anything to get that back.

"Oh my God, I miss you too Val!"

"Now look, you know I ain't ever been good with that sappy shit, like never. But first, I wanna say I'm sorry for the way I treated you that night at the club. I'm sorry for the things I said and just how I was acting. It wasn't cool and you didn't deserve that. I was dealing with my own shit and I took it out on you. And it definitely wasn't cool that I didn't show up for your dad's funeral. I would be lying if I said I wasn't at least a little bit envious of you Lita. I mean damn, I know you got your fair share of issues too but, you have a family. And I ain't just talking about Mike and the kids but you got your sister, aunts, uncles, cousins, hell you even got Lamont with his drug dealing turned producer ass. You have goals and things you're trying to accomplish and I just feel stuck. I mean I have a great job but half the people there don't even like me and I'm pretty sure it's no secret at Global Connections that I have a very healthy sexual appetite that has resulted in me sleeping with far too many people in that industry. But you said something to me a while back about talking to a professional and I was like yo Lita, fuck you in so many words. But I took your advice and I've been seeing a therapist. Now, I can't lie, he is fine as fuck! But I've been keeping my clothes on 'cause right now my goal is to get on top of these issues and work this shit out. I can't be trying to get on top of my issues and having the sexy therapist on top of me at the same damn time. That would be counterproductive right? Hell, I don't know. I'm just trying to deal with this shit from my past and the craving I've had for a sense of belonging since I was a little girl. Shits hard man, I swear."

"Awww Val!"

"What I tell you about that sappy shit Lita, stop it!"

"You know you're my girl! I can't help but be happy hearing about your growth."

"And that's why I love you, 'cause you always loved me for who the fuck I was. I just feel like a lot of people tolerate me but they don't embrace me like you do. Like seriously, thank you, Lita."

Val's voice was a little shaky but I knew how she felt about getting emotional so I didn't want to put her on the spot and ask her if she was okay. I could tell she was fighting back the tears and trying to refrain from being vulnerable with me.

"It's all good, you know I got you." I stated in a way that Val was comfortable with because being emotional was actually very hard for her.

"So enough about me, what's been up with you?" Val changed the subject to deflect from her vulnerability.

"Girl! Now that's gonna take a whole night and a glass of wine."

"Shiiiiitttt. I gots nothing but time. You gotta head back home?"

"No, actually I don't. Mike has the kids with him this weekend."

"Why you make it sound like Mike done moved out the house? Oh my God, did he?"

"No, not exactly. We are separated though."

"Oh hell naw! Why?"

"Like I said, break out the wine. I'm heading over."

* * *

"Look at yo sexy ass, Lita! I missed you!" Val gave me a long, tight hug when I showed up at her house. She had her hair pulled up in a messy bun, and wearing loungewear. Val was barefoot exposing her fresh pedicure and her Polynesian tattoo on her right foot which she said was symbolic of bravery and sexuality; two of the traits she said she always possessed. I loved when she wore her hair up because you could see her entire face.

She had the smoothest skin which obviously didn't require much effort on her part to maintain seeing that she drunk and ate shit most of the time. I always had to work at keeping my skin this clear. But then again, Val would say the same thing about me with regards to losing weight. I had always maintained a steady fit, size twelve frame while she typically struggled to lose weight and wore a size twenty. We both had our flaws so to speak but we would always find the beauty in each other.

"Thank you, thank you. You're looking pretty hot yourself but you always ooze mad sex appeal."

"Ha, well a bitch likes sex so I guess that sounds about right. But come sit down and tell me what's been going on!" Val sounded eager and excited to see me at the same time.

"Okay, but first the wine."

"Awwww, shit okay. I got you." Val brought over two glasses and a bottle of Sweet Red from Cooper's Hawk. Do we need to roll one up too while we're at it?"

"Naw, I'm good."

"Well, I'm about to, more for me. So Lita!!! What's going on boo?" Val asked while rolling her blunt to perfection.

"Girl, where do I start? First, let me just start by pouring one up for Daddy, goddamn I miss him. Everything happened so suddenly."

"I know honey. When Don made the announcement at work, he mentioned that your dad had lung cancer!"

"Yeah, he did but he didn't tell any of us and his doctor mentioned that he refused treatment because he didn't want the focus of his life to be his sickness."

"Honestly, I probably would've done the same thing."

"I hear you, it just hurt so bad. And he was actually experiencing shortness of breath and Mike knew about it and never told me. That really pissed me off."

"Why didn't he tell you?"

"He said my daddy asked him not to tell me because he didn't want me to worry."

"I tell you, men can be so fucking irritating at times. They can be so stubborn."

"At the time, my daddy didn't know he had cancer but when he found out, he didn't tell anyone not even Mike. He died six months after he was diagnosed."

"Wow, Lita. I'm so sorry honey. At least he didn't suffer you know? Your daddy seemed like he wanted to be in total control of his life and not leave it up to some doctors. I can respect that."

"Yeah, honestly, I'm understanding that more everyday but the shit still hurts you know?

"Well, of course, yo daddy was your ride or die. Is that what caused you and Mike to separate?"

"Actually, no. You know we had been going through some things for a while. Between me wanting to start my marketing firm, Mike and I arguing about every little thing, him not being home or just always working and us just not connecting, my daddy's death was just the tipping point."

"So you said he hasn't moved out?"

"Naw, we talked about that but we both agreed we would live in the same house and we would at least be cordial for the kids. Basically, we out here lying and shit."

"So are ya'll still fucking?"

"You're too funny. But nope no fucking going on with the Paynes."

"Aww hell naw! How have you been surviving? That whole not getting any is hard."

"Well…"

"Well, the fuck what? You trying to say you getting some on the side?"

"You can kind of say that." I said with a mischievous smile.

"Kind of my ass, either ya fucking or ya ain't."

"Ha, well you know I ain't as crass as you but yes, a sister's back has been blown the entire fuck out on a few occasions."

"Shut the fuck up! You let Law get some of that Lita?"

"I sure did and that shit was fantastic you hear me?" We high-fived each other.

"Oh shit! I mean you always had that freak in you but I didn't know it was going down like that? How the hell did this happen, when did this happen?"

"We actually started sleeping together before my daddy passed. Long story short, I went over his house one night in Hyde Park. He owns a townhome there that's so beautiful. His style is so incredibly fly and he treated me like royalty. We just had a good time sipping wine and talking. Before I knew it, I was giving him that good good."

"Wow. Now you know I gotta ask." We both giggled like middle schoolers talking about boys we had crushes on.

"Trust and believe, that shit was wide and long."

"Aaaayyyyyeeee!" Val started twerking in her seat.

"And for a man that's almost sixty, he definitely was able to maintain his stamina and I doubt he takes Viagra. The hardness of that dick was a natural progression."

"Ha! I love it! You know I live for stories like this honey."

"Well, he knows what the hell he's doing goddamn. I was feigning after that and I still be feigning."

"Umm, so why the hell are you over here and not getting you some of that?"

"Hello? I needed some girl time with my Val. I missed you."

"Of course! I missed you too but I'm just saying good dick can be very comforting especially when you got a lot of shit going on."

"Yeah, I hear you but I've been kind of taking a break from Law for a minute."

"You got me confused now. What's up?"

"Well, Mike and I haven't been separated that long and lately Law has been wondering where my head is regarding my marriage and if I'm thinking of staying or leaving. It's just too much pressure on me right now."

"Well, can you blame the nigga? You gon put that Lita on him and just chill?"

"But he told me he would give me space on that and not pressure me."

"Chile and you believed him? These niggas catch more feelings than a motherfucking episode of This Is Us."

"Ha! You are a whole fool."

"You know I'm right, goddammit. These men try to get all up in us and then they the ones that start getting all butt hurt when you ain't running up behind they ass."

"I mean, Law has been cool. He ain't been too over the top but I feel like it could go that route so I'm just laying low for a while."

"Yeah, that's probably best."

"So Sheree has been wanting to spend more time with Lamont especially since he visited Chicago that same night of the Old School/New School Hip Hop concert."

"Aww that's cool. Lamont has always been a good daddy so I know he was happy to hear that."

"Yeah, I even took her out to Atlanta to visit him."

"Oh cool. Did you make any business connects while you were out there?"

"Most definitely. I also kicked it with a college friend of mine that lives out there and we even went to a few day parties."

"See that's what I'm talking about. It's about time you did more things for you. So did you stay at your friend's house while you were there?"

"Actually, we stayed with Lamont."

"You did?" Val sounded surprised while inhaling the smoke from her blunt.

"Yeah, he offered and he's been renting a nice, spacious house out there so we stayed. I let them have their time together for the most part."

"Soooo, if my memory serves me correctly, Lamont is still digging you, right?"

I let out a long sigh. "Girl... I know."

"Aww shit, what happened?"

"That's a long story too but we ended up fucking." I kind of put my head down.

"You have got to be fucking kidding me! Ha! You getting more ass than me these days. How the fuck you getting your groove back and I'm going to therapy? Something is seriously wrong with this picture."

"Honestly, that was so not planned. You know Lamont and I have been co-parenting for twelve years and ain't nothing like this ever popped off."

"I know what happened. Lamont looking like a snack these days that's what happened."

"Girl ain't he? But I don't think it was just that. It's just, ever since me and Law hooked up, I feel like it's been easier for me to cheat. Basically what I'm saying is, once I got over the initial thought of doing it and then actually doing it, it became easier. And I'm not saying I'm just out here looking for fuck buddies. I think I'm just more open to the possibilities of things happening in life and I'm not closing myself off anymore if that makes any sense? And Mike just seemed so complacent in our marriage. Hell, he could be getting it in as far as I know. It ain't like he's been getting it from me!"

"I mean anything is possible. But Mike does really love you. Like not even trying to be funny, he's kind of a punk for you so who knows? I've just never caught that vibe from him that he would go all the way. Now you on the other hand…"

"What, seriously?"

"Hell yeah, Lita. I know you love Mike and you never been the one to just be out there with a whole lotta dudes, but you got a lot of free-spirit tendencies in you that you try to keep under wraps which is understandable."

"Hmmm, I guess. I don't know. Maybe an open marriage might work?"

"Ha! Mike ain't going for that shit and honestly, that ain't all it's cracked up to be."

"How do you know? Girl, why did I even ask?"

"You asked because you know I'm gonna give it to you straight, no chaser. I was once involved with a guy that claimed he had an open marriage. But then his wife started calling me trying to hook up with me!"

"Now Val, you know you like kissing the ladies here and there." I laughed.

"I know what I said but the thought of putting my mouth on another woman's pussy just don't get me excited at all. I mean, don't get it twisted.

His wife snuck me a few naked pics before and her body was banging! But the thought of eating pussy gives me hives so I'll just stick with a little kissing and cuddling women for now."

"Yeah, well maybe an open marriage ain't the answer."

"But why even an open marriage? Do you actually still want to be with Mike?"

"It's like there are times that I do. We just have so much history together and being able to raise the kids with Mike has always been something I've wanted for them."

"But there you go again, talking about everyone else. I'm talking about you. What do *you* want?"

"I guess I just don't know. Mike is what I've known for the past ten plus years and even though I have truly benefited from this marriage in more ways than one, I feel like I've lost the essence of who I am which sometimes feels like that outweighs many of the benefits. I've morphed into transforming my life to accommodate Mike and our kids. Thank God I never quit my job when I got married and had the boys because I would've been miserable being a stay at home mom. But I still feel like Mike wants me in a certain box that suits him. I can work and even travel from time to time with my job but he's so connected with the execs at Global Connections that it seems like he knows my every move. He didn't want me to start my business and then had the nerve to get upset when I took money from my pay increase to fund the initial startup. That was some serious bullshit. And then on top of that, the sex had been subpar at best."

"Aww damn, yeah that's a lot of shit going on. See this is why I can't do that whole marriage thing. I mean seriously, why do us women have to always change for these men? Even with Don, I always made sure not to make him look bad and I worked around him to suit his needs. That shit gets old."

"You're right about that." Val and I clicked our glasses together.

"So was Lamont just a one-time deal?"

"Yeah, definitely. Don't get me wrong, the sex that night was off the chain but I ain't trying to kick it with him like that. I know Lamont has grown and things seem to be going pretty well for him right now, but Lamont really doesn't hold my attention. That whole nightlife/producing lifestyle is not my scene. I mean I can fuck with it sometime but not all the time. I still like my fine dining experiences, deep conversations, shopping on the Magnificent Mile, luxury condos, jazz music and yoga. You know simple shit."

"Ha! Simple shit? That's that bougie shit and I ain't mad at you at all. Lamont is definitely not about that life. He is definitely yo weed and Hennessy kind of dude but a good lay from him every now and then could do the body some good."

"Ya damn right about that."

"Well, I guess you got a lot of decisions to make. One thing is for sure. You have some beautiful kids who have only known what you and Mike have provided for them so just give it some more thought before you change their world you know?"

Wow, maybe Val's therapist was really doing his job? Two sappy moments in one day was a record for Val, but she did have a point and I know her perspective was coming from an honest place with everything she experienced growing up.

"I definitely have which is why I've been chilling from Law. He's definitely a drug for me. It's so hard being around him. He says one word and my panties are on the floor!"

"Man, that's how it was with me and Don. I would do anything for him. My head was so far stuck up his ass but I'm moving on."

"How has that been for you guys at work?"

"Well, you know we never really saw each other at work unless it was planned with him being up on the 19th floor and all. He would send me texts to come and meet him in his office or one of the other secret offices in the building. It was so habitual that as soon as his text would come through, I would just politely take my thong off, put them in my purse and go skipping to wherever he was. You know that's a damn shame. But these days, I avoid him like the plague, especially after that Natalia fiasco. I'm through."

"Well, I'm just glad he's not hurting you anymore."

"I'm glad too. Believe it or not, I've come a long way since then. My therapist has really been helping me see how much of a crutch Don was for me. I always ran back to the familiar which was being abused and hurt by someone but I'm really trying to grow from that experience. I ain't even had sex in a long time." Val whispering that she hasn't been fucking in a while was quite humorous but I didn't show it.

"Wow, you haven't had sex since, Don?"

"Girl hell naw, but it's been about a week," Val whispered again like she was letting me in on some huge secret. Now in my book, no sex in a week didn't actually constitute a long time but I knew in Val's book it did.

"Well, I'm super proud of you honey for wanting to clear out your energy field for a minute to regain a sense of control over your life."

"See, that's why I fuck with you. My therapist said the same damn thing!"

"Well, you know a bitch gots many talents." I said proudly.

"And see, you make me so proud when you start talking like me!"

Val and I hugged, drank more wine, laughed and told more stories. Val was one of the most important adult relationships I had in my life and I was so glad we were friends again like old times.

* * *

I hadn't talked to anyone about the time I had spent with my mom while she was in Chicago a month ago. The only person who knew I'd seen her was Niecey but we really didn't go in depth about our conversation. I guess I just needed some time to sort things out and possibly even decide if I wanted to continue a relationship with Lorraine.

Niecey and Lorraine had already talked about what happened all those years ago so she was up to speed on why Lorraine left but I still didn't talk too much about our conversation to Niecey. I'd never really felt as close to Niecey as I would've liked. I felt more like her mother than her sister. I mean yeah, we watched each other's kids, we talked about family stuff and went over each other's houses from time to time but that was about it. Niecey was always caught up in some drama whether it was with her baby's daddy, someone at her salon or some street dude. Niecey was always loud as fuck, would get overly emotional about things, and always had something negative to say or felt like someone owed her something. She just never took responsibility for anything.

We didn't hang around the same circles at all. I mean, I know my friends had hood in them but they knew when to turn that shit off and be a goddamn professional. Niecey, on the other hand, was trying to serve dark liquor at her daughter's christening. I just couldn't with her. But I wanted to talk to someone about Lorraine that I felt would understand at least a little and considering her and I did grow up together, Niecey was really my only choice.

"Hey, Lita." Niecey said with a long sigh like she was irritated to hear from me.

"Damn Niecey, it's like that? Can't I get a more excited response from you when I call?"

"It ain't nothing personal. I just got a lot of shit on my plate." I knew whenever Niecey started talking like that, she basically got herself involved in some mess again.

"What is it now Niecey?"

"Damn, why you gotta say it like that? Like I'm always in some shit. I know it seems like that most of the time but it ain't always like that. And goddamn, didn't you call me? It ain't like I called you, bugging you!"

Niecey had a point there and maybe I shouldn't have said it like that.

"I'm sorry Niecey, I really am. I shouldn't have responded to you like that. What's going on? Is there something I can help you with?" Sometimes I had to prepare for our talks on the phone because Niecey stressed me out most of the time but I was really trying to give my best effort and be more patient with her.

"Well, it's not something really major but, do you remember when you wanted me to talk to Mike's friend Drew about that auditing situation at the salon a while back?"

"Yeah?"

"Well, he helped me out a lot and for once I didn't go in a situation just letting a guy fuck, you know? I mean, I was throwing out all the cues at first but he wasn't taking the bait at all. But then he called me out of the blue one day asking me out on a date. It was so formal the way he stepped to me. I wasn't used to that you know? I asked him why all of a sudden he wanted to go out with me now even though I was giving him all the signals back then."

"So what did he say?"

"He said at the time, he was on again off again with his girl and he didn't want to start anything with anyone just yet even though they were broken up. He said since he didn't know how things were going to turn out with the bitch he would just wait before trying to link up."

I couldn't help but laugh out loud.

"Damn, Lita, I'm trying to be serious right now. Why are you laughing?"

"I'm sorry Niecey, I didn't mean to it's just, how you gonna call the girl a bitch and you don't even know her?"

"Aww damn, did I? I guess it's just a habit but anyways, we're supposed to go out tonight and I don't know what to wear, how to do my hair or how to act. I mean, I know he's used to all that prim and proper shit like Mike. But hell, after you married Mike you learned how to be bougie as hell so maybe there's hope for me."

"Why the entire hell does everyone keep calling me bougie?"

"Cause ya is, get over it, Lita. But this ain't about you right now. It's about me. What imma do?" Niecey sounded really concerned.

"Just be yourself baby sis."

"Oh, so you just gon let me be out here with a body-con dress on and my twenty pound layers of weave trying to go see Drew? I doubt he's into that. He seems like he's into them prissy bitches with they real hair that shop at Whole Foods and shit and hang out at the gym for lunch." Niecey seemed really down on herself.

"Niecey, stop it. He likes *you*. He wouldn't have asked you out if he didn't want the real Niecey. Don't start changing who you are now for some dude. You must really like him the way you're getting all worked up about this."

"I can't front. I really do. When he helped with the auditing, he was so nice and attentive you know? He was mad respectful towards me. I need that kind of chivalry in my life. There was this one day I forgot to have some files ready for him when he came over to my salon so I told him I would bring it to his house after work. Girl, when he answered the door in those grey sweatpants, I was in heaven. I'm like damn Zaddy Drew, come through with the package!"

"Ha! You crazy Niecey."

"But on the real, it just ain't about that. He just seems like a really good dude and I really want him to like me."

"Niecey, look at me." I grabbed Niecey's hands. "Trust me, he will."

"I mean, I know I can be a bit loud at times, I know I can drink any nigga under the table, and yes, I do hang out at strip clubs sometimes for the pure enjoyment of it cause them bitches got talent on the pole. But I can be a little subdued at times."

"Take it from me Niecey, don't change who you are to accommodate anyone. You want him to know who *you* really are today so you don't grow resentful tomorrow."

"Wow, that's some deep shit. Did you get that from them Deepak Chopra books you be reading?"

"Naw Niecey, just speaking from experience."

"What experience you talking 'bout?"

"It's nothing to get into right now."

"You and Mike okay?"

"Naw not really but we're maintaining."

"Look, I know I don't know what it's like to be married but you can talk to me you know?"

I never really talked to anyone about being separated from Mike except for Val and Law. But maybe I should open up to my sister more. It could possibly bring us closer.

"It's a long story Niecey but Mike and I are separated. We're living in the same house still playing this game but I need to make some decisions."

"Damn. I had no idea. That's why you didn't know about me and Drew. I thought Mike would've told you by now but now it makes sense. Oh, I'm sorry girl."

Niecey reached out and gave me hug. I felt her sincerity but I wouldn't dare tell her about Law and Lamont because she would mess around and accidentally tell one of her clients and my business would be all out in the street in a matter of seconds.

"I'm good. We're just on two different pages right now. I'm not sure if I want to make our marriage work or move on."

"Well, hell if your shit ain't work how the hell do I think imma ever find somebody?"

"Uh uh Niecey, don't do that. Don't determine your life based off of mine. I'm in a certain stage in my life right now that could go either way but that doesn't mean you're doomed in the relationship department. Life is what you make it. Hell, look at Lorraine. She even changed her life and met a great man and started a whole other family."

"Well, you're right about that. For someone going through what you're going through right now, you actually seem quite calm."

"I mean, I have my moments but I've been doing a lot of self-reflecting regarding some of my decisions and where I wanna go from here."

"That's what's up. So you never told me about your talk with mama even though I asked her all about it."

"Yeah? Well, what did she tell you?"

"She told me what I knew was gonna happen. You finally broke down and you let her in. I knew mama always loved us."

"But honestly Niecey, how did you know that? All those years we were out there to fend for ourselves."

"Well, not really, we always had Daddy and plenty of people who helped raised us on the block."

"Yeah, I feel you but I needed Lorraine."

"I get that. But I don't know, I guess I saw at a young age mama was not like the other moms. I knew something else had to be wrong. I just didn't know what it was but I never held that against her."

Wow, Niecey had a leg up on me with that one. This was a side of her I had never seen before. She seemed so mature in that area. Niecey was always the caring type. She was loud and confrontational but she would give the shirt off of her back and give you money if she had it and you needed it. She always took care of my niece, Deja with ease, and even though I felt Deja's father didn't deserve it, she checked up on him and made sure he was cool, and she always made sure Daddy was good. And she never judged Lorraine and even welcomed her back with open arms. But I also felt that all that giving came with a price tag of people taking advantage of her and I just hated being in that position with people so I guarded myself.

"That's always been a challenge for me Niecey but I really love that about you."

"What's that?"

"You love hard. I know my attitude can suck at times and I know we go back and forth, but you're always here for me."

"Shit, no doubt. That's what Daddy taught us and I'll ride for you 'til the day I take my last breath."

"I really love you Niecey."

"I love you too big sis."

CHAPTER

11

Mike and I pretty much avoided each other when we were at home unless the kids were present but I couldn't keep doing this anymore. Mike said he wanted to work things out but every time we would try to have a decent conversation, he would say something that irritated me and then he would get frustrated with my response. Part of me wanted to just tell him I cheated so it would give us a reason to go ahead and get a divorce. The only thing is I truly missed what we shared but I knew we could never get that back.

I walked downstairs to the basement which I pretty much allowed to become Mike's man cave. He was bench pressing shirtless while listening to DMX. Mike always enjoyed listening to nineties hip hop while he worked out. He was definitely in his zone because I called his name three times and he never answered.

"Yeah, what's up?" Mike stood up while wiping the sweat from his forehead and chest. He didn't seem too eager to talk to me.

"I was wondering if we could talk?"

"You picked a pretty good time to talk. I was kind of in the middle of working out."

"I know, and I didn't mean to interrupt, it's just that it's pretty hard to catch up with you these days. Maybe we can talk later this evening?"

"Hmmm, yeah that's probably not gonna work. I was gonna kick it with Drew and the fellas tonight."

"Oh?"

"You sound surprised."

"Well, usually we fill each other in if we're going out so one of us will be home with the kids or if we need to get a sitter."

"It's funny you mentioned that because you didn't really seem to have a problem leaving me in the dark about that ten thousand dollars you withdrew from our account."

Mike was starting to hit that nerve because he kept failing to realize I didn't have to ask his permission for a damn thing but I took a deep breath and tried to remain calm.

"I honestly don't want to fight. I just wanted us to talk about our marriage."

"I'm trying to figure out what's left to say. You talk to the kids, you talk to your girls on the phone or you go out with them, you go to work and you're building your business. You don't say shit to me when we're here so what could you possibly have to say now?"

I could tell Mike was not only upset with me but he almost seemed to have made his decision about our marriage without even saying it.

"Is there someone else?"

"What? You got a lot of fucking nerve Lita, seriously."

"I mean, it's just a straightforward question. We haven't had sex in a long time and you haven't been trying to get it from me. I mean, you are a man. I can't see you holding out this long."

"So, you come down here and interrupt my workout to ask me some shit like that? I should've known when you said you wanted to talk it was only to benefit you."

"What the hell are you talking about? Asking you if you've been with anyone else has to do with *our* marriage."

"No, you just wanna know if I'm fucking anybody else. You know what I think? I think you're the one out here fucking and you're trying to ease your guilty conscience by trying to find some shit on me."

I grew silent almost immediately. I didn't expect Mike to respond like that. I was speechless. And as much as I tried to hide it, it appeared that Mike was actually well aware and in tune with me at that moment.

"Mike, I'm not trying to upset you."

"It's too late for that. Like I said, I'm going out tonight and it ain't no need for you to wait up. The look on your face says more than you know. Tomorrow morning, I'll call an attorney and start figuring this shit out since everything points to you wanting to be single."

Mike walked right past me like I was just a random person in our home and went upstairs to take a shower. For the first time since our separation, I cried and I cried long and hard. I couldn't believe what was happening. All this time, I entertained the thought of being single again, but after the talk I just had with Mike, it was starting to feel like it was becoming a reality.

I wanted to call Law for some reason. I always felt like he could console me no matter the situation and I felt like this would be no different. I sent him a text.

By any chance will you be free to talk in a couple of hours?

I patiently awaited Law's response. I couldn't quite call him yet seeing that Mike was still home. Time continued to pass and there was still no response from Law until almost an hour later.

Are you okay? Sorry, I'm just now seeing your text.

I could be better but will you be available to talk in about an hour?

Yep.

Okay great, I'll call you in about an hour.

Okay.

Something seemed different about Law's texts this time around. He didn't seem as excited to hear from me. His responses were quite short. I mean, I know we hadn't talked in a while but I didn't think the last time we talked was on bad terms? I was waiting for Mike to leave so that I could finally call him.

Mike didn't leave the house until about ten-thirty and I kind of wondered where he was going at that hour but I knew I wasn't at liberty to question him about anything at this point. I finally got the kids to go to bed and I took a bath before I called Law.

"Hello."

"Hey, handsome." I said flirtatiously.

"How are you, Lita?"

"Why so formal?"

"Well, it's just kind of odd to hear from you almost a month later and at this hour no less. Let me guess, you were waiting for your husband to leave the house?"

"Is everything okay Law? You sound upset about something."

"Honestly, I'm not upset but I am a little disappointed. Clearly, you've been pretty busy for the past month."

"Well, yeah, kind of? Between the kids, work, and my business, my schedule has been pretty crazy. And I didn't get a chance to tell you this, but I actually reconnected with my mother after all these years." I thought me explaining my schedule to Law would allow him to ease up on me a bit.

"That's good news for you and your mom. I'm happy for you. Really, I am. I always thought you owed it yourself to connect with her if you could."

"Yeah, you're right about that. I'm still not exactly sure of the kind of relationship I want to have with her but at least I'm thinking about it."

"I don't want to come off rude or insensitive as I'm definitely happy to hear the news about your mom but why did you call?"

Law was always straight forward and he definitely wasn't beating around the bush with me right now. That was one of the traits I liked about him but being in the hot seat right now wasn't as comfortable.

"I guess I'm just a little bit out of it."

"What's going on?"

"Well, first let me start by saying that I really miss you and I didn't mean to let so much time pass without even sending you a text." It was pretty quiet on the phone as if Law was waiting for me to say something else. "I mean, it's just been crazy around here on the home front."

"Let me help you out a bit because I know sometimes getting straight to the point is not exactly your strong suit. You're trying to figure things out in your marriage right now, and trust me, I've been there so I totally understand. When we first hooked up, I told you I would be there for you no matter which path you chose. I told you I would not pressure you about that, but you need to figure out what you want to do. One thing I will not do is accept the back and forth much longer."

"Wow, Law. You sound a little hostile. And if I recall, you told me you wouldn't pressure me about leaving my husband but that's exactly what it felt like you were doing, hence the reason you hadn't heard from me in a while."

"So, let's talk about that. You just said you hadn't contacted me in a month because of work, kids, and pretty much life right? But now you're saying it's because you felt pressured by me. All I can say is I've been straight forward with you about everything since we've been involved. I have not said one thing to you and meant another. I've expressed my feelings for you on numerous occasions. I don't have a problem with the fact that you may not be ready to leave your marriage, hell, that's a big decision but all you had to say was you didn't see a divorce being in your near future and you want to work some things out with your husband or see where things go. I would've respected you for that and even if you still wanted to see me, I would've been open because at least I would've known exactly where your head was and I could act accordingly. But every time you would talk to me, you would always express your frustrations about your marriage and how you felt it was time to leave. Those are two different viewpoints. I'm not here to tell you what to do, but you've got to figure out what you want baby and you need to be honest with yourself and others."

"I'm so sorry. I just don't know what I want right now." I started feeling the tears swell.

"And it's okay baby that you don't know but I have to look out for myself as well you know? If you're trying to have someone to dip off with and have sex with from time to time, no strings attached, you have to be comfortable saying that. I wouldn't view you as anything less. I would actually respect you more because you're being who you are at the moment and you're being upfront. Now, I'll be honest, I dig you a lot more than just hitting it and walking away but I understand you're trying to figure things out. But you gotta let me know baby. And if you just need me to get you right from time to time, just know that will be a different dynamic regarding our relationship. We may not be as intimate with our thoughts and feelings because of the parameters. Again, I like you more than that, so ideally, that's not what I want."

I had so many preconceived notions about Law regarding my current situation but surprisingly he was so much more mature about all this than I could've imagined. I guess I was trying to have my cake and eat it too so to speak but Law was right. He was saying in so many words I needed to put my big girl panties on and figure my shit out.

"Well, with that being said, I am trying to figure some things out in my marriage right now and I think I owe myself that much."

"And that is definitely your decision and all I can do is respect that."

As much as I wanted to be able to call Law for impromptu booty calls from time to time, I just didn't want to appear to be *that* woman. I know he said he wouldn't look at me any differently but I just couldn't juggle the double lifestyle any longer. I had decided when Mike came home, I would really try to repair our marriage and try to hear him out more. Maybe *I'd* been selfish where Mike was concerned. I mean he is an amazing man and maybe we just had to be more creative and diligent in working on our marriage. But at this point, Mike seemed like he really didn't want to even be in the same room with me.

"I appreciate you Law for understanding."

"Well, it's not the easiest thing to do. I mean I really like you and I like being around you. And yes, I like making love to you and I would be lying if I said I wouldn't miss that."

I was starting to feel that strong desire for Law again by the way he was talking to me. It was always so hard to focus on my marriage knowing that Law was an option. How would I be able to shake this feeling?

"Well, I'm missing it already. This is tough for me."

"But that's something to think about Lita. If this is so hard for you, do you feel like you're being honest with yourself about wanting to work on your marriage? Do you love him?"

"I mean, we share a life together, we have children, we have history."

"And the question remains, do you love him?"

"Yes." I felt that I loved Mike but I wasn't in love with him anymore but I knew if I had started explaining what I meant by that, I would've allowed Law to talk me right back into his bed. I had to stay strong and focus on my marriage.

"Well, that sounds like something I can't compete with at the moment so I'll respect your decision and I'll fall back. I guess I'll talk to you if you reach out to me first."

I could hear the disappointment in Law's voice and I was hoping I was making the right decision by cutting the relationship off.

"Okay. I really value the experiences you've brought to my life. You mean a lot to me."

"Thank you for that. It's probably best now that we move on. I want to respect your wishes because if I keep talking to you, I'm going to invite you over and I'm going to have you screaming my name. I'm just expressing how I feel."

For the first time, I noticed Law's mischievous side. He didn't have to tell me he was trying to have me all up in his bed like that. He knew exactly what he was doing.

"Well, you're right it's best if I go. I'll talk to you later."

"One more thing before you go Lita, I love you."

"What?"

"I think you heard what I said, I know that probably threw you off guard."

Maybe, I did need to leave Law alone. Why all of a sudden he wants to tell me he loves me? Was he just trying to keep me from going back to Mike or did he really mean what he was saying? I couldn't decide if I trusted him or not.

"That's a very serious statement to make. I'm not sure how to respond."

"You don't have to respond. I just wanted to at least let you know how *I* felt. Take the time you need to sort things out. I'll be here either way."

Either Law was definitely into me or he was laying the game on very thick. Who knew?

"Okay, I'll be in touch."

"Okay, talk to you soon."

We hung up from each other and all I could think to myself was why did I leave that door open for Law? If I was looking to work things out with Mike, I probably should've completely cut things off with Law but part of me couldn't because I still wanted him in my life.

* * *

I knew Mike said he didn't want me to wait up for him but I couldn't help it. I wanted to talk to him and get some insight on what was happening with us sooner rather than later. I guess a part of me wondered if he was cheating as well and then I would have a "reason" to move forward with the divorce without him finding out about my infidelity. I started feeling my eyes getting heavy but I wanted to be awake by the time Mike got home.

It was three in the morning and I was alerted on my phone that Mike was coming in the house because of the smart locks we had installed on all of our doors. I tried to pretend I was asleep but when Mike walked upstairs, I moved around as if I was waking up because I heard his footsteps. Mike was no longer sleeping in our bedroom but in the guest bedroom down the hall. I was hoping he needed to get something from our room like a pair of boxer briefs or a t-shirt just so that we could talk but he never came.

As I was just about to get up, I heard his footsteps coming closer to our room. He knocked on the door.

"Yes?"

"I thought I heard you moving around. Are you awake?"

"Sort of." I lied.

"Can I come in?"

"Sure."

When Mike opened the door, he stood there looking at me. I knew that look all too well. That was the look he gave me on our wedding night before we basically broke the headboard. It was that look that said he wanted to explore every inch of my body; a look that I hadn't seen in a long time. Mike didn't say a word. He walked into the room, locked the bedroom door and walked towards our bed.

"Do you have any panties on?"

"No." I said confusingly.

"Good."

Mike crawled under the covers and began giving me the best head ever. What had gotten into him? Mike hadn't been this assertive in a long time.

"What are you doing?"

"Shhhh." Mike said quietly while briefly holding his head up from in between my legs. Once Mike returned to pleasuring me, I wondered what was going on but I was enjoying myself too much to care.

The sex Mike and I had was phenomenal but after he practically fucked my brains out, I thought he would've stayed the night in our bed. He got up and started putting his clothes back on.

"Where are you going?"

"I'm heading back to my room?"

Okay, I was really confused. What was Mike trying to prove?

"Okay, why? We just made love?"

"No, we fucked." Mike said in a serious tone as he was putting on a pair of jogging pants.

"What is going? Is everything okay? I thought maybe you wanted to work things out?"

"Well, you shouldn't have assumed. I'm still calling the attorney later and we can start figuring out how we're going to divide everything up."

"Mike! I don't understand what's going on right now? You're acting really different and I can't follow your mood. Did something happen?"

"You wanna know what happened? I went to the strip club tonight with the fellas and I got horny as hell looking at all those butt ass naked women. Instead of spending my money on some hoe at the club, I thought I'd fuck one for free so here I am."

"Who the fuck are you calling a hoe? I don't deserve the treatment I'm getting from you right now!"

"Let me fill you in on a little something. I was riding through Hyde Park one evening on my way home from work.

Clearly, it was one of those nights you asked *my* mother to watch the kids because you weren't gonna be home. When I was in Hyde Park, I thought I saw your truck parked on Cornell so I backed up and recognized your license plate. I knew Val didn't live in Hyde Park but I brushed it off thinking you were at one of your other girlfriend's house. But that night you came home, you seemed a little different. I just couldn't put my finger on it."

My heart began racing because I could tell where this conversation was going and that it wasn't going to end well.

"But after I left the house last night to go hang out, you must have been very eager to call your little boyfriend because you didn't even notice that I walked back in the house to get my wallet that I had left on the kitchen counter. I walked upstairs to tell you we could have that talk later but when I got close to our bedroom door, you were so engrossed in your conversation with Law? Is that the motherfucker's name?"

I couldn't believe this was happening and I definitely didn't want Mike to find out about Law, especially not like this. And I definitely didn't want him to connect the dots that Law was the same man he met at the gala.

"Let me explain!"

"There's really nothing to explain. First and foremost, you might want to close the door when you're talking to the other nigga you're fucking considering one of our children could've walked in on you."

"Mike, please let me just say something!"

"Lita, hell naw! All this time, I been turning down all kinds of ass for you. Do you understand me? All kinds of women; Black, Latina, White, Asian, short, tall, skinny, thick and everything in between. I could have had any one of them bent over my desk in a minute but I was trying to be a good husband to you. Damn, I know I don't always do shit perfectly but I have always been here for you and our kids. I have given you the absolute best life that I could have provided and it just wasn't enough. Fuck, I ain't trying to throw ten years away but you put me in a straight up bogus position Lita. Clearly, you're searching for something. Maybe you're trying to discover a new you or some shit like these new age women talking about these days. I don't know what the fuck it is but you need to go find that shit. The only reason your ass ain't out of this house right now is because of our kids. I love them too damn much to treat their mom like shit. So like I said, I'll be filing those divorce papers. That'll help make your decision a whole lot easier because I don't deserve this shit."

And just like that, Mike slammed the door.

* * *

"Hey Lita, honey!"

"Hey, mama."

"Wow, you called me mama?"

"I know, that kind of shocked me too. When you picked up the phone, that was the first thing that came to mind."

"Are you okay? I'm detecting something in your voice."

"Wow, for us not having a relationship for the past twenty years, I'm actually surprised you were able to detect that."

"Well, no matter what, a mother will always feel some sense of connection to her child, no matter how many years goes by. So what's wrong honey?"

I couldn't say a word, I just began crying uncontrollably.

"Oh baby, I wish I could hug you right now. You know I would fly out there in a minute if you wanted me to?"

"You know, I never would've thought after all these years, I would hear you talk to me like this."

"Well baby, I've made many, many mistakes in my life but as long as I'm living, there's always a chance to make things better. I'm just glad that I've had the opportunity to change things in my life and have an opportunity to make things right with you. I will forever be grateful for your forgiveness."

"But who will forgive me? I've made some mistakes myself."

"Baby, whatever it is, you can tell me. Nothing is ever too bad to share with your mama."

"Trust me, for lack of better words, I fucked up."

"What happened?"

"Well, long story short. I cheated on Mike, numerous times and he found out."

Lorraine let out a long sigh.

"Lita, I know it feels like the end of the world, but it's really not. You have to give these kinds of situations time."

"He's already called his attorney and they're drawing up papers as we speak. What do I tell the kids?"

"Slow down for a minute. Do you love Mike?"

"Of course, what kind of question is that?"

"It's a legitimate question because you opened yourself up to someone else. There's always a reason for that."

"So you're blaming me?"

"Please listen to me. I'm not blaming you for anything. I just want to help you sort some things out and get to the root of what's going on. So yes, you love Mike, but do you want to continue your marriage?"

"Mama, Mike and I had been at odds for a while now. He never really tried to take into account my feelings about things that I was passionate about like starting my business, we were arguing all the time about everything, and I know this might be TMI but he wasn't willing to try new things and please me sexually. And then I met this guy Law at the bookstore. I promise I wasn't looking for anyone else but when I met him, I was so drawn to him. So much so that I actually kind of made the first move by stating to him how attractive he was. I don't know what came over me. As much as I tried to stay away from him, I couldn't. He excited me, he made me think about things and I admired how he chose to live his life. He seemed so in charge of his world and wasn't concerned about pleasing others."

"So you never said if you still wanted your marriage."

"I love Mike, I promise I do, but I haven't been in love with Mike for a long time. We are great together when it comes to the logistics of raising a family and our financial obligations but there's no spark. There's no excitement anymore and I just feel like we naturally grew apart. So honestly, I can't see myself being married to Mike anymore but again, I never wanted to hurt him."

"And I believe you but you have to be honest with yourself. I think a lot of the things that were happening in your marriage and the things you were upset with Mike about were not really about Mike. What you seemed to have been experiencing is the evolution and discovery of Lita. When you met Law, that was more of a wake-up call that change needed to happen. And that may not necessarily mean that you will end up with Law but it does mean that there were some things that needed to come to a head for you. The way you described Law just really sounds like a man that was reflecting back to you what you saw in yourself and what you wanted to be. As women, we tend to lose ourselves a lot in our relationships because we give so much until we're depleted. I'm so sorry honey you're going through this."

"Well, I made this bed and I have to lie in it. It's not your fault."

"I'm apologizing because I know in your own way, you took on my role when I left. You became the one that stepped in and took care of everyone. I'm still amazed at how you raised Sheree while attending school and pursuing your goals. You never had the opportunity to be taken care of. You had to be extremely responsible at such an early age. There were some things you never had a chance to explore and for that, I apologize."

I never really made the connection of my mom not being in my life to what's been going on with me presently. But there was no excuse for hurting Mike the way I did.

"I have to own my mistakes."

"And I'm in total agreement with you on that one. You've always been mature in that respect even when you were a little girl but you can't deny how you feel. And if you really feel like your marriage has run its course, you have to allow Mike to go in peace."

"You've said a lot of things that brought a lot to my attention. What made you think of that?"

"Well, I've spent plenty of years in therapy honey and even more time reflecting and working on myself. But just give Mike some space. Just be still for a moment and don't rush into anything. You may just need some time to re-evaluate. Even though he's contacted the attorney, you still haven't received any divorce papers yet. Just be sure that you really want this divorce and if you still feel that way after some time has passed, then you have to do what's best for you. Either way, I love you and I support you."

Being able to talk to my mom this way helped me so much. All my life, I never had her guidance and direction. It was nice to experience that for once.

CHAPTER

12

I couldn't believe this day had finally come. I was sitting in a conference room across from Mike with our attorneys who were doing their best to divvy up our assets as amicably as possible. The conference room was about as cozy as the doctor's office where I typically got routine pelvic exams. It felt cold and sterile. How did we get here? I knew deep down inside I loved Mike, but I thought long and hard about our marriage over the past few months and felt it was best. Mike didn't seem angry with me anymore about my infidelity but I could tell he was still hurt.

When we informed the kids that we were getting a divorce, Tariq and Rashad were upset but were more concerned with who they were going to live with and if there would be enough money for video games and the latest gym shoes. Clearly, our boys never really knew how well off we were. Sheree, on the other hand, stated to me she could sense things between Mike and I for a while and often wondered if we would stay together. Sheree also said she was hoping she could go and visit Lamont more now even though I explained to her that she could do that whether Mike and I were married or not.

I had launched my business but I hadn't really turned a huge profit yet. With regards to the divorce, I was actually kind of glad because I didn't want Mike to feel entitled to any portion of that. Since no real profit was made, there wasn't much to share with him in that respect. I had heard about people turning into complete monsters during the divorce proceedings and I had hoped that wouldn't be us. Thankfully, Mike was cordial but he mainly talked to me through our lawyers.

"Mrs. Payne, my client and I have discussed the terms of the custodial arrangements regarding the children." Ron stated sternly.

Ron Weiss was Mike's attorney who had represented various high profile clients in the Chicagoland area that included surgeons, school superintendents, politicians, you name it. Ron was very skilled at gaining not only financial security for his clients but also assisting parents with gaining the visitation, custodial, or full custody rights of their choice. Clearly, Mike was using his money and influence to afford one of the most prominent attorneys on retainer.

"I'm confused, Ron, what terms are you speaking of? I'm their mother and my children will be living with me."

My attorney, Rick attempted to remind me that I should speak through him and let him handle the various custodial terms and conditions. He could not have been handling much if the custody of my children was even a topic of discussion.

"Mrs. Payne, my client is asking for joint custody."

"I'm sorry, I can't do that." I immediately responded.

"Lita, please consult with me." Rick whispered.

"Listen, I'm not going to allow Mike's attorney to take my babies away from me. He's rarely even home due to work. I run my own business and before you know it, I'll be working solely for myself and my kids won't ever have to worry about me not being available, unlike Mike." I whispered back at Rick.

"Due to your client, Michael Payne's grueling work and travel schedule, we are asking that Mrs. Payne remain the custodial parent, along with creating a visitation plan that works for my client as well as yours. He may be the custodial parent during the summer months when the children are on break from school."

I gave Rick the most serious stare down in history for even suggesting that without consulting me. I leaned over to Rick to whisper in his ear.

"What the hell do you think you're doing?"

"Lita, you've got to trust me on this. If you force their hand, Mike will definitely be advised to go after full custody by his attorney. I've seen Ron at work in divorce proceedings, he can be a serious beast. I know his game and how he plays it so I'm just trying to make sure he doesn't try to take you to the cleaners."

"On what grounds though? This is insane!" Rick and I were still attempting to whisper to each other back and forth.

"Excuse me, are you all done or do you need extra time?" Ron asked impatiently.

"We're done Ron. So what has your client decided?" Rick respectfully asked.

Mike began engaging in deep conversation with Ron and finally stated his answer.

"I'm in total agreement with me being able to visit my children during the school year and them staying with me during the summer." Mike said confidently.

I was not fond of the arrangement but it was better than me gambling the possibility of not having my kids with me at all.

"I'm in agreement as well." I stated.

After the meeting was over and papers were signed, we all dismissed ourselves from the conference room. I was a bit thirsty so I stopped off at the vending machine to get a bottled water while my attorney was making a phone call. I noticed Mike in my peripheral.

"Lita, I hate that it had to come to this."

"Well, I know my role in this whole ordeal and I guess I left you no choice."

"Not exactly Lita. I was so upset with you that night when I found out about your affair but after I said I wanted a divorce, you really didn't even try to work things out or plead your case. You appeared ready for this as well so I felt no reason to hold each other back."

"All I can say is, I am so sorry for how I hurt you. It was not my intention whatsoever."

"I actually understand that now. And what I understand even more so is that you've been changing Lita and I ain't saying that's a bad thing because I know we all change. But the change in you just doesn't seem like it wants to be aligned with me anymore and I refuse to lie to myself and think this is what you want when it's not."

"It's amazing that after all these years, you seem more in tune with me now than you ever have."

"Well, life-changing situations can do that to a person."

"So do you really honestly believe we can pull off this co-parenting thing without ripping each other's heads off?"

"I know I'm going to make a conscious effort. What about you?"

"We're finally agreeing on something because I feel the same way."

"Damn Lita, for a while we had something good. This fucking sucks big time." I could tell Mike was becoming a bit emotional but trying to contain himself.

"It does suck but maybe marriages can really just run its course after a while. I know we all say 'til death do us part, but do we really mean that when we say it?"

"Well, I did. I really thought I was everything you needed and wanted. But you have to discover you and what works for you. I never would've thought when we got married that you would've cheated on me. You were always the *responsible* one I guess you can say. You just always walked around like you wouldn't be affected by these distractions out here. I just always put you up on a pedestal in that way."

"I have to correct you there. I still wasn't affected. I just finally opened myself up to what my heart desired and stopped trying to play by the book. I've always had a desire to run my own business and what happened between me and Law—"

"Please don't say his name. I still wanna beat his ass."

"Well, what happened between him and I, was more so about things that I'd always wanted but took too long to share with you and I grew resentful. By the time I'd met him, it was already too late. I was ready to stop putting what I wanted on hold. I know it's not right but that's how it happened."

"Don't tell me you're trying to hook up with this guy for the long term because I'm really not trying to have some man around my kids who slept with my wife knowing good and damn well she was married."

"I know we're trying to have the most appropriate conversation we can have under the circumstances but I don't know what the future holds and who I will be dating. I'm pretty sure you're not aware of that on your end as well but what I do know is I don't want us to be angry forever. I want to continue to discover me and I want you to be with someone who will give you what you need."

"You seem pretty calm about all this."

"I'm just not trying to continuously beat myself up over what has transpired between us."

"So, what now?"

"I'm not sure. I just want to love on the kids so much more with everything we're going through. I'm gonna grind hard so I can get this marketing firm where it needs to be and eventually phase out of my job at Global Connections. I'm going to spend more time with my sister and my mom now that she's back in the picture. And, I don't know, maybe take up a new hobby like painting or take vocal lessons. I've always loved to sing."

"Damn, was I really holding you back from all of that?"

"No, not at all but I held myself back. All my life, I focused on making sure everyone else was good. Even the way I hustled to get through school and eventually get that position at Global Connections. That was all for Sheree because I felt she deserved the best life. I decided not to start my business sooner because I didn't want to "rock the boat" with you so to speak. It just became all too consuming."

"Well, it seems like you got this all figured out." Mike sounded disappointed.

"I really don't, but I'm trying to make a real effort in being honest with what I want and what makes me happy."

"Are you in love with that guy?"

"No."

"Are you still seeing him?"

"No. I haven't seen him in like four months.

"Look, we had something good for a while. I mean I know our shit ain't been perfect but ain't nobody shit perfect. And if I'm honest with myself, I have to take some responsibility for my part in that as well. Since we've been married, you never had to want for anything financially. Even though you've been able to hold your own, I always took care of you in that way and I know you appreciated that. But I dropped the ball when I didn't support your dreams and when I put my job before you. I could've cut back on my hours but it was easier to spend more time at work than coming home and dealing with our issues. I fucked up big time in that respect because it caused you to go seek comfort and support elsewhere."

I couldn't believe the conversation Mike and I were having right now. I never really heard Mike talk to me like this before let alone apologize for not giving me what I needed.

"I think we're starting to reflect so much more now that we are getting closer to finalizing our divorce."

"But that's the thing, Lita. Do you *really* want this divorce because I'm looking at you right now and thinking about everything we've built together and I'm trying to figure out if there is even a small chance of us staying together."

I was really in shock with the words that were coming out of Mike's mouth. We were literally in the middle of getting a divorce and he was actually insinuating us staying together even though I was the one who cheated on him. I couldn't believe it.

"If there is truly a chance of us working this out, I would much rather keep our marriage together. I just want your support. I want you to love me the way that I am and as I continue to evolve. If that is something you're not willing to do, I will not force you."

"Then fuck it, let's make this shit work Lita. Let's just start over. We both had our faults, we ain't gotta remind each other about that shit. I love you, Lita Baby. You are my world and I'm sorry for not showing you that but I want you back in my life."

As Mike looked at me, a tear slowly dropped from my eye.

"Lita Baby, don't cry, we can do this."

"I'm just crying because I'm sorry for lying to you. I'm sorry for cheating on you. I'm just sorry."

"Look, I can't lie to you. That shit still hurts. And I ain't gonna forget that it happened but, I know that's not you. I said some real hurtful shit to you that night. I called you the worse thing I could've ever called you and I'm sorry. There was no excuse for me to be that way towards you. I just want you to know this ain't all your fault and I swear, if you're down for trying this again, I'll give you everything you need and more."

Mike grabbed me and hugged me and I cried some more. And then I whispered in his ear. "Thanks for forgiving me, Mike. I love you and I would love to give us another try."

Mike held me even tighter. He grabbed my ass and whispered to me.

"Lita, I wanna take you home and make love to you."

We left the building without uttering a single word to our attorneys. We couldn't get home fast enough.

CHAPTER

13

"So do you need me to throw you a divorce party or what?" Val said before I could even say hello when I picked up the phone.

"So umm, yeah about that. Mike and I decided not to go through with the divorce."

"What? Child, you know you always confusing me these days."

"I know." I laughed.

"Well, it sounds like a lot of happiness is flowing through your voice."

"That's because it is." I was smiling over the phone.

I filled Val in on what happened the day Mike and I met with our attorneys and what Mike said to me.

"Well, I'm really happy for you Lita. You sound so vibrant like Mike been breaking you off a little somethin' somethin' over there."

"Girl, that's an understatement. We can't keep our hands off of each other. He's been on a whole other level with it these days. He even asked me if I wanted to skip work one day and he took off work too. We dropped the kids off at school and came back home and got it in all day and in every part of this house!"

"Ha! Okay, I see you and Mike!"

"Yeah, it's been really good. It's like we have a whole new marriage."

"That's what's up! Low key, I was kinda hoping ya'll got back together. Don't tell nobody, I'm kinda a sucka for love."

"First of all, why are you whispering? Secondly, you didn't think I knew that?"

"Aiight whatever Lita. Now you know I can't let these niggas know my soft spot 'cause they'll try to run all over me."

"Yeah, I hear you. Hey, so how are things going in therapy?"

"Well, a sista got some pretty good news of her own."

"Ooh, do tell."

"Well, after six months of therapy, I've actually sort of graduated."

"Oh my God, that's so great!"

"Yeah, I'm pretty proud of myself too. There's so much that I got a chance to work through and just deal with. I never realized how angry I was and how that played out in my relationships. But I'm feeling good these days."

"I love it, Val! Damn, I'm so happy for you."

"Thanks love and…"

"And what?"

"Well, since I'm no longer working with my therapist, he actually asked me out on a date."

"Wow! Get out! How did you feel about that?"

"Well, I was real happy. Shit, I was feeling him from the start. But I really started liking him during the time we were working together. But Lita you would be so proud of me. I never once made a pass at him. He was the one that actually pursued me after our professional relationship had ended."

"That's crazy. My mom said that happened to her. She ended up actually marrying her therapist."

"Well, I don't know about wedding bells in my future but I really, really like him. I just don't wanna fuck it up."

"You won't honey."

"Well, I hope not. He is such a cool guy. I mean, we kind of have the same thought process and we're a lot alike. He's about five years older than me. He doesn't have any kids as he said he never really wanted any. He was

more into his career and traveling. He loves going to the movies like me, he likes to gamble from time to time, he smokes cigars, and dammit, he told me he loves sex! Like, really good sex, not that boring shit. He can get with me hanging from a chandelier here and there, he didn't mind that I liked kissing girls sometimes, he said he likes costumes and a little bondage. Girl… I'm like this may be the one honey!"

"Ha! Yes, you sound like you have definitely met your match."

"But you know what's so cool? I haven't had sex with him yet and we've already been on three dates!"

"Yeah, that's definitely different for you. What's up with that?"

"Well, believe it or not, I just like being around him. Don't get me wrong, he is so sexy but every time he's taken me home from a date and walked me to the door, he never once forced himself in and I didn't force him in either. I'm just letting things flow naturally. But man, the last date we went on, girl after he kissed me I damn near had an orgasm. Now ain't no man had *that* effect on me. Clearly, he'll be getting it soon. But I'm liking the change of pace. I'm liking this whole courting thang. It's kind of cool."

"I am so happy for you honey."

"I know you are and I'm happy for you and Mike. Sometimes shit gotta fall completely apart to be rebuilt."

"That's some good advice."

"Well, I can't exactly take the credit, that came from my therapist. His name is Terrance by the way."

"Ooh, you giddy! I hear it all in your voice."

"Girl, yes I am and I don't give a damn. I like this cute butterflies in the stomach type shit."

"Well, enjoy it. You deserve all the happiness Mr. Terrance brings to your life."

"Thank you, mama. And Lita, I love you so much."

"I love you too Val."

* * *

It was the night of my thirty-fifth birthday bash at the Waldorf Astoria Chicago Hotel. I was wearing a cream colored backless sequin mini dress with Ferragamo pumps to match. Mike was wearing a dark grey Dolce &

Gabbana three piece single-breasted suit that was tailored to perfection. He looked extremely handsome and as I watched him talk to the guests that night, I kept having flashbacks to the time we had almost gotten a divorce three years ago.

Wow, so much had changed. I was no longer working for Global Connections as my marketing firm took off during our second year of being in existence. My client list was insane and my firm was quickly becoming the who's who so to speak with regards to marketing and public relations in a metropolitan area. Mike and I obviously reconciled and he definitely played an integral part in me building my business as he supported me financially but also helped funnel clients my way.

Over the years, Mike and I made a continuous effort with regards to making our marriage work. But it wasn't all smooth sailing after him and I reconciled. We still struggled at times with how we communicated with each other. I even noticed Mike kind of getting pretty close with a new female employee at his job so I actually suggested trying an open marriage. Needless to say, that didn't last long. We just had too much on our plates to open our marriage up to catering to someone else's needs. Open marriages seemed like they were more work than anything. We always try to keep an open mind about things but the one thing we've been really trying to focus on is being honest with each other so that we're not blind-sided. The look on Mike's face when he found out I cheated on him is one that I never want to see again.

So many great things were happening in my life and the people around me. My mom and her husband bought some property here in Chicago. She had been expressing some interest in pursuing real estate as another stream of income so she's been out here more often looking at properties. We were definitely rebuilding our relationship and it felt so good. I really wished Daddy had shared with me years ago that my mom's behavior was a result of her illness but I understand why he didn't. I just hate how the guilt of feeling responsible for what happened to her ate away at him. It's sad to know that he carried that for so many years. I sure wished he was alive to see us now. I miss him so much but I'm so glad he was there for us and that he did the best that he could.

Niecey and Drew had gotten married a year ago and were now expecting a child. Ever since Drew had been in Niecey's life, she was lot calmer and relaxed. I just couldn't believe she stopped drinking Hennessy and smoking weed! She just decided she didn't want it anymore and stopped cold turkey. Drew had also helped her open up another salon in Texas as he has family from there. Her business was really taking off and no longer did she feel pressure to do something illegal to keep her doors open.

And my girl Val was just beaming. Her and Terrance decided to buy a home together and they have a golden retriever named Teuila. Val said she chose that name because it was a Pacific Islander name of course and that it rhymed with Tequila which was one of her favorite drinks. Val and Terrance were not exactly fond of the institution of marriage and decided against it but they said they had their own commitment ceremony of some sort with just the two of them. They also didn't want children but made a pact to always contribute to various organizations that supported orphans and children in the welfare system. I was so happy for them because they were truly on the same wavelength and they seemed to make each other happy.

As for me and Law, I'll never forget the time I walked into that bookstore and we locked eyes. Even though we rarely had contact these days after I decided to stay with Mike, he changed my life. He helped me to discover a part of me that was hidden for so long. He accepted every part of me and reminded me that I was more than a wife, a mom or an employee. Law reminded me that I was a living, breathing woman who had desires, who could be contradictory, who was passionate and sensual and that I could still be beautiful with all that wrapped up in one. Law was actually my soulmate. He came into my life and was a direct reflection of me. Yes, that relationship was seasonal but it was so necessary. The last time I spoke with Law, he stated that he had been considering moving to Vancouver where one of his other offices were located. He said that he would let me know once he decided. I was still attracted to him but for some reason, I just knew that time we shared was over. I was in a different place and so far that place seemed to be with Mike.

Lamont and I are still in contact of course due to us co-parenting Sheree but now that she's older, I typically send her to Atlanta to see him by herself. There was no need for me to tag along and honestly, Lamont and I really had nothing else to talk about if it didn't concern Sheree.

Our arrangement was for the best and I just didn't feel the need to be having casual sexual encounters with him. That didn't really serve a purpose for me. He had always been a fun, wild ride but that ride was truly over.

I never started those vocal lessons but I sure did start painting. Painting was one of those hobbies I could get lost in. I could be as creative as I wanted to be and I didn't have to rely on it to make a living. When I first started taking painting classes, my instructor would peep over from his canvas and smile at me from time to time and always use my work as an example of how graceful my strokes and use of colors were. He would always tell me I was a natural. Needless to say, when Mike and I decided to try an open marriage, Felipe, who was my instructor was that guy that I would indulge in from time to time. The sex was magical, whimsical and downright exciting, but the more I thought about it, being with Felipe was more so a reflection of my art. When I painted, I could feel Felipe inside of me and when I was with Felipe, I felt creative and high. And that's when I realized my self-discovery was an ongoing process. I was discovering life through my creativity, my work, how I related to my kids and even the choice I made to stay with Mike. And there were days that self-discovery was a challenge but as long as I was feeling these things, I was alive and not just existing. I stopped seeing myself as being "right" or "wrong", I just saw myself as being. It was very freeing.

Who knows what the future holds for me but I decided to focus on the now and tonight felt mystical. Everything felt aligned the way it should be.

"Hey Lita Baby, come here."

Mike grabbed my waist and then my hands and we started stepping Chicago style to the music.

"You look so beautiful tonight baby, you look happy which looks even more beautiful on you."

"Well, you play an integral part in that Mr. Payne."

"I would hope so." We both laughed. "Hey, you know what Lita?"

"What's that Mike?"

"Do you remember we had our first date in this area at that fancy restaurant around the corner? It's no longer there but man, I was definitely trying to impress you back then."

"Oh, I definitely remember. It was nice being exposed to the finer things in life."

"But at the time, I had no clue you were a single mom doing the best you could just to stay afloat. You always had it together whether you realized it or not. It's just always been something in you. You never let people see you sweat. You've always done what you had to do. Back then, I assumed you were some rich heiress the way you carried yourself."

"Ha! Well, clearly I wasn't. But it's nice to know you thought so highly of me back then because man the struggle was real."

"I know it was and that's why I was so proud to be your man. I felt like I was really contributing something huge to your life. All a man wants is to be respected and to be able to provide for his family."

"And a woman wants to be desired in every way. I know we lost that for some time, but it's nice to be in this space with you now Mike. We've come a long way."

"Yes, we have." Mike and I were starting to step a little more intricately as the DJ was playing one of Mike's favorite songs.

"So what now?"

"You know, you asked me that same question when we were going through our divorce."

"Well, I just wanna know what's on your mind. This is the big thirty-five for you. I know you got something brewing."

"Well, right now, I'm just extremely content with the way life is and having all of my close family and friends here with me tonight. And most importantly, I love you for saying fuck it, Lita, let's give this shit another try." We both laughed as we were reminiscing.

"Yeah, those were some times for sure. But hey, I had to realize your self-discovery was not an insult to me whatsoever. I can't even lie, allowing you to be free to be comfortable in discovering more about yourself has actually benefited me too. You just seem more happy and excited and that flows into our marriage you know?"

"I definitely feel you on that. I never would've thought we would be here but we are and it feels damn good."

"It sure does." Mike spun me around and before we knew it, we were the center of attention in the middle of the floor. Then the DJ switched up the music and we began doing a series of line dances. Thank God for my natural hair because I started sweating like crazy.

We continued to dance, take pictures, and enjoy the night. We held up our glasses in memory of Daddy because he loved big events like these and he loved to dance. But I thought about what Mike asked me. Hmmm, what was next? I didn't know, but I was finally able to say I was no longer avoiding discovering the ride.

THE END

Made in the USA
Lexington, KY
08 November 2018